TWOSPOT

Books by Bill Pronzini

"Nameless Detective" Novels:

The Snatch
The Vanished
Undercurrent
Blow Back
Twospot (with Collin Wilcox)
Labyrinth
Hoodwink
Scattershot
Dragonfire
Bindlestiff
Quicksilver
Nightshades
Double (with Marcia Muller)
Bones
Deadfall
Shackles
Jackpot
Breakdown

TWOSPOT

Bill Pronzini
&
Collin Wilcox

SPEAKING VOLUMES, LLC

NAPLES, FLORIDA

2011

TWOSPOT

ISBN 978-1-61232-069-4

To Lee Wright, with love

PART ONE

The Private Detective

1

The old-fashioned arched sign over the entrance to the private road read:

CAPPELLANI WINERY

I swung my car off the Silverado Trail and took it beneath the sign and past another one that appeared in my headlights: GUIDED TOURS. VISITORS WELCOME • TASTING ROOM OPEN 10–4 • The road was narrow but well graded, and it began to climb and dip almost immediately through low rolling foothills. The hillsides were carpeted with curving rows of grape vines, most of which had been stripped clean of fruit because it was the first of November and the harvest season was all but over. Here and there were some of the big truck gondolas the pickers used, and oaks and madrone and eucalyptus dotted the terrain, but there was nothing else to see except the black-shadowed vineyards and a black moonless sky. The winery was tucked farther back in the foothills, a mile and a half from the Silverado Trail and a few miles southeast of the village of St. Helena.

It was just past nine o'clock and the night was cool, but I rolled my window down a little so I could smell the good vinous, earthy scent of the vineyards. A summer fragrance, though, not an autumn one, because the drought that had plagued California for more than a year continued to linger with no signs of abatement. Even the grape leaves had not taken on their fall colors—yellow, scarlet, purple—as they would have by now if the rains had come as usual.

Alex Cappellani had told me it had been a poor harvest, one of the poorest in the Napa Valley in years. The big wineries which owned the bulk of the 16,000 acres of vineyards in the valley would survive all right on volume; but unless the drought ended soon, Cappellani and the other small cellars could be in serious trouble. They made most of their profits on vintage-dated varietals —Pinot Noir and Grignolino and Grey Riesling—and without a yield of high-quality grapes with which to manufacture these wines, they had little hope of competing in the marketplace.

This was the latest in a long series of problems that had beset the Cappellani Winery since Alex's great-grandfather founded it in 1878. Poor harvests and labor squabbles had almost closed it down in the 1890s and in the early 1900s; Prohibition *had* closed it down for the duration, and there had been an added difficulty when Alex's grandfather was arrested in 1923 and fined a substantial sum of money for illegally conspiring to produce alcoholic beverages; Alex's father, Frank Cappellani, had apparently been more interested in reactionary political causes, and as a result of apathetic management the winery had nearly gone into receivership in the early '60s. Frank's death of a heart attack in 1964 put the cellar in full control of his wife, Rosa, who had turned out to be a capable and hard-nosed business woman. With the help of Alex's elder brogher, Leo, and later Alex himself, Rosa had gotten the winery back into the black: until the drought it had been flourishing.

But the drought and poor harvest were not the only things Alex was concerned about these days, and had nothing to do with why he'd hired me three days ago in San Francisco. What he had come to me about was a man named Jason Booker, an enologist—a wine and winemaking scientist—whom Rosa Cappellani had signed on six months ago. Booker was forty-six, nine years Rosa's junior, but they had evidently become intimates; and although Rosa insisted there was nothing serious in their relationship, Alex was convinced that Booker was pressing her to marry him. He was also convinced that Booker was a shady opportunist who cared not at all for Rosa, who wanted only to gain control of the winery through marriage. So he wanted me to run a check into this Booker's background to see if there was anything there that would corroborate his suspicions.

You can find out a lot about a man in three days if you have a basic fact sheet on him to begin with—where he went to school, where he has lived and worked, things like that—and Alex had provided me with a copy of Booker's job application and references from the Cappellani offices in San Francisco. Since Booker had lived in California all his life, the first thing I had done was some routine checking with police and credit agencies. Which got me nothing much; he had an average credit rating and no police record of any kind. Then I had driven up here and spent the past two days talking to people at the four wineries which had employed him during the last twenty years, two in Napa Valley and two in the Valley of the Moon. The consensus was that he was a good enologist but nothing much as a man: arrogant, ambitious, charming when he wanted to be, ruthless when he saw an advantage to be gained.

One other thing I learned was that, his job application to the contrary, he had not worked anywhere for an eight-month period in 1970. This morning, I had found out why: a viticulturist at the Sonoma winery which employed Booker prior to that eight-month gap told me Booker had left there without giving a reason but that he had let it slip he was planning to get married. There had been nothing on the job application about a marriage—he had listed himself as a bachelor—and so I had gone to Santa Rosa and checked the Sonoma County records. Married, all right, to a woman named Martha Towne in February of 1970. According to the marriage certificate, she was sixteen years older than he and a resident at that time of Petaluma.

The Petaluma address turned out to be an expensive home in an affluent west-side neighborhood. It also turned out to still belong to Martha Towne—a bitter Martha Towne who was more than willing to talk about Jason Booker, to me and to anyone else who might want to listen.

It was an old story, old and sad and ugly; and it pretty well corroborated Alex Cappellani's suspicions. Martha Towne had been recently widowed and had inherited a considerable estate from her late husband when she met Booker at a party. She had also been lonely, and flattered and overwhelmed by his attentions, and she had married him three months later. Only to discover, after five months together, that he was far more interested in her money than he was in her. He had gotten her to open joint checking and savings accounts and had then appropriated fifteen thousand dollars for personal investments about which she knew nothing. When she found out she told him to pack his bags, and divorced him and managed to get a sympathetic judge not to grant him a community property settlement.

She had not remarried again, and all you had to do was look at her to tell that she never would. Booker had taken a lot more from her than the fifteen thousand dollars; he had taken her faith and her trust, and she had never recovered them either.

I asked her if she would sign a formal statement of what she had told me, if it proved necessary; I also told her why I might want it, omitting the names of the Cappellani family. She said she would, gladly, and her eyes shone with a kind of malice when she said it. I did not blame her much, but I got out of there pretty fast just the same.

It was after six when I called the winery from a pay phone and asked for Alex. But the woman who answered said he wasn't there; he was expected at eight o'clock. So I ate cannellone and drank a couple of beers in an Italian restaurant on Petaluma's main drag and then drove the fifty miles to St. Helena and called the winery again from there. Alex was in this time; he asked me to come straight out and to meet him at the office in the main cellar building.

The road wound across a stretch of bottomland, where the vines were laid out in long straight rows. I still could not see the winery from there, but beyond the crest of another low hill there was the faint glow of lights against the dark sky. The night seemed vast and still and touched with a kind of old-world serenity, and you could imagine that this was a foothill vineyard in France or Italy or Switzerland at the turn of the century. That same flavor of Europe long-ago permeated the Napa Valley; you felt and saw it not only in the vineyards and the old stone wineries, but in the quiet villages and the ancient mills and factories and railroad depots, and in the attitudes of the people who lived there.

All the driving I had done today was beginning to make me a little logy. I rolled down the window another couple of inches, to let in more of the cool night air, and yawned, and the yawn triggered a series of small dry coughs that brought a tightness into my chest. When the coughing stopped I took several slow deep breaths. The tightness eased then, but a dull ache lingered in the region of my left lung.

There was a lesion on that lung. It was benign, as I had learned after an agonizing week this past summer, just prior to my fiftieth birthday; but there was still the possibility that it would turn malignant, or that other malignant lesions would form on one or both lungs. That was what a doctor named White had told me—and he had also told me that if I wanted to keep on living, I had to give up smoking cigarettes.

So I had given them up. Cold turkey. I had consumed an average of two packs a day for thirty-five years, and had tried to quit several times with no success; but when a doctor tells you point-blank that you're going to die if you *don't* quit, you do it and you stick to it. I had not had a single cigarette in five months. Every time I thought about having one, which was less and less frequently now, I reminded myself that it would be like putting a knife in my own chest. And the craving would go away.

The lesion, and the specter of death, had changed me in a lot of ways over these past five months. In the beginning, while I was waiting for the pathology report on whether the lesion was malignant or benign, I had been obsessed by death—so obsessed by it that I was having difficulty functioning. But then, as a result of a complicated case I had been on in the Mother Lode, I had finally come to terms with my own mortality. I was no longer afraid of the specter of death; I had made peace with myself and with the world around me. I was no longer inclined to view certain things and certain people with cynical eyes. I was no longer inclined to care too much and too deeply about the lives and the suffering of others—what the unemotional and intellectual types like to label dismissively as weltschmerz, as if it were some sort of curious affliction. Not that I have stopped caring; it is just that human pain and human folly do not hurt me so much anymore.

When I got to the top of the low hill beyond the bottomland, the winery buildings appeared in another shallow valley below. What looked to be the main cellar was off to the south, built before a cut in a limestone ridge; nightlights shone across its stone facade and its huge domed roof, illuminated part of a wide gravel yard and a parking area for visitors. Vineyards stretched away on its far side, and at an angle beyond the cellar's north side were a couple of smaller stone buildings that probably housed bottling and shipping facilities and some of the winery's smaller cooperage.

A stand of oak trees and two hundred yards of open ground separated those buildings from an old stone house, shaded by more oaks, that had the appearance of a nineteenth-century Italian villa. There were lights visible in some of the house's facing windows.

I took the car down there, past where the road made a loop toward the main cellar and a gated lane branched off it and led up to the house, and pulled it into one of the slots in the parking area. There was no sign of activity around there; pick-up trucks and a big diesel rig and a handful of empty gondolas sat dark and silent around the north side of the yard. If this were the height of the crush, or if the harvest yield had been a good one, there might have been some nighttime work going on. As things were, it did not seem that anyone was collecting overtime pay tonight.

I got out and walked across the yard to the cellar. The cool air was pungent with the heady odor of crushed grapes and fermenting wine, and I had the thought that maybe I ought to change my drinking habits too, learn how to enjoy good wine. Wine, at least, did not give you a belly that was starting to hang over the belt, the way beer had with me.

The only doors in the front wall of the cellar were a pair of brassbound black-oak jobs, set into an archway, that looked as if they had come off a church or a European castle. Above them was a redwood sign that gave the winery's name, and beside them was a bulletin board that told you the tasting room was inside and what the hours were. I looked for a bell-push of some kind, but there was nothing like that set into the stone wall. So I reached out and tried the doors, and one of them swung inward beneath my hand.

Inside, the temperature was several degrees colder and the fermenting-wine smell several degrees sharper. There was a dankness too, created by the stone floors and walls and the high stone ceiling. A pale light burned in the tasting room straight ahead, and another glowed in the foyer where I stood, and there were still others spaced at wide intervals along corridors that extended the width of the building on both sides; but they were only diffused pockets of light that made the shadows around them seem deeper, that gave heavy old wood casks and tables and beams an unreal cast, like half-formed lack ghosts.

I moved forward a couple of paces. From somewhere in the building I could hear the faint hum of machinery; otherwise there was nothing but silence. The corridor to the south, I saw, led into an area filled with huge redwood aging tanks. The one to the north went past a dark enclosure with windows on two sides and rows of wine bottles glistening dully on shelves inside—a sales room—and then past another enclosure that had a palely lighted window, as though from a desk lamp inside. That was probably the office, I thought, and when I glanced up at the foyer wall an arrow sign there confirmed it. I took a step in that direction.

And something made a scraping sound down there, the kind of sound a person makes when he drags a heavy object across a stone floor.

I hesitated, listening, but the noise was not repeated. Sounds in the night, I thought, and shrugged, and started down the corridor. My footsteps echoed on the floor, were magnified by the stone walls until they reverberated like the hollow clopping of wood on wood.

The light in the office went out.

That brought me up short again. A faint uneasiness began to work inside me, an intimation of something being wrong. Why would Alex Cappellani shut off the light when he heard someone approaching? Unless he planned to come out and greet me—but the office door remained closed.

I listened. Silence. All right then, he was waiting in there, or somebody was. For what? To find out who was out here?

"Mr. Cappellani?" I called. And identified myself.

Silence.

The uneasiness grew stronger, but the need to know what was going on carried me forward, on the balls of my feet now, until I was standing just beyond the dark office window. It was pitch black in there; I could not even make out the shapes of furniture.

"Mr. Cappellani?"

Nothing but the echo of my voice.

With the hackles coming up on my neck, I eased forward to the door and put a hand on the knob and turned it. It opened inward an inch or two. I shoved it wide with the tips of my fingers, tensing, looking inside but not moving my body.

Breathing—somebody breathing just inside the door.

The scuffling of a shoe sole.

Those sounds warned me, but not in time to do anything more than take a half-step backward. The dark shape of a man lunged into the doorway, and I had a fleeting perception of something upraised in his hand, something swinging down toward my head, and got my arm up in panicked reaction—and the object glanced off my wrist, glanced off my right cheekbone, brought a bright flash of pain and confusion and sent me sprawling backward across the cold stone floor.

2

The blow and the impact with the floor created a wild roaring in my ears, distorted my vision, but neither stunned me enough to put me out or keep me down. I slid a couple of feet on my back, caught my momentum and scrabbled around on reflex until I was up on one knee, turning back toward the office. I saw the man-figure standing there, two of him, through wavering shadows and a blurred nimbus of light, saw him move and the object he had hit me with leap free of his hand. Reflex made me duck this time, and over the roaring in my head there was the explosive crash of glass shattering on the floor close by. Wetness and glass shards spattered my hands and arms, I could smell the sharp sourness of red wine—the son of a bitch had tried to brain me twice with a goddamn bottle of *wine*—and I let out a sound that was half grunt and half bellow of rage and pain, and heaved up onto my feet like a wounded bear.

The man-shape had spun and was running away along the corridor.

Shaking my head, pawing at my eyes, I staggered after him. Bounced off one of the stone walls before my vision wobbled back into focus and I could see where I was going, where the guy was. Hunched shadow forty yards away, racing past the entrance to the tasting room, heading toward the narrow corridor that led into the area where the aging tanks were. I locked my teeth against the pain in my head, the pain in my wrist, and kept on lumbering in pursuit.

He was halfway through the forest of redwood vats by the time I cleared the foyer. But then he seemed to slip on something and reeled into one of the tanks, almost fell, got his balance back and threw a look over his shoulder. I was thirty yards behind him then, but I could not see enough of his face in the murky light to get an impression of what he looked like; it was just a dim blur, and he was just a man-shape in dark clothing. I shouted at him, for no rational reason—I was still groggy, still caught up in emotional reaction—but he had already pushed away from the tank and was running again, this time in quick choppy steps like somebody trying to run across ice.

I saw the reason for that when I came into the vat area: the floor there had been hosed down sometime during the afternoon and the stones were wet and slick and puddled with water. I slowed in time to keep myself from slipping the way he had, adjusted my own strides to match his. The distance between us was still thirty yards.

There was an archway at the far end of the area, and beyond it, in another room, were the steel vats the wineries use for aging white wines. The floor in there was wet too, but the guy got across it all right and into a third room, this one lined on both sides with horizontally laid oak casks that had been stained a glistening black by millions of gallons of fermenting red wine. A rubber hose was stretched out loosely and carelessly along the stones, and I got my feet tangled in the damned thing and cracked my elbow against the rounded edge of a cask. I finally managed to kick loose just as the guy reached the far end of the room and vanished into a right-angle corridor toward the rear of the cellar.

The roaring in my ears had diminished and I could hear the hollow drumming echoes of his footfalls and of my own as I ran up there. When I swung around the corner he was just going into a big room with a shadowy maze of overhead refrigeration piping and metal catwalks, and a cluster of stainless steel fermentation tanks. I pounded after him, breathing through my mouth now because the dankness and the overpowering wine smell were beginning to make me nauseous.

In the room down there the guy broke stride and I saw his head jerk from one side to the other, as if he were looking for a place to hide or some sort of escape route. Then he made a quick glance back toward me again, and must have decided there wasn't time to do whatever it was before I caught him or got close enough to identify him; he shifted back into a hard run. And when he got to the far end he made another turn, to his right this time and without slowing, into a second north-south corridor.

What turned out to be down there were areas filled with more oak casks, with smaller aging cooperage stacked in tiers on wooden chocks, with some type of shadow-obscured equipment. He went straight through them all, and I still could not get any closer to him than thirty yards.

Another archway loomed ahead. A few feet beyond it was a blank stone wall: he had reached the end of the building. But along that end wall was yet another east-west corridor, and the guy veered into it to his right, and two or three seconds later I heard a clattering metallic sound, followed by a sharp creaking—the creaking of hinges. There was a sudden draft of cool fresh air.

Panting, I stumbled to the archway and lunged through it. A heavy wooden door stood open five yards away; the corridor was empty. I thought something obscene, ran through the door onto the gravel surface of the yard. At first I didn't see him and I thought he had gotten around to the front or the rear of the cellar; the night seemed dark and still and deserted. Then there was movement off to my right, in the shadow of a black oak growing between the south edge of the yard and a wide, shallow-looking pond. I picked him out then, running toward the pond or toward a dirt-and-gravel road near it that curved up through the open vineyards beyond. He had better than sixty yards on me now.

I went after him—across the yard, past the oak, over toward the pond. Once he got to the road he ran straight up the center of it, head down and body bent forward, feet kicking up thin puffs of dust. I came onto the gravelly bed and plunged upward in his wake.

It was rough going. The road climbed steadily up the hillside to a broken line of eucalyptus trees across the crown, and the loose gravel made it difficult to maintain traction. The night air was sweet after the winey dampness of the cellar and it had cleared the last of the grogginess from my mind; but it did not help the throbbing pain where I had been clubbed, or the tightness that was building in my chest from too much exertion. I could feel myself slowing up, starting to stumble like a drunk trying to follow a straight line. But he was slowing up too, I could see that—because he was somewhere around my age or because he was not in the best physical condition. It was all coming down to which one of us gave out first.

We were well up into the vineyards now—rows of old gnarled leafy vines curved out on both sides—and the guy was coming in on the line of eucalyptus at the brow of the hill. The road hooked near there, through the trees; I could not see from where I was the point at which it came out of them and went down the far slope. Which meant I was going to lose sight of him pretty soon, if only briefly.

And that was what happened: one second he was there, running through the curve, and the next he was gone into the deep shadows cast by the eucalyptus.

A bird screeched in a startled way up there, as if it had been disturbed from its sleep; the only other sounds were the scrape of my shoes on gravel and the wheezing rasp of my breath. I staggered finally through the hook in the road, to where it leveled off at the crest and the trees began. Then I could see the direction it took, and beyond the eucalyptus, in another hollow, I had an impression of lights glowing against the sky; but I still could not see the guy.

I started into the trees—and off to my left there was the faint rustling of leaves, the sound of a snapping twig.

I pulled up sharply, turning in that direction, sleeving sweat from my face and eyes. Blackness, crouching shadows. But then I heard the rustling again, and it was no more than fifteen yards away, back toward the slope I had just come up; he must have gone in there to hide and been too exhausted or too panicked to bring it off. A second later there was movement that I could perceive even in the darkness, the crunch and slide of retreating steps. He knew I had heard him and he was making a run for it again.

All right, you bastard, I thought. I veered off the road and cut into the trees, and I had glimpses of him dodging and weaving with more agility than he had shown before. Maybe he had gotten a second wind—but there was a smoke-and-fire pain in my lungs and my chest felt as though it were being squeezed in a vise. I would not be able to keep on like this much longer. If I was going to get him at all, it would have to be now, right now.

The eucalyptus were beginning to thin out and between their trunks the black rows of grape vines were visible ahead. He saw that too, cut sharply to his left and came out into the open, down onto the clotted black earth between two rows of vines. Running downslope on that surface was even harder than running up the gravel road; he stumbled, lurched sideways, and fell jarringly to his hands and knees. He struggled up immediately—but the fall had cost him the last of his advantage.

I had him then. I had him good.

I threw myself forward with my arms outstretched and hit him in the small of the back with the fleshy joining of my upper chest and upper right arm. The air went out of him explosively, like a balloon bursting, and my momentum knocked him sprawling into one of the vines and carried me down on top of him. A vine branch splintered and caught me a scraping blow across the temple, showered me with juice from a burst cluster of grapes. None of that did any damage but it made me lose the grip I had on the guy's clothing. He kicked out from under me and tried to pull away, making little mewling gasps the way somebody does when he's had the wind knocked out of him.

I twisted around and got another grip on his jacket. He lashed out in a frenzy, all arms and legs and hard edges of bone; I had to keep my head tucked in against my chest to protect it from the blows. But I seemed to have more weight and more strength and I managed to pull myself over him again, smothering his movements, and then cuffed him a couples of times awkwardly with my free hand.

Only then I became aware of his body beneath mine on the loose earth, squirming, and there was something about the touch of him that was not quite what it ought to be. I reared back, straddling him now, holding him down with the one hand while the other one cocked back on reflex. And got a look at the white face and a pair of wild glaring eyes. And realized with astonishment and another sudden rush of confusion just what it was that was wrong.

It was not a man I had under me, it was an outraged *woman*.

I stared down at her, shock-frozen, and she used that moment to lunge upward with her head and shoulders and sink her teeth into the flesh below my collarbone. I let out a yell, pushed at her head and wrenched it aside; skin came tearing loose with her teeth, there was more stinging pain and the wetness of blood. She kept on struggling frantically, dangerously, and I had no choice except to force her back down again and hold her pinned until I could get my breathing and my thoughts under control.

"You son of a bitch," she said. It came out in thick stuttering pants. "If you try to rape me I'll be the last woman you ever do it to."

I said, "Jesus Christ."

She was not the one who had clubbed me back in the cellar, not the one I had been chasing; he had been a man, all right, I was sure of that. He must have stayed on the road, gone down into the hollow on the other side of the hill. Long vanished by now. The woman was somewhere under forty, slender and muscular and small-breasted, and her hair was cut very close to her head in one of those mannish styles; she was also wearing a dark shirt and jacket, dark trousers. All of which, along with the black night, explained why I had mistaken her for the guy.

But what the hell had she been doing up in those trees?

She was still struggling, still glaring up at me. There did not seem to be much fear in her; just fury and determination. She called me a couple of things, still fighting for breath, and told me what she would do to me if I tried to rape her. Hardboiled language, and all of it razor-edged.

"Listen," I said, "listen, I'm not trying to rape you."

Her mouth worked and she let go with a blob of spit that splattered across my cheek.

"Goddamn it, I tell you I'm not trying to rape you." I was having trouble drawing enough air, just as she was; my lungs burned malignantly. "I was chasing somebody else, a man, I thought you were him in the dark."

I had to say it again before she finally stopped thrashing around. She lay there tensed and wary, breasts heaving, hating me with her eyes. "Why were you chasing somebody out here? Who the hell *are* you?"

"A friend of Alex Cappellani's," I said. "I drove out to the winery to see him and this guy came out of the cellar office and tried to brain me with a wine bottle. So I went after him."

"What guy?"

"I don't know. I didn't get a look at him. He shut off the light in the office when he heard me coming."

"None of that makes any sense."

"Yeah," I said. "Look, I'll let go of you, let you up, if you don't try to mix it up anymore."

"That depends on what *you* try."

"A little more conversation, that's all."

"Then let me up."

I released one of her arms and she did not move. So I let go of the other one and slid back off her and made it up painfully onto my feet. My legs felt weak now, and I seemed to have half a dozen pulsing aches all over my body; the place where she had bit me stung like fury. I wiped her spittle off my cheek, stepped back and over to one of the vines and rested my weight on a grape stake there.

The woman got up slowly, not taking her eyes off me. She brushed the dirt off her clothing in an angry way, put a hand up and ran fingertips across her jaw where I cuffed her. "You play pretty damned rough, don't you," she said.

"I'm sorry. Are you all right?"

"I've been treated worse." She slapped again at the front of her jacket and the blue jeans she was wearing. "You said you were a friend of Alex's. What's your name?"

I told her.

"I never heard that name before."

"I only met Alex a few days ago." My respiration was just about back to normal, but the constriction in my chest had not lessened any yet. The damned cough started up again, thin and dry.

She stood there watching me, speculatively now, not saying anything.

When the coughing quit I said, "What about you? Do you live here?"

"No, I don't live here." She hesitated then, but only for a moment; most of the anger seemed to have gone out of her. "I work for the Cappellanis, in their San Francisco office. I've been staying up here as their guest since last night."

"Why were you in those trees?"

"Because the guest quarters are over on the other side of the hill and I was walking over to the main house. On the road. Somebody came running up from the other side, and as soon as he saw me he veered off into the trees. I thought that was pretty odd so I went in there a little ways to try to see who it was. Then I heard you, and you heard me and came after me, and I reacted stupidly and ran. I didn't know what the hell was going on."

"You didn't get a look at the guy?"

"It was too dark. Look, you said he shut off the light in the cellar office and then came out and hit you with a wine bottle. Why would anybody do a crazy thing like that?"

"I don't know," I said. "Unless he's a thief and he panicked. Or—"

I stopped abruptly, because for the first time since I had been attacked I was beginning to think logically instead of emotionally —and I was remembering all at once that scraping sound I had heard, the sound of something heavy being dragged across the stone floor.

The woman said, "What's the matter?"

"Alex Cappellani," I said. "He asked me to come out to see him tonight. He was supposed to be in that office when I got here, waiting for me."

She understood right away what I meant. "My God," she said, "you don't think that man might have done something to Alex?"

I did not answer her; there was nothing to say. I just turned and started back toward the dirt-and-gravel road, not running because of my lungs but moving pretty fast just the same. After the first few steps the woman was right beside me.

3

When we got down to where I could see the yard in front of the cellar, the figure of a man appeared there, walking toward the entrance doors from the direction of the Cappellani house. I tensed a little—but there was nothing furtive about his movements. He noticed us at about the same time, slowed and then stopped in the light from one of the night globes burning above the archway.

The woman and I left the road and hurried across the yard. The man stood with his arms at his sides, watching us approach. He appeared to be in his forties, wiry and pinch-faced, and he was wearing a sports jacket and an open-necked shirt and slacks, all of them dark-colored. His expression was one of curiosity at first, but as we came up and he got a good look at what was in our faces, at the condition of my clothes, it changed into an anxious frown.

He blinked at me and said to the woman, "Shelly? Is something wrong—?"

I went right by him, and she did the same thing without offering a response. The dark winey coldness enveloped me again as I stepped inside; I had to breathe through my mouth to keep from gagging. I went at an angle across the foyer, into the corridor to the north and along it to where the office was. Echoes from my footfalls and the woman's bounced hollowly off the stone walls. On the floor up there the spilled wine gleamed blackly, like blood, amid the shards from the broken bottle.

When I got to the open office door, the woman—Shelly—said, "There's a light switch on the wall inside, to your right."

I reached in there, fumbled around and located the switch and flipped it. Bright fluorescent light from a pair of overhead tubes consumed the blackness; the sudden glare made me squint. Behind me I hear the sharp intake of Shelly's breath.

Alex Cappellani was lying face down in the middle of the floor, and there were streaks of crimson matting the curly hair on the back of his skull.

I moved to him and went down on one knee, pressed fingertips against the artery in his neck. There was a pulse, irregular but strong enough. I let out the breath I had been holding, started to shrug out of my jacket.

Shelly leaned down next to me. "Is he—alive?"

"Yeah. But he needs a doctor, fast. That head wound—"

"Good God!" a man's voice said. It was the pinch-faced guy; he had followed us inside, and he was standing now in the doorway with his eyes wide and shocked. "Alex! What's *happened* to him?"

"Somebody cracked him over the head," I said.

"Hit him? But who? Why?"

Shelly said, "Logan, for Christ's sake." Then, to me, "I'll call the hospital in St. Helena."

I nodded as I covered Alex with my jacket. "But we'd better not touch anything in here. There another phone close by?"

"In the sales room."

The pinch-faced guy was still standing in the doorway, gawking. He said to Shelly, "Who is this man? What's he doing here?"

"What are *you* doing here?"

"I came down to talk to Alex." He looked me up and down. "He's been in a fight—"

"Never mind that now," Shelly said, and crowded past him into the corridor. "Mrs. Cappellani had better know what's happened. And Leo."

The guy blinked at her. "Yes, you're right."

"Then don't stand around here, go tell them."

He did not like her commanding tone—the resentment was plain in his expression—but he didn't give her any argument.

When she turned toward the sales room, he glanced at me again, briefly, and then hurried after her along the corridor.

There was nothing else I could do for Alex. You don't move somebody who has been badly hurt, if you have any sense, and you especially don't move somebody with a head injury. I straightened up and backed over to the door, stopped there to look around the office. Cluttered mahogany desk set against the far wall, between two filing cabinets; an oversized phone on the desk with two rows of buttons on its base unit; a couple of round-backed chairs and a table with a wine rack on it full of dusty bottles. The wine rack told me where the bottle came from that the attacker had used on me, that he had probably used on Alex as well. But there did not seem to be anything out of place in there. The file drawers and desk drawers were closed, nothing was strewn around anywhere on the floor, and the clutter of papers on the desk had a natural appearance, not as if someone had been rummaging through them.

So maybe I had interrupted the assailant before he could steal anything. Or maybe he had found what he was after with a minimum of mess. Or maybe he had not come to steal anything in the first place. That scraping sound—why would a thief, why would *anyone,* have been dragging Alex across the floor?

Well, Alex himself had the answers, if anyone did. It was not up to me in any case; the matter was a police one.

I went down the sales room. Lights blazed in there now, illuminating shelves and displays and stacked cases of wine, and Shelly was behind a counter along one wall, speaking into a telephone receiver. That telephone, too, was oversized and had the two rows of buttons on its base; when I came up and looked at the buttons I saw that two of them were marked "Open Line" and the rest were numbered. Which meant that the winery buildings, and no doubt the main house too, were interconnected by a series of private lines, so you could call directly from one extension to another.

When Shelly finished talking to the hospital I took the handset from her and dialed O and told the operator I had a police emergency. She put me straight through to the sheriff's office. I identified myself to the officer who answered, gave him a brief account of what had happened; he said they would be out as quickly as possible.

Somebody had left a package of Kools on the counter, and Shelly helped herself to one and then extended the pack to me as I dropped the handset back into its cradle. I looked at it longingly for a moment, felt the lingering tightness in my chest, and thought: Just like putting a knife in my lungs, just like committing suicide.

"No thanks," I said. "I don't smoke."

She lighted hers, blew a long sighing stream of smoke at the ceiling. "I suppose it was necessary to call in the sheriff," she said, "but I wish you hadn't done it."

"Why is that?"

"I don't like cops much."

"Oh? Any particular reason?"

"I was married to one once."

She said that as if it were a complete and final explanation. But her voice was matter-of-fact, without any trace of bitterness. I wondered, not altogether relevantly, what she would say if and when she found out I was a cop of sorts myself.

This was the first chance I had had to take a close look at her, and I saw that she was around thirty, that she had gray-green eyes, that her close-cropped hair was a dark auburn color and very fine, like a child's. But there was nothing childlike about her features. They were strong, intelligent, maybe a little hard around the mouth—the face of a woman who has not had an easy life but who knows exactly who she is and what she wants. A survivalist. Tough and probably cynical about some things; nothing much in this world would suprise her anymore. For all that, though, she was more than a little attractive. Not beautiful, certainly not pretty, but very damned attractive.

I realized that she had been studying me too—but there was nothing in her eyes to indicate what impression she had formed, or if she had formed any impression at all. In that same matter-of-fact voice she said, "You've got blood on your shirt where I bit you."

I looked down at the area under my collarbone; the shirt there was torn and stained a dark red. The bite still stung, and as soon as my mind focused on the stinging I grew aware again of the throbbing in my head and the dull ache in my wrist and the bunched muscles in my legs. Christ, a walking-wounded.

She said, "Does it hurt?"

"A little. It'll be all right."

"I guess we both played rough up in the vineyards."

"Yeah, I guess we did."

Neither of us said anything for a time, thinking our own

thoughts. I broke the silence finally with a question: "The pinch-faced guy—who is he?"

"Logan Dockstetter," she said. "He's the winery's sales manager. And a fag, if you hadn't already guessed."

That last comment was uncalled for; Logan Dockstetter's sexual preferences had nothing to do with anything. But I did not say that to her. Apparently she did not like homosexuals any more than she liked cops, and there is never any point in calling someone on his prejudices.

I said, "Is Dockstetter staying here too?"

"No. He came up from San Francisco tonight, along with his boyfriend, Philip Brand. Brand is the Cappellanis' accountant. The two of them—"

She broke off because there was an abrupt commotion out in the foyer—the echo of hurrying footsteps, the excited babble of voices. I shoved away from the counter, and Shelly came around from behind it, and together we went across to the doorway and out into the corridor just as five people came crowding up.

Three of them were men, Logan Dockstetter among them, but it was the older of the women who was in the lead. Rosa Cappellani, I thought. But she was nothing at all as I had pictured her, nothing at all like the popular conception of an Italian matriarch. She had a lean but heavy-breasted body that seemed well preserved in a blue pants suit; silver-streaked hair, and features that were too angular to be called anything other than handsome. Those features were set now in firm lines that gave her an imperious, no-nonsense demeanor, and though she had to be pretty upset she gave no outward indication of it. My immediate impression was that here was a woman who was always in perfect command of her emotions, who possessed a good deal of strength and self-assurance.

She went past Shelly and me without looking at either of us, as if we were not even there. Which gave us no choice but to turn and follow her, along with the three men and the other woman. When she got to the office door she stopped and stood stiffly, staring inside. I saw her face in profile, and nothing changed in it; she did not even blink.

I stepped up to her. "I checked his pulse and it seems strong and fairly stable," I said. "It would be best not to touch him."

She pivoted to me, acknowledging my presence for the first time, and gave me a long probing look. Then she said, "I had no intention of touching him," and she had a voice to match her demeanor. "Has an ambulance been called?"

Shelly said, "Yes. I phoned for one a few minutes ago."

"And the police?"

"Yes," I said.

"Good." Mrs. Cappellani took her eyes off me and put them on one of the men—a guy about her own age dressed in work clothes and a poplin jacket, with eyes set deep under a craggy forehead and a nose as sharp as a rock spire. "Paul," she said, "find a blanket somewhere. A heavy blanket. We won't touch Alex but he has to be kept warm."

He nodded and hurried off.

"Where's Leo?" Shelly asked.

"He went out for a walk," the other woman said. "I don't know where he is." She was in her early thirties, attractive, with thick coils of dark hair and breasts even larger than Mrs. Cappellani's. There was vulnerability in her face and a kind of detachment in her manner, as if she had withdrawn into herself as a defense mechanism against all the things which could hurt her. The exact opposite of Shelly. I thought that she was probably Leo Cappellani's wife; Alex had told me Leo was married.

The third man said, "Do you want me to see if I can find him, Mrs. Cappellani?" He had a deep and very precise voice that surprised you a little because of his physical appearance: round soft face, bright eyes, prim mouth. He was about Dockstetter's age.

"Yes," she said. "Do that, Philip." Philip Brand, I thought. "And take Logan and Angela with you."

She looked at me again as Dockstetter and Brand and Angela Cappellani went toward the foyer. "Now suppose you tell me who you are and what happened here."

I told her. But I did not say that I was a private detective hired by her son, because of the nature of my investigation and because it was not up to me to discuss my findings with her. And I did not say anything, either, about the scuffle with Shelly up in the vineyards; I was embarrassed by it, and it had no particular relevance anyway. I said only that in the darkness I had mistaken Shelly for the man I was chasing and that he had gotten away for that reason.

"You have no idea what this man looked like?"

"No, ma'am. He was just a dark shape, average height and build. But Alex probably saw him and can identify him."

"Yes. I'm sorry for what happened to you, but I'm grateful just the same that you arrived when you did. You may well have saved my son's life."

There was nothing I could say to that, and the craggy-featured guy saved me from having to find words by coming back with a folded Army blanket. Rosa Cappellani took it from him, went into the office and shook it out and draped it carefully around Alex's inert form. Then she straightened up, but she did not come back out of the office; she just stood there, stoically, staring down at him with her hands clasped in front of her.

The wine smell had begun to get to me again; I could taste sour bile in the back of my throat. I said to Shelly that I was going out for some air, and went into the foyer and through the double doors. As soon as I stepped outside I could hear, in the distance, the faint ululating wail of an ambulance siren. They made good time out of St. Helena, I thought—and I hoped the county sheriff's people were as efficient. The sooner they got here, the sooner I could find a hotel or motel and get some rest.

I took a couple of deep breaths, and the doors opened behind me and the craggy-featured guy came out. He paused to fire one of those misshapen Italian cigars called a Toscana, that smell like smoldering manure, and then walked over to where I was.

"Paul Rosten," he said, "I'm the winemaker here."

I nodded, gave him my name.

"What the hell happened in there?"

Before I could answer that there was abrupt movement to the north, over by the two smaller cellars, and three figures materialized there and came running toward us. When they pounded up into the glow of the nightlights, I saw that two of them were Dockstetter and Brand and that the third was obviously Leo Cappellani; Angela had evidently remained at the house. Leo had the same dark angular features, the same wide mouth and curly black hair as his brother. But he was a few years older, a few pounds heavier. He also had quite a bit of his mother's imperiousness, something which Alex did not have. You could tell that about him right off.

He gave me a once-over look and said to Rosten, "Alex—how badly is he hurt?"

"We don't know yet," Rosten said grimly. "It looks like he was hit pretty hard on the back of the head. He's probably got a concussion, if not worse."

"Christ. Is he conscious?"

"No."

Leo glanced at me again. "Who are you? Why are you here?"

I did not want to go over it again before the police arrived, but he had a right to know, and the others too. So I gave them a somewhat abbreviated version, while the shriek of the siren got louder and eventually headlights—three sets of them, in tandem—appeared at the top of the far hillside.

When I was done, Leo shook his head and said, "Doesn't make any sense. There's nothing in that office worth stealing, no money or anything else of value."

"The police will get to the bottom of it, Mr. Cappellani."

"I hope so."

He turned abruptly and went inside the cellar. Rosten went with him, but Dockstetter and Brand stayed where they were and looked alternately at me, as if I were some sort of curious specimen, and at the headlights coming down the road toward us.

The siren cut off as the ambulance rolled into the yard, but the flasher light on its roof kept going, streaking the darkness with stroboscopic red patterns. The other two vehicles were Napa County sheriff's cars, neither of which had flasher lights or sirens. They all came to stops near where we were standing, and a couple of interns jumped out of the ambulance and opened the rear doors and hauled out a wheeled stretcher. Three uniformed deputies came running up; one of them asked where the injured party was. I said inside, and Dockstetter said he would show them where and led the interns and two of the deputies into the cellar.

I identified myself to the third deputy, a guy about my own age. We went over by the county cars and I explained to him what had taken place; I had told the story enough times now so that it was like delivering a set speech. Then I admitted to being a private investigator, showed him the photostat of my license, and said that I had been doing some confidential work for Alex Cappellani. The deputy wanted to know what work, if it could have any bearing on the attack on Alex. I told him I had no ideas on that. But I gave him a rundown of Alex's reasons for hiring me and of what I had learned about Jason Booker. When I asked him if he could refrain from saying anything to Rosa Cappellani or any of the others until he was able to talk to Alex, because it was a delicate family situation and maybe *not* related to the attack, he agreed to handle matters with discretion. He seemed to be a decent sort and I thought that he would keep his word.

While we'd been talking another set of headlights had appeared, this time up in the vineyards to the south, coming down the same dirt-and-gravel road that I had been running on earlier. Now the car, a dusty station wagon, pulled up on the edge of the yard and a man got out and jogged toward us. He was a slender fortyish guy wearing slacks and a turtleneck sweater, with a handsome ascetic face and a Kirk Douglas cleft in his chin that you could spot at ten paces even in the spinning flasher light.

Just before he reached us, looking half agitated and half perplexed, the cellar doors swung open and the interns came out wheeling Alex on the stretcher. Rosa Cappellani, and Leo, and Shelly and Rosten and the two deputies, followed in a bunch. The slender guy went straight over there, gaped at the stretcher, and then moved quickly to Mrs. Cappellani's side and put a hand on her arm.

I heard him say, "My God, Rosa, what's going on? What's happened to Alex?"

"Someone attacked him, Jason," she said in her brusque way. "One of the others will explain."

Jason Booker, I thought. I watched him stand there scowling as Rosa stepped away from him. The interns were loading the stretcher into the back of the ambulance now, and Mrs. Cappellani stood in a rigid posture with her arms folded across her breasts until they had closed the doors and started around to the front. Then she turned abruptly to Leo.

"We'll follow them to the hospital," she said.

Leo said something I didn't catch, and the two of them hurried off toward the house, Rosa without looking again at Booker.

Her apparent indifference to him made Booker scowl all the harder. He spun around and went over to Shelly and got into a conversation with her, presumably to find out what was going on.

I glanced at my watch as the ambulance pulled away, and the time was a few minutes past eleven. I asked the deputy beside me if I was going to be needed much longer; he said he didn't imagine I would be. But then one of the other deputies joined us, and he had questions, and I ended up having to tell my story still another time while he took notes and copied down my name and address and investigator's license number. It was eleven-thirty before they finally decided it was all right for me to leave.

I thanked them and started wearily to my car. Halfway there, a voice called my name behind me. Shelly. I stopped, turned to her as she came up.

"Leaving us?" she said.

"Yeah," I said. "It's been a long night."

"That it has." She watched me for a moment and then smiled faintly. "Maybe we'll see each other again, one of these days."

"Maybe we will."

"Ciao then, big man."

"Sure," I said. "Ciao, Shelly."

And I left her and got into my car and went away from there.

4

I spent the night in a hotel in St. Helena.

When I woke up a little after seven on Friday morning, after a good deep sleep, I felt better than I might have expected. I still had a headache, but it was muted and tolerable; the pain in my wrist was gone, and my lungs were clear of phlegm and my chest felt normal. I was even pretty hungry.

In the bathroom I had a look at myself in the mirror. Nickel-sized bruise on my cheekbone—but it hurt only when I touched it. The bite wound under my collarbone also hurt when I touched it. It was some bite too: torn skin, raw flesh, the teeth marks sunk so deep they were visible even now. The iodine I had swabbed on it last night before going to bed, from the first-aid kit I keep in my car, made it look even worse. I put more iodine on it and covered it with a gauze bandage, to guard against infection; the bite from a human, I had heard somewhere, can be even more dangerous than one from an animal.

After I was done with that I shaved off the gray stubble on my cheeks. Then I put on a change of clothes from my overnight bag, went out and hunted up a copy of the San Francisco *Chronicle*—morning habit—and took it into a cafe on St. Helena's picturesque main street.

Over eggs and toast and coffee I had a look at what was going on in the world. Most of the front page concerned Fidel Castro, who had been in Washington the past three days for talks with the President—his first visit to the United States in nearly twenty years, and naturally a controversial one. There had been another demonstration by Cuban exiles protesting his presence in the country, but like the others before it, it had been small and well controlled. The President was quoted as saying that the talks were proving successful, which the political columnists were interpreting to mean that re-establishment of diplomatic relations with Cuba was imminent. Castro and his entourage were expected to leave Washington today for a swing through other parts of the U.S., including a brief one-day visit to San Francisco on Monday. On the local scene, the mayor was being roasted by right-wing opponents for inviting Castro. And there was more flap over water rationing; and the Gay Task Force was planning another human rights demonstration. I read Herb Caen's column: he was grousing again about the infighting in San Francisco's city government. I turned to the Sporting Green, and one of the columnists there was alleging that the 49ers would be a .500 team at best this year because of poor coaching and dissension between players and management.

So much for the news. And so much for breakfast. I finished the last of my coffee refill, left the paper to enlighten somebody else, and walked back to the hotel. It was eight-thirty and time to put in a call to the hospital to find out what the situation was with Alex Cappellani.

But I did not find out much, as it developed. The nurse who answered my call said that his condition was "satisfactory," a term which can mean anything at all; that was all she would tell me because I was not a relative and because the injury to Alex was a police matter. When I asked her if he could have visitors, or at least take a call, she advised me firmly that the family had issued instructions that he was not to be disturbed.

I hesitated, thinking: Now what? I could leave a message and then hang around here for the day, on the chance that Alex was well enough to want to get in touch with me and to see me. But that would mean paying out another twenty dollars for the room, and it might also mean a wasted day. I decided the best thing to do was to go back to San Francisco and get a report ready for him of my findings on Jason Booker. So I gave my name to the nurse and requested that Alex be told when possible that I had called and that I could be reached either at my office or at my flat.

I got my things together then and checked out and headed home for the first time since Tuesday.

The Napa Valley is some seventy-five miles northeast of San Francisco, a good two-hour drive, and it was eleven o'clock by the time I came across the Golden Gate Bridge. The weather had been warm and clear in St. Helena, but in the city it was cold and foggy—one of those thick, wind-blown fogs that blanket the hills and drift like wisps of smoke through the streets. I drove straight downtown, left my car in the parking lot on the corner of Taylor and Eddy, and hurried over to the tired old Victorian building on the fringe of the Tenderloin where I have my office.

There was nobody in the dark lobby. One of the other tenants, a guy who ran a mail-order business, had gotten mugged in there six months ago—the Tenderloin has one of the highest crime rates in the city—and ever since then I make it a point to look around when I come in. I opened up my mailbox and pulled out three days' accumulation of mail: two letters and two pieces of junk advertisement. A sign on the elevator grill said that the elevator was out of order. Again. So I climbed the stairs to the third floor, and there weren't any muggers up there either.

The office was just a single room, with a little alcove off of it that contained a sink and some storage shelves; if you needed the toilet, there was one down at the end of the hall with a broken seat and a paper dispenser that never had any paper in it. A low rail divider separated the room into two halves. My desk was behind it, in front of the windows facing Taylor Street, and there were a couple of client chairs over there, and a filing cabinet with a hotplate on top of it. On this side of the divider was an old leather couch and another chair and a table with some magazines that had never been read. Except for the poster I had had made during the summer and tacked up on one of the walls, it was pretty much the same arrangement and the same decor I had opened business with after leaving the San Francisco cops fourteen years ago.

The poster was a blow-up of the cover of a 1932 issue of *Black Mask* and depicted a guy holding a couple of guns and standing in front of a suit of armor; it also featured a story by one of my favorite pulp writers, Paul Cain. It looked a little gaudy up there, and was probably inappropriate for a business office; but what the hell, everybody has a hobby and pulp magazines—reading them and collecting them—are mine. I have been fascinated by the pulps ever since I was a kid, and it was that fascination that led me into police work, led me eventually to become a private investigator: I wanted to be a detective just like the ones I read about in the pulps. Up until this summer, when my outlook on so many things had begun to change, that fact had nagged at me—that I had built my whole life as an emulation of the fictional private eye, made myself into a kind of functional cliché. Now, it did not seem to matter. It was *my* life and I enjoyed what I was doing. What difference did it make how or why I had become what I was? And if I were to lose a client because I collected pulps and had a *Black Mask* cover on my office wall, then I was better off without that kind of client.

The steam radiator was clanking away and it was warm in there, but a little musty from being closed up for three days. I unlatched the window and raised the sash a few inches. Then I put fresh water into the coffeepot, the pot on the hotplate, and sat down at my desk to look at my mail.

A fifty-dollar check from a furniture store that had hired me to do a skip-trace on one of their clients, and a letter from a guy who said he was the vice-president of the Northern California Chapter of the Mystery Writers of America and wanted to know if I would be a speaker at one of their monthly meetings. I put the check into my wallet and the letter into my basket until I had time to answer it; the idea of speaking to a group of mystery writers appealed to me.

I called my answering service, and there were a couple of messages. The one that interested me most was from Leo Cappellani, who had called at nine-forty this morning and who wanted me to get in touch with him at the winery's San Francisco office as soon as I came in.

I frowned a little as I put down the phone. How had Leo found out I was a private detective? From Alex, maybe? I lifted the receiver again, started to dial the number the answering service girl had given me.

And the office door opened and Leo Cappellani walked in.

I blinked at him, cradled the handset and got up on my feet. He glanced around the office, took in the *Black Mask* poster on the wall; but there was nothing in his face to show what he thought about any of it. He was wearing a conservative brown business suit today, and he looked crisp and successful and a little imposing, like a banker or a corporation lawyer. I noticed as he came up to the rail divider that his eyes were sharp and peremptory—as his mother's were, but nothing at all like Alex's mild expressive brown eyes.

"Good morning, Mr. Cappellani," I said. "I just came in, just got your message. I was about to call you."

"Yes," he said. "Well, I was on my way to an early lunch and I thought I'd stop by on the chance you'd returned."

I invited him to have a chair, and he came in and took the one in front of my desk. I said then, "How is Alex?"

"Not seriously hurt. He has a scalp wound and a mild concussion."

"Then he was able to talk to the police?"

"Yes. But he had nothing to tell them about the man who assaulted him. He was sitting at the desk with his back to the door, and the door was open. He heard a sound just before he was hit, but he didn't get so much as a glimpse of the man."

"He doesn't have any idea who it could have been?"

"None."

"Was anything taken from the office?"

"No. Nothing at all." Leo crossed his legs and watched me with those sharp black eyes. "Now you can relieve my curiosity, if you don't mind."

"About what, Mr. Cappellani?"

"About why you didn't tell any of us last night that you're a private detective."

"It didn't seem to be relevant," I said.

"That remains to be seen. Are you working for my brother?"

"Did he tell you I was?"

"No."

"Was he the one who told you I'm a detective?"

"No. One of the sheriff's deputies let that slip to Shelly after you'd gone. The deputy didn't say you were working for Alex, but the implication was that you are and that you told the police why he hired you. I'd like to have that same information."

"Why?"

"Because my brother is headstrong and inclined to act at times without good judgment."

"And you think hiring a private detective is a lack of good judgment?"

"If his reason involves family matters, yes."

"What sort of family matters?"

"Any sort. Alex may not value our privacy, but my mother and I do. If he has hired you to poke around in our affairs, we have the right to know about it."

Sure, I thought, and you're going to know about it pretty soon. But not from me. "Look, Mr. Cappellani," I said carefully, "I'm sorry, but if I am working for your brother, and he didn't want to discuss the matter with anyone, then I'm afraid I can't discuss it either. You value your privacy and I value the ethics of my profession; I can't breach a confidence."

His mouth tightened a little. "You've already breached confidence, it seems, by talking to the police."

"That's not quite the same thing. Whatever I might have said to the police, it was in the interest of helping to get to the bottom of the attack."

"Are you saying whatever Alex hired you to do has a bearing on what happened last night?"

"No, sir, that's not what I'm saying. I don't know what has a bearing on the attack last night. I'm bound by law to inform the police of anything, anything at all, that *might* be related to a felonious act; but I'm not bound to inform anybody else without the consent of my clients. I don't mean that to sound tough and unsympathetic to your feelings. It's just that I have to run my business my way, as you have to run your business your way."

He kept looking at me, frowning, and it got pretty quiet in there. But then, abruptly, his mouth loosened and his face smoothed, and he said, "All right, you've made your position clear." He stood up, turned toward the divider.

I said, relenting a little, "Mr. Cappellani?"

He pivoted to face me again.

"I wouldn't worry too much about your brother's motives," I said. "And I don't think it'll be long, either, before he decides to confide in your and your mother."

That got me another long, searching look. "I'll accept that," he said finally. And then he gave me a faint smile. "You're an interesting man. It's not often you meet someone with convictions these days."

There was nothing I could say to that.

Leo said, "I didn't intend to come on like a hardnose, or to seem ungrateful for all you did at the winery, and I apologize. The past fourteen hours have been bewildering, is all."

"Sure. I understand."

He nodded, and turned again, and went across the office and out through the door.

I thought as he closed it after him: you're a pretty interesting man yourself, brother. The difference between him and Alex was like night and day. Leo was one of these complex types you can never quite get a handle on, with hidden qualities and changeable moods and what seemed to be a strong sense of family pride and of personal conviction; and Alex was easygoing, extroverted, not particularly proud, not particularly dogmatic. I wondered if Alex favored his father, as Leo appeared to favor his mother.

The coffee water had come to a boil. I made a cup of instant and then dragged my old portable typewriter in front of me and began to type up my report on Jason Booker. I was half through it, hunting and pecking with my forefingers, when the telephone rang.

I hauled up the receiver and identified myself, and a woman's voice said, "This is Shelly Jackson."

Neither the name nor the voice registered immediately. "Shelly Jackson?" I said.

"How soon they forget. Last night, at the winery."

"Oh—Shelly. Excuse the blank reaction; I never did get your last name. Are you still up in the Valley?"

"No. I'm back here at the winery offices. So you're a private detective, huh?"

"Yeah," I said.

"I've never met a private eye before," she said. "How about getting together for lunch today?"

"Sure, all right. But I thought you didn't lik cops."

"I don't. You know The Boar's Head, on Vallejo?"

"I know it."

"One o'clock okay with you?"

"Fine."

"See you then, big man."

I replaced the handset. Well, I thought—and wondered why she wanted to have lunch with me. Because she was curious, as Leo was, why a private detective had been up at the winery to see Alex? Probably. But then again, maybe she had something else on her mind.

I locked up the office and went to find out.

5

The Boar's Head was a popular restaurant and tavern at Vallejo and Sansome, not far from the Embarcadero and the ugly elevated freeway that spoiled the view of the waterfront piers, the Ferry Building, the Bay beyond. The area used to be industrial and was dotted with old brick warehouses that, in recent years, had been converted into office buildings. One of those ex-warehouses, a block and a half away on Vallejo, housed the San Francisco offices of the Cappellani Winery.

The place was modeled after a British pub: black-beamed ceiling, heavy wood tables and chairs and booths; walls decorated with boar heads and dart boards and old English hunting prints. The bartenders and waiters all wore derby hats and dispensed Guinness stout and English beer and ale, along with thick meat and poultry sandwiches from a long chef's table up front.

Most of the lunch crowd had already gone by the time I came in at five of one, but it was still far from empty. I looked around for Shelly, did not see her; I did, however, notice two other people I knew—Logan Dockstetter and Philip Brand—sitting in a booth toward the rear and having what appeared to be an argument. I sat down in another booth diagonally across from them, where I could see the entrance. Neither of them noticed me. They were too wrapped up in whatever it was they were arguing about, Brand making angry gesticulations and Dockstetter stiff-backed and glaring.

The waiter appeared beside me, and I ordered a pint of Bass ale, and he went away again. Brand and Dockstetter were still going at each other across the aisleway, not making much effort to keep their voices down. Because of that, and because there was no one else carrying on a conversation in the immediate vicinity, I could hear most of what they were arguing about.

"I tell you, Logan," Brand was saying in his deep, precise voice, "we damned well *are* in trouble. I ought to know, for God's sake I'm the accountant."

"You're also a silly pessimist," Dockstetter said.

"You're the one who's silly. You won't admit what is staring you in the face. Sales are down, we've had complaints about the quality of our estate-bottled varietals, we've had a miserable harvest. And now God knows what more complications there might be with Alex."

"Alex? What happened to him last night has nothing to do with the winery."

"How do you know that? None of us knows *what* the attack on him has to do with." Brand made another waving gesture. "The point is, we're in trouble and the sooner we all admit it, the sooner something can be done about it."

"Such as what?"

"Such as getting rid of Paul Rosten and Jason Booker, to begin with. Rosten has turned into an incompetent winemaker; he's old-fashioned and ultra-conservative and he's gotten careless. I don't know why Mrs. Cappellani keeps him on, unless it's because he's been with the family for so long. Or because he's been sleeping with her all these years."

Dockstetter said something I didn't catch.

"Well, it wouldn't surprise me," Brand said. "And Booker—all *he's* interested in is getting next to Mrs. Cappellani himself. A disgusting man. You can almost feel the friction between him and Rosten, or at least anyone with perception can feel it."

Silence from Dockstetter.

Brand said, "And I still say we ought to increase our production of generic table wines . . ."

There was more, but it was all shoptalk that did not mean much to me. In the middle of it the waiter returned with my pint of ale.

I took a long draught, lowered the stein again, and with its bottom made interlocking circles of wetness on the table while I listened to Brand finish his diatribe over there.

Dockstetter said stiffly, "I've told you and told you, Philip, I don't agree with any of that. Mrs. Cappellani is an intelligent woman, she's done a marvelous job with the winery since that bastard husband of hers died. If you were right, she would have taken action herself long ago. Or Leo would have."

"Mrs. Cappellani is becoming less and less involved with internal matters every year. And Leo—and Alex too—is too busy with his private life to pay proper attention to what's going on."

"That's some way for an employee to talk."

"It's the only way for an employee who gives a damn to talk," Brand said. "If you'd accept the facts of the situation, we could go to Mrs. Cappellani and between us make her understand that changes have to be made before it's too late."

"I won't help you make unnecessary waves."

Brand stared at him with a mixture of exasperation and contempt. "No, of course you won't. Hear no evil, see no evil, speak no evil—that's your credo. You've got no backbone, Logan, none at all."

"I don't have to take that from you."

"No—you don't have to take *anything* from me."

"What is that supposed to mean?"

"What do you think it means?"

Brand slid out of the booth, got on his feet.

"Where are you going?"

"Away from you."

"Damn it, Philip . . ."

"Oh go diddle yourself," Brand said, and turned and stalked over to the entrance.

Dockstetter glared after him. In profile his face was white and so pinched now it looked deformed. He sat there rigidly for several seconds; then he got out of the booth in slow, measured movements, took a couple of bills from his wallet and put them on the table, and walked out after Brand. His back could not have been straighter or stiffer if he had had a steel rod strapped to his spine.

I watched him go, wondering if he was right about the status of the Cappellani Winery, or if Brand was. Well, in either case the

Cappellanis appeared to have more than their share of problems. Dissension in the ranks along with everything else.

I looked at my watch, and it was ten past one. So maybe Shelly had gotten tied up at the office, or maybe she was one of those people who are chronically late for appointments. Not that it mattered much, except that I could smell the aroma of barbecued meat coming from the chef's counter and it was making me pretty hungry.

Waiting, I sipped my ale and glanced around at the boar heads and the other wall decorations. Now that I was alone with nothing to occupy my attention, the place gave me a certain nostalgic feeling. Five years ago, when I had been in love with a woman named Erika Coates who worked in the financial district not far away, I had had lunch with her here on several occasions. Good, intimate lunches that seemed, in retrospect, to have been filled with warmth and laughter.

But it had not been quite that way. Erika had plenty of good qualities, but she was also an uncompromising, unyielding person: if you wanted to play with her, you had to play by her rules. Two of those rules were that I had to give up smoking for my own good, and that I had to give up my profession because it was shabby and pointless and I was living a lie by trying to emulate the detectives I read about in the pulps. She had been right about the first and wrong about the second, as I had finally proved to myself, but the combination of the two had built an unmendable rift between us.

It took me a while to get over her—and I suppose I never really *did* get over her, despite not seeing her once in those next five years. I might have gone on that way, plagued by vague ghosts, if it had not been for the things that happened this past summer and the changes they had brought about in me. But with all of that, I had decided at last to put away my pride and get in touch with her if I could. I did not believe there was anything left between us; what has been lost and buried in the passage of time can seldom be resurrected. And yet I felt I had to *know* for my own peace of mind.

I had no trouble locating her; she still worked for the same company, and she was still unmarried. At first she had not wanted to see me, but because it was my fiftieth birthday she had finally consented to have dinner. And it had turned out to be a strained evening, both of us reserved and uncomfortable. When I told her about the lesion on my lung, she was sympathetic but she could not resist an I-told-you-so. When I tried to explain about the changes in me, she said they were a step in the right direction but until I quit being a private eye I was still living in self-delusion. Uncompromising, unyielding—the same old Erika.

At the end of the evening I told her I would call her, but we both knew I would not and that we wouldn't see each other again. I did not know her and she did not know me; we no longer had anything at all in common.

I had no regrets about seeing her, though, because in doing so I had gotten rid of the vague ghosts and put my soul at ease. Still, sitting here now in The Boar's Head, with memories on the walls and memories playing across the screen of my mind, I felt just a little sad for what once was and for what might have been.

I finished my ale, looked again at my watch. One-twenty. I considered calling the winery office—and while I was considering the street door opened and Shelly came inside.

When I leaned out of the booth and waved at her, she saw me and then came over wearing a lopsided grin. "Sorry to be late," she said. "A couple of last-minute things to take care of."

"No problem," I said.

The waiter showed up as soon as she sat down, and we got our orders out of the way: two roast beef sandwiches, another Bass ale for me, a pint of Black-and-Tan—half Guinness and half lager —for her. After he drifted off, Shelly brushed a hand absently through her fine, short-cropped hair and looked at me in a frankly appraising way. She was dressed in a tailored three-piece wool suit and a blue silk blouse; the outfit, and some carefully applied makeup, made her look less hard-edged than she had last night. And even more attractive.

"So," she said. "Tell me what it's like to be a private eye."

I shrugged. "Like any other job. Interesting sometimes but mostly pretty dull."

"Which category does what you're doing for Alex fall into?"

"What makes you think I'm working for Alex?"

"Aren't you?"

"If I am, I'm not at liberty to discuss it."

"Top-secret stuff, huh?"

"Nope. Professional ethics."

"Uh-huh. Well, I'll bet it concerns Jason Booker."

"Why do you say that?"

"Because it's pretty obvious that Alex hates Booker and that he's afraid Booker will marry Rosa. It would be just like Alex to hire a private eye to get something on Jason, or beat up on him, or whatever else it is you do."

"I don't beat up on people," I said a little sharply.

Her gray-green eyes were amused. "No? How about me last night?"

"That was a different matter altogether."

"God, you're sensitive, aren't you?"

"A little, I guess. People always seem to have the wrong idea about the kind of work I do. I don't strong-arm people and I don't 'get things' on people. I operate strictly within the law."

"I stand corrected," she said. Her gaze had turned speculative, as it had a couple of times up at the winery; but she did not seem to be put off. "Okay?"

I smiled at her. "Okay."

Our sandwiches and drinks arrived, and we went to work on them. I said between mouthfuls, "If Alex hates Jason Booker, how does Leo feel about him?"

"Booker? The same, I gather. But Leo says Rosa has no intention of marrying anybody and she's too tough and too sharp to let Booker talk her into anything she doesn't want to do. Alex is the only one who's worried."

"What's your opinion of Booker?"

"He's a turd," she said.

"That bad?"

"At least. He tried to get me into bed with him not too long ago, at the winery; big macho come-on, as if there wasn't a woman in the world who could wait to screw him. I laughed in his face." The lopsided grin again. "He's never bothered me since."

"Nice guy, all right," I said.

"Yeah. You don't suppose he could be the one who clobbered Alex—and you—with that wine bottle?"

"It's possible, I guess."

"It wouldn't surprise me," Shelly said. "He's the type that's capable of doing anything to get what he wants." She paused. "If it was Booker, you know, he might try to go after Alex a second time."

"He might, yeah."

"So are you planning to stay on the scene?"

"I don't quite follow."

"Keep on working for Alex. Give him protection."

"We don't know that he needs protection. The man who hit him could still have been a sneak thief."

"That doesn't answer my question."

"I can't answer it," I said. "I haven't talked to Alex."

"Make you a bet that when you do, he'll want you around. He needs people to lean on, particularly in a crisis. He's not at all like his mother, or like Leo. Why do you think he'd hire a private eye in the first place, instead of working things out himself?"

"If he hired me."

"Sure, right."

"Anyhow," I said, "this whole business will probably be over before much longer. The Napa sheriff's people should see to that."

"But will they?" She laughed ironically. "I doubt it. They haven't found out a damned thing so far."

"You really are down on cops, aren't you?"

"You bet I am."

"Then how come the lunch with me?"

She gave me a long look over her stein of Black-and-Tan. "Two reasons," she said. "One is that I'm curious as hell about you and Alex and what happened last night. As if you hadn't already figured that out."

"Uh-huh," I said. "What's the other reason?"

"Chemistry," she said.

That gave me pause. "Pardon?"

"Oh come on, big man, don't play dumb. You know what I mean."

I knew what she meant, all right. I had been too tired and too battered to attach much significance to it at the time, but I remembered now the way she had looked at me inside the winery sales room, and later, just before I was ready to leave: the sort of looks a woman gives you when she's interested in what she sees.

So maybe I was interested too. She was a damned good-looking woman, and I do not know very many good-looking women who find me interesting—not at my age, and not with my shaggy looks and my overhanging belly. No great passion on either side, but you don't need great passion to begin a relationship.

Shelly said, "Mutual, right?"

"Mutual."

"Good. Now we can go on from there."

We went on from there. I told her a little about myself, and she reciprocated. She was from Florida, she said, and she had been married to a county sheriff whose idea of fun was to get drunk twice a week and rape her—not make love to her, forcibly rape her. She divorced him finally, knocked around Miami and Fort Lauderdale for a while, came to California a few months ago to visit a friend, decided to stay on, and got the job with the Cappellani Winery through another acquaintance who knew Leo. What she did there was handle marketing matters. She thought San Francisco was a good place to live, "except that there are too goddamn many fags here," but she would probably go back to Florida eventually because of the climate there.

It was a relaxed and casual conversation, without much intimacy—just two people getting to know each other a little better. When she said at three o'clock that she had to get back to the office I was sorry to have it end. I liked her, despite her narrow opinions on some matters; she was frank and open, and she did not seem to play games.

We left the Boar's Head together, and out on the street Shelly said, "Call me tonight or tomorrow night, big man. I'm in the book. On Beach Street in Marina."

"Count on it," I said.

We touched hands. Standing close to her that way, I found myself wondering what it would be like to go to bed with her. Typical male: get to know a woman and right away you think about getting laid.

The only thing was, there was a look in Shelly's eyes which might have meant she was wondering the same about me.

6

It was three forty-five by the time I got back to my office. I checked in with my answering service—no calls—and then finished the report on Jason Booker and wrote a letter accepting the Mystery Writers' invitation to speak at one of their meetings. At five o'clock I closed up for the day, stopped at a store on Van Ness to buy some groceries, and eventually drove up to my fog-bound flat on Pacific Heights.

The telephone started ringing as soon as I keyed open the door.

I had an armful of the groceries and a handful of my overnight bag and my house mail; I kicked the door shut, put the groceries down on the highboy along the inside wall, the bag and the mail down beside them, and clicked on the light switch so I could see my way through the bachelor's clutter of newspapers and magazines and clothing on the living room floor. I keep the phone in the bedroom and I hustled in there past the laminated wood bookshelves that contain my pulp collection, caught up the receiver on the fourth ring.

"Hello?"

"Good—you're in," a man's voice said. "Alex Cappellani."

I sat down on the rumpled bed. "How're you feeling, Mr. Cappellani?"

"Lousy. But not as bad as I'd feel if you hadn't showed up at the winery last night."

"When will you be able to leave the hospital?"

"I've already left it. Earlier this afternoon."

"But I heard you had a concussion--"

"Mild concussion. They wanted to keep me in there for observation, but I wasn't having any of that. I don't like hospitals."

I could appreciate that; but I did not say anything.

"Look," Alex said, "what is it you found out yesterday about Jason Booker?"

"You want me to give you the full report now?"

"Just the meat, that's enough."

"Okay," I said, and told him about Booker's marriage to Martha Towne, about the fifteen thousand dollars of her money that he had appropriated for private investments of his own.

"I knew it," Alex said grimly. He paused for a moment. "All right. Can you meet me in twenty minutes?"

"Twenty minutes? Aren't you calling from the winery?"

"No. I just got into the city, I'm in a service station down on Lombard."

Well, Christ, I thought. Leo Cappellani had said Alex was headstrong and sometimes exhibited a lack of good judgment; driving seventy-five miles with a concussion and a bad scalp wound was a prime example of both.

I said, "Why do you want me to meet you?"

"Because I'm going to have a showdown with Booker and I want somebody there. I don't trust him and I don't trust myself."

I frowned. And Shelly had said he always needed somebody to lean on in a crisis: here he was wanting to lean on me, all right. "Why don't you trust him, Mr. Cappellani?"

"For all I know he's the son of a bitch who hit me last night, that's why. Maybe he found out somehow that I'd hired you to check into his background."

"That's not much of a reason for attempted murder."

"Not for you and me, maybe. But how do we know how a bastard like Booker thinks? He stands to gain access to a lot of money if he's able to convince Rosa to marry him. The kind of guy you proved him to be, if he realized how much of a threat I am he might have figured his only chance was to get rid of me."

You're going off half cocked, I thought. But I said, "You wouldn't be planning to accuse him, would you?"

"That depends. Probably not; I don't have any proof. But I damned well do want the satisfaction of telling him to his face what I know about him and what I think of him."

"That might not be a good idea," I said. "Wouldn't it be better if you talked to your mother first—?"

"I'll talk to my mother later," he said stubbornly. "Listen, you probably saved my life last night and I'm damned grateful—but I'm not after advice from you. All I want is for you to back me up when I see Booker."

I hesitated. Did I want to get mixed up in an emotional and potentially volatile scene between Alex and Jason Booker? The answer was no. But then again, if I refused and he saw Booker alone, there was no telling what might happen. Hell, Booker *could* be the one who had taken that wine bottle to Alex in the winery office . . .

He said, misinterpreting my silence, "I'll pay you for your time, don't worry about that."

"I wasn't worrying about it," I said. "I wasn't even thinking about it."

"Okay—sorry. Will you meet me?"

"Yeah, I'll meet you. Where's Booker?"

"At our town house, up on Russian Hill. He told my mother he had something to do down here and she gave him permission to spend the night at the house."

"Anybody else there? Servants?"

"No."

"What's the address?"

"Chestnut and Larkin." He gave me the number.

"I'll see you out front, then. We'll go in together."

"Right. Twenty minutes?"

"As soon as I can get there."

We rang off, and I sighed a little and went into the bathroom and took four aspirin for my lingering headache. Then I got the groceries and carried them into the kitchen, talked myself out of taking time to have a beer and look through my house mail, and left the flat.

When I got to my car a block away—parking on Pacific Heights is always a hassle—I found that in the half-hour since I had left it somebody had slammed into the rear end. There was a piece gone out of the left taillight and a big dent in the trunk lid. I scowled at the damage, went finally around to the front. And saw with amazement that there was a note on the windshield, under the wiper blade. I took it out and looked at it, and the amazement went away. Uh-huh, I thought.

What the note said was, "Whoops, sorry about that."

The house on the corner of Chestnut and Larkin was a big white neo-colonial set a little way back from the sidewalks behind shrubbery and a five-foot brick-and-wrought-iron fence. There was a driveway on the downhill Larkin side, leading to an attached garage, and in the driveway was the dusty station wagon that Jason Booker had been driving last night. Through a shifting curtain of fog, I could see blurred light beneath the closed garage door and in one of the side windows; the rest of the house appeared dark.

I found a parking spot near the driveway. On a clear day you would have some view from up there: the broad sweep of the Bay, the Golden Gate Bridge, Alcatraz and Angel islands, the Marin hills, part of the East Bay. Which was the main reason why Russian Hill was one of San Francisco's moneyed neighborhoods; panoramic views do not come cheap. But tonight, about all you could make out down below were the vague misty lights that marked Fisherman's Wharf and Aquatic Park and the Presidio.

There were other cars parked in the area, but all of them were dark and nobody got out of any of them to approach me. So I stepped out myself after a moment, into the icy wind and the wet brackish-smelling fog, and walked up to Chestnut and down the sidewalk in front of the Cappellani house. More cars parked there, and all of them deserted too.

Where was Alex? It had been a good thirty minutes since he called me, and he had said he was in a service station on Lombard Street; it should not have taken him much more than ten minutes —fifteen, maximum—to get from there to Russian Hill. Unless he had stopped somewhere on the way, for some reason.

I came back to the corner and stood next to a lamppost there, hunching my shoulders against the wind. A pair of headlights appeared behind me, but they drifted on past, went down to where Larkin hooks into Francisco, and disappeared. Out on the Bay, a foghorn echoed in its mournful way; and over on Hyde, a cable car bell clanged tinnily. Otherwise the night held a kind of eerie stillness, the way it does in one of San Francisco's heavy blanketing fogs.

Five minutes went by without another car showing up, without any sign of life on the streets. Then there were two sets of fuzzy headlights on Chestnut and another set on Larkin, each of which vanished again without slowing as they passed me. I was getting damned cold, standing there, and not a little irritated. Where the hell *was* he?

It occurred to me then that maybe he was already here. I did not know what kind of car he was driving; it could be any one of those parked nearby. And in spite of our agreement he could have gone into the house without waiting for me to show up. But was he that impulsive, that foolish? It would have defeated the whole purpose of getting me up here.

I gave it another two minutes. Nothing, no other car. All right, damn it, I thought—and I went over to the front gate, through it and up the front walk to the house's pillared entranceway. There was a doorbell button set into a recessed niche beside the door, and I pushed that and heard the distant peal of chimes inside. But I did not hear anything else in there: no one came to open the door.

I began to feel uneasy, as I had up at the winery cellar—an intimation that something was wrong. Booker was supposed to be here, *should* be here; that was unmistakably his station wagon over in the driveway, and there were those lights showing in the garage and in the side window. But if he was here, why hadn't he answered the door chimes? And where was Alex, if not inside the house?

Maybe the two of them went off in Alex's car, I thought. Only that did not make much sense. There didn't seem to be any reason for either of them to have wanted to do that; and Alex couldn't have gotten here more than fifteen minutes before me, which was little enough time for him or Booker to decide to go for a ride.

I pressed the doorbell button again, listened to more chimes echo and then fade into unbroken silence. On impulse I reached down and tried the doorknob. Locked.

The uneasiness took me away from the door, around the corner, and down to the driveway. A car came uphill through the fog, and I turned to watch it whisper past; it slowed at the top of the hill, but then it continued along Larkin and its taillights were swallowed by the mist. I went into the driveway, stopped beside the station wagon and glanced inside. It was empty. When I put my hand on the hood the metal turned out to be cold: it had been some time since the car was last driven.

I stepped off into the shrubbery and went up to the lighted window. Past thin curtains I could see that the room there was a study, with a desk and some leather chairs and a leather sofa and wall shelves holding books and military-type curios. Like the car, it was empty—but draped over the sofa was a man's shearling coat, and on the desk was a man's tweed hat.

Turning, I moved back to the driveway, walked along it to the closed garage door. No handle on its surface, which meant that it was probably remote-controlled. To the left, I saw then, away from the house, was a narrow concrete walk that led between a wooden property fence and the side wall of the garage. I went over there, onto the walk. It ended three-quarters of the way back at a raised wooden platform on which were two metal garbage cans; but halfway along was a side door set into the garage wall.

The door was unlatched: a tiny strip of light shone between its edge and the jamb.

I came to a standstill, and there was a clenching sensation in my stomach. Something wrong here, all right—the same kind of something, maybe, that had been wrong at the winery. I listened again, tensely. Silence, except for the wind rustling the shrubbery.

Get it over with, I thought. And went up to the door, hesitated again, and then put my palm flat against the panel and shoved it wide.

Worse than last night, much worse.

Because the first thing I saw was the dead man lying on his side on the concrete floor.

I said "Jesus" under my breath, went in there a couple of paces. He was sprawled out in front of an open door into the house, with one arm extended beyond his head. In that hand was a .32 caliber blued-steel automatic. But he had not been shot; the side of his head had been brutally caved in.

Jason Booker.

To one side of him was what looked to be a homemade black jack—a man's sock filled with something like sand or buckshot—and it was matted with blood and hair: the murder weapon. Spatters and ribbons of blood stained Booker's face, the back of his sports shirt, the floor around him. It had congealed, but still glistened wetly; he could not have been dead much more than half an hour.

Alex, I thought. Alex?

I started to take another step toward the body, stopped abruptly when I realized there was still more blood, a small puddle of it, down near my right shoe. Booker's too? But the puddle was a good twenty feet from where he lay. I stared at the gun in his hand, and sniffed the air, and thought I could smell the faint lingering odor of cordite. Had Booker managed to shoot his assailant? before he died, or before a final death blow was struck?

There were plenty of signs of a struggle. Firewood had been knocked from a stack along the wall to the left of the open house door, tools had been dislodged and scattered from a workbench to the right of the door. Half a dozen coins were strewn among the dislodged tools: two nickels, two dimes, a quarter and a penny. There were also a matchbook and a nearly empty package of Camels—and a piece of paper that looked as if it had been part of a 5×7 notepad, center-folded and resting tented on the fold.

I could make out typeprint on the paper, and I detoured around the puddle of drying blood and went over to it and sat on my haunches. Without touching the paper, I leaned down to look at the words. They were in elite type, and they spelled out the address of this house. That was all, except for a single word in capital letters at the bottom, like a signature, that meant nothing to me at all.

The word was *Twospot*.

I straightened up, frowning. You could put together some of what had happened here, but there were other things that did not seem to add up. If Alex had murdered Booker, what was the sense in the piece of notepaper? He would have had no conceivable reason for carrying around the address of his own family's house. It could belong to Booker, but the same thing applied: he would not have needed an oddly signed paper to tell him where the house was situated.

But if Alex was not the murderer, then why had Booker been killed? And by whom? And why hadn't Alex kept his rendezvous with me?

You're wasting time, I told myself. Get the police out here, leave the speculating to them. I went to the open house door, entered a small storage pantry, passed through it into a central hallway. The house was deeply hushed, contained an almost palpable aura of emptiness. Light from the study I had seen from outside spilled into the hall, creating pockets of heavy shadow; I located a wall switch, flicked it with the back of my hand to keep from smearing any fingerprints that might be on it, and turned into the study.

A telephone sat on one corner of the desk. I took out my hand-kerchief, wrapped it around my hand. Then I lifted the receiver and dialed the number of the Hall of Justice.

When the switchboard operator came on I asked him if Lieu-tenant Eberhardt was on duty; Eberhardt was a close friend of mine, had been ever since we had gone through the Police Acad-emy together after World War II. But he said no, Eb was gone for the day—did I want to talk to anyone else? I knew several other detectives, one of whom was a Homicide Lieutenant and a casual acquaintance I had played poker with on a number of occasions. I asked if he was on night watch, and the operator said he was and transferred the call.

An unfamiliar voice said, "Homicide, Canelli speaking. Can I help you?"

"Yeah," I said. "Let me talk to Frank Hastings."

PART TWO

The Police Lieutenant

7

I watched Canelli bring my cruiser down the spiral parking ramp. The car bounced to a jerky stop at the broad yellow line at the bottom of the ramp—then stalled. Through the windshield, I could see Canelli's lips moving as he restarted the car. To myself, I smiled. As long as I'd known him, Canelli had been on the losing side of a long, grueling battle with machines. Anything mechanical defeated him. A typewriter ribbon or a cassette cartridge left him helplessly muttering. Cheerfully, he volunteered to get coffee from the machine—but often returned to the squadroom apologetically carrying cocoa, or tea, or soup. Yet, before he'd wandered into police work, he'd been a skilled electrician. Electricity, he said, made sense.

Finally the car stoppd at the curb in front of me, and the door swung open.

"I think this car needs a tune-up, Lieutenant," he said earnestly.

Not replying, I closed the door, fastened my seat belt and motioned for him to get under way. "Go to Van Ness," I said, "and turn right."

"Yessir."

Concentrating on his driving, Canelli maneuvered the car out of the garage and onto Sixth Street. The night was cold and damp;

the fog was so thick the pavement glistened. On Folsom Street, the garish glow of neon signs was softened to misty pastels. As Canelli switched on the windshield wipers he asked, "Where're we going?"

"Chestnut and Larkin. The corner."

"Hey, that's a pretty fancy part of town. One time when I was an electrician, I worked in a house on that block that had an observatory on top of it. Honest to God."

"An observatory?"

"Right. No fooling. It had a telescope that I bet was ten feet long, at least. I was working on the servo system, that operated the overhead doors. They were half clamshells, I remember, just like the big observatories. It was unbelievable. Except that the servos shorted out when it rained."

I didn't reply, but instead let my head fall back against the seat. I was tired and sleepy. At ten o'clock last night, Ann had called. She'd been deeply disturbed, almost in tears. She'd just had an unexpected call from her ex-husband, a society psychiatrist named Victor Haywood. The purpose of the call had been a demand that she "do something" about their younger son's grades. In Haywood's terms, the boy was a "low achiever." Ann, a fourth-grade teacher, had protested. Billy was bright and happy: an imaginative, lively boy. A bitter argument had flared, during which Haywood had superciliously questioned Ann's choice of a "bed partner." Translation: Haywood thought I was a low achiever, too. Ann had hung up on him—and then called me. We'd finished talking at midnight. At 2 A.M. I was still awake—still angrily brooding.

Beside me, I heard Canelli elaborately clearing his throat. He couldn't tolerate long silences. He couldn't tolerate curiosity, either. So he began to probe:

"The guy that called it in—" Canelli hesitated. "I had the feeling that he knows you."

"He does. We've played poker a few times."

"Is he on the force?"

"He used to be. Now he's private detective. He's an old friend of Lieutenant Eberhardt's. They served together on General Works."

"As long as I been on the force," Canelli said, "I never knew a private detective. Not personally, I mean. But whenever I run across one in the line of duty, so to speak, I gotta say that they give me the creeps, sometimes. I mean, there's this one guy I met that seems to make his living snatching kids from one parent to give to another parent. And he seemed to be proud of what he was doing. And he also seemed to be getting rich from it, too. He was driving a Mercedes, I remember. And he even said he had an airplane, too." Canelli shook his head. "I couldn't get over it."

I pointed ahead. "Van Ness is next. You'd better get in the right lane."

"Oh. Right." Canelli glanced hurriedly over his shoulder and abruptly jerked the steering wheel to the right. His broad, swarthy face furrowed as a horn blared from behind.

"Those sportscars," he muttered. "They're always coming up on you from out of nowhere."

I often wondered why I'd chosen Canelli as my driver—or, for that matter, why I'd picked him for my squad. At age twenty-eight, at a suety two hundred thirty, Canelli looked and acted more like an overweight fry cook than a homicide detective. His brown eyes were innocent. His normal expression was either puzzled or beguiled, depending on the problem. His only professional asset was a perpetual run of incredible good luck. If the entire squad spent days sifting through garbage for a murder gun, Canelli would accidentally stumble over the weapon lying under a rosebush. His luck protected him behind the wheel, too. In hot pursuit, Canelli drove with a kind of inspired lunacy—all the while muttering to himself. Once, mopping my face at the end of a chase, I'd told Canelli that he reminded me of W. C. Fields in *The Bank Dick*. Canelli's large brown eyes had reproached me for days. He was the only detective I'd ever known who could get his feelings hurt.

"If he's a friend of Lieutenant Eberhardt's, I suppose he's all right," Canelli ventured. He was probing again.

I shrugged. "He seems all right to me. He's one of these people who doesn't talk unless he's got something to say. And, if it'll reassure you, I don't think he's got much money."

"That probably means he's honest."

"It probably does."

My poker-playing friend—they called him Bill—was standing just inside an elaborate wrought-iron gate.

"Hello, Frank. Good to see you."

I smiled and offered my hand. "Good to see you, too."

I introduced him to Canelli and turned to look at the house. It was an impressive sight: a two story neo-colonial with a pillared portico, Williamsburg-style windows and a gabled roof. The property was surrounded by an ornate iron fence supported by traditional brick pillars. The grounds around the house were meticulously landscaped. Situated on some of the most desirable real estate in San Francisco, the property could easily be worth a quarter of a million dollars. Seen shrouded in the fog that was blowing up Russian Hill from the Bay below, the house and grounds seemed strangely isolated, revealing nothing.

I turned to Canelli. "You go inside and secure the premises. Then make the calls. When you call, make sure you get the best personnel available, even if they come from home. I want Parrington from the lab and Walton from the coroner's office—plus enough assistants to get the job done. I'll call the D.A. myself, as soon as I get the details straight."

"Yessir." Canelli turned to Bill. "Which phone did you use?"

"The one in the study. The front door's locked, so you'll have to go in through the service door to the garage. It's on the downhill side. That door was ajar when I came. So that's the way I left it."

"Once you've made the calls," I said to Canelli, "you may as well open the front door. Leave it wide open, and tag it in that position for the lab." I hesitated a moment, surveying the large corner lot, with only the five-foot iron fence for protection against the curious. "Better call for three black and white units," I added. "At least."

"Right." Canelli lumbered down the sloping sidewalk toward the driveway.

I turned to Bill. "Before the troops get here, I'd like you to give me everything you've got that's relevant. We can talk there—" I gestured to the porch, where we would be sheltered from the fog. As I preceded the private detective, he carefully closed the gate behind us, using a handkerchief.

For the next few minutes he talked and I listened. Midway through the report Canelli opened the front door, and I gestured for him to join us.

Bill's report was a good, solid one: concise but not too sketchy, perceptive but not too speculative. When he finished, I regretfully shook my head as I looked him straight in the eye.

"At this point," I said, "the man we want to question most is your client. He's the one who's missing—and probably running. I guess that's obvious."

His only reply was a brief, rueful smile. But the expression on his squared-off face was easily readable. He was a serious, conscientious man—one who cared what happened to his clients. He hated the idea of his client in custody. But he wouldn't ask me for a break. He was too proud.

As two black and white cars pulled up in front of the house, Canelli asked the private detective whether he'd ever served in Homicide. The rueful smile returned.

"I was never asked," he replied.

I faced the two of them. To Canelli I said, "I want you to take him into a bedroom, or somewhere, and make notes on everything he'll tell you—names, times, addresses, everything. It'll be part of your report. I don't have any of his information on paper. So it's your responsibility. Clear?"

Canelli nodded. "That's clear."

"If you want," Bill said, "I'll send you a written report."

I nodded. "Fine. Thanks. But I still need Canelli's."

We shook hands, and I watched the two big men turn and walk into the house together. Their movements were as different as their personalities. Despite his size, Canelli's gait was loose and ambling. Bill's movments were solid and decisive. Canelli was still deciding who he was and where he was going. The older man already knew.

I turned to the four uniformed men who had assembled behind me on the walk, waiting for orders. I recognized a sergeant, and made him responsible for securing the perimeter of the property. As we talked, a third black and white car drew up at the curb. Across the street, a press car was parking illegally. Up and down the block, window drapes were drawn aside; front doors were opening. In the cold, fog-smudged darkness, shirtsleeved people were materializing: silent, disembodied, two-dimensional figures. Whenever someone died, wherever the place, the same silent shapes appeared. The shades, someone had called them. From Greek tragedy.

"Don't let anyone in except through the front door," I ordered, still speaking to the sergeant. "You'll be on the front door. Clear?"

"Yessir."

I nodded, then walked through the door and into a small entryway. I was facing a central staircase that curved gracefully as it swept up to the second floor. From above, I could hear voices. Canelli was taking his notes.

The first floor was arranged around a large hallway. Through an ornate archway to my left I saw a large formal living room. The room looked as if it waited for a *House & Garden* photographer, not for its owners. Each piece of furniture gleamed; each book was perfectly aligned on its shelf. Magazines were arranged on the coffee table in a symmetrical fan. I looked carefully at every sofa and chair. All of the cushions were plump, unmarked.

I turned to an open door that led into a small study, where I saw a tweed hat resting on one corner of an elaborately carved desk. An expensive shearling coat was thrown carelessly across a leather couch. If Jason Booker had parked in the driveway and entered the house through the front door, as Bill had surmised, then Booker must have come directly into this room. Because the clothing, Bill said, almost certainly belonged to the victim.

Careful where I walked, I entered the study and stood in the center of the room. Like the living room, the study was a stereotype: an expensive decorator's idea of how a study should look. Everything was in its calculated place. Behind glass doors, floor-to-ceiling bookcases held leather-bound books that probably hadn't been read for years—if ever. Except for the tweed hat, nothing on the desk was disturbed; a calendar, a desk pen, a notepad and a phone were arranged with thoughtful symmetry. Still standing in one spot, I leaned forward to look at the tooled leather calendar. There were no notes, no dates circled. Nothing.

I stepped to the sofa and carefully patted down the shearling coat's big patch pockets. I couldn't feel anything: no weapons, no billfold, nothing bulky. After the photographers had finished, I would go through the pockets.

I turned next to a big leather armchair. This was where he'd sat; the heavy leather clearly retained an impression of a body. A side table was placed beside the chair. A large crystal ashtray rested in the exact center of the table.

In the ashtray I saw three filter-tip Winston cigarette butts, smoked almost to the nub. Statistically, the average cigarette represented approximately thirty minutes of "presence," assuming the subject was an average smoker and was under moderate strain. If the statistics were right, Booker had been on the premises at least an hour and a half before the murder.

Waiting for his murderer—someone known to him, perhaps.

Alex Cappellani?

I made a slow, careful circuit of the room, but saw nothing else. Stretching out full-length on an Oriental rug, I looked under the desk, the sofa, the big leather chair. Nothing. I got to my feet and re-entered the central hallway. Eberhardt's friend had told me what to do next. A polished walnut door, half open, led to small storage pantry. I stopped in front of the door, turned, looked back at the study.

Was this the way he'd come?

How long ago?

In response to what cue—what ominous sound—what tremor of fear?

I slipped through the doorway and stood in the darkened pantry. The pantry's second door was open wide, and through it I saw garden tools hanging on a garage wall. For the first time, I caught the odor of death: drying blood mingled with the stench of excrement.

I drew a deep breath and stepped into the garage.

The murder scene was precisely as Bill had described it. Point by point, I recalled the private the detective's theory. He'd speculated that Booker could have been in the study when he'd heard a noise in the garage. He could have left the lighted study and entered the darkened hall. Then Booker could have crept through the storage pantry and pushed open the door leading into the garage. With a gun in his hand, he could have cautiously entered the garage and switched on the overhead light. Standing where I stood now, he could have been struck by an assailant who'd crouched down behind a shoulder-high stack of oak firewood piled close beside the door.

Why?

Had Booker been an intended murder victim?

Had Cappellani made an appointment with him for six-thirty—then arrived earlier, surreptitiously coming through the garage, instead of the front door?

Or had Booker surprised a burglar—and died by accident, not design?

The facts seemed to fit the latter theory best. If Alex Cappellani had planned to murder Booker, he wouldn't have called a private detective to witness the crime.

Three strides took me to the body. This would be my last time alone with him—my last chance to touch him with my imagination, and try to learn the secret of his death. I squatted beside the body—and found myself staring straight into Booker's dead eyes.

He'd been a handsome man. The gray in his hair and the coarsening texture of his skin put his age in the early forties, but a leanness of cheek and jaw gave the face a younger look, and made an intriguing study of opposites. Even with lips distended in death's last agony, the mouth was well shaped. The chin was cleft. The nose was straight. It was the face of a gracefully aging poet.

He was wearing an expensive silk sports shirt, checkered slacks that were probably pure wool and Wellington boots that could have cost a hundred dollars. He was lying on his right side, with his arm draped languidly over his torso at the waist. His right arm was extended above his head, pointing toward the service door set in the opposite wall. In his right hand he held a small blue-steel automatic. Leaning forward, I sniffed the barrel. The gun had been fired.

A package of king-size cigarettes was tucked in the pocket of the silk sports shirt. I pushed up the package from the bottom until I could read the label: Winston.

Blood matted his hair and streaked the shirt. He's bled so much that blood was pooled beneath the handsome head. The blood was already coagulated. The private detective had been right: Booker had probably been dead for about an hour.

Still squatting, I minutely scanned the concrete floor of the garage. A blue sock filled with sand lay about a foot from the automatic. The sock was saturated with blood. Judging by the position of the firewood that had been tumbled to the floor, and by the hand tools that had apparently been swept from the top of a nearby workbench, there'd been a struggle that had started the moment Booker stepped into the garage. At least one shot had been fired. The assailant had escaped, probably through one of the two garage doors.

I took a moment to verify that the victim's wallet was in his hip pocket. The pocket was buttoned; the wallet apparently hadn't been touched. I stood up and began pacing across the cement toward the open service door. Carefully, I examined the scattering of matches, coins, the package of Camels and the cryptic "Twospot" note—all described by Bill. The items made a random pattern on the floor between the murder weapon and the door.

If Booker smoked Winstons, the murderer must have smoked Camels.

And, if the Camels belonged to the murderer, his prints could be on the cellophane wrapper of the cigarette package.

Still pacing, I saw the small circle of blood that stained the concrete just inside the service door.

Logically, it was the murder's blood.

As I was about to go through the service door, I heard someone call my name. Turning, I saw Parrington, from the police lab, and Walton, from the coroner's office. Both men stood in the doorway of the storage pantry, waiting for permission to enter the area. Each man carried a satchel. I told them to stay where they were, and asked Parrington for a piece of chalk. I marked off a "safe" corridor that led to the rear of the garage. Walking between the chalk lines, the two men followed me to a six-foot circle that I chalked on the oil-stained concrete. As we assembled inside the circle, a police photographer ventured into the open doorway. I waited for hum to join us before I explained to the three men what I expected from them.

"Especially," I finished, "there are three things I want you to do. First—" I pointed toward the service door. "I want that blood typed. It might not be Booker's. Second—" I pointed to the package of Camels, then turned to the photographer. "I want to make sure those cigarettes show up clearly in the pictures. I think they might've belonged to the suspect. And also—" I turned to the lab man. "Also, I want that cigarette pack fingerprinted by the best man available. Which means you. Clear?"

Parrington was young and eager. He wasn't able to surpress a smile at the cryptic compliment. Perhaps to conceal the smile, he solemnly nodded.

"That's clear," he answered. "What's the third thing?"

"The third thing is the bullets. I want every square inch of this place searched for expended bullets." I pointed to the automatic. "That gun's been fired. I want to know where the bullets are."

"One of them might be inside the murderer," the coroner's man said laconically. "That's what you think, isn't it?"

I nodded. "That's what I think." I edged past them and walked between the parallel chalk lines to the door. Then I turned back. "When you're ready to move the body, let me know. I'll be in the hallway, probably. Don't hurry, though. I requested you men for this job because I want it done right. The reason I want it done right is obvious." I pointed to the dead man. "We've got a victim who wore hundred-dollar shoes and who was a good friend of the woman who owns this house. And the woman who owns this house is a very important person—as I'm sure you'll be reading in tomorrow's papers." I looked at each man in turn. "Clear?"

They nodded.

8

I was yawning as I unlocked my office door the next morning.
Canelli and I had arrived at the murder scene about seven-fifteen
the previous evening. The technicians hadn't arrived until quarter
to eight, and hadn't finished the first phase of their investigations
until almost nine. They were still on the premises when the second
wave arrived: the D. A.'s man, the light crews and the additional
lab men who would search inch by inch for evidence. At the same
time, three men from my own squad arrived, called from their
homes. Their responsibility was the interrogation of witnesses. I
put them under Canelli's command while I performed the on-site
investigation's final ritual. Before witnesses, I moved the body and
searched his pockets. I found sixty-three dollars in cash inside his
wallet, together with the usual credit cards and identification. He'd
carried his wallet in his hip pocket. In another pocket I found less
than a dollar in loose change and a Swiss Army knife. A third
pocket yielded a key ring and ten .32 caliber cartridges. None of
the keys fitted any of the locks in the Cappellani house or garage.
However, when I searched the victim's shearling coat, still in the
study, I found a separate key to the front door. At about ten P.M.
I told the D. A.'s man that, based on my tentative appraisal of the
physical evidence, I'd concluded that Booker had arrived on the

premises at about four-thirty, driving his own car. He'd probably been alone. Using a key, he'd entered the house through the front door. He'd bolted the door behind him and gone directly to the study, where he'd possibly waited for an hour and a half. At about six, he may have heard someone entering the garage through the service door. Since we'd found no jimmy marks, we assumed that the intruder's entrance had been effected by a key—unless he'd come through the overhead garage door, using an electronic door opener.

The assistant D. A. had been satisfied—and anxious to return to a Friday-night party. My next problem was the reporters: one each from San Francisco's two daily papers, and two TV reporters. I made them wait until the body had been taken away, then allowed them to photograph the scene of the crime. An informal press conference had taken three-quarters of an hour. By that time, additional information had been developed. One neighbor thought she heard a shot "sometime during the six o'clock news." At about the same time, a teenage boy had seen a man run from the garage and get into a compact car. At the place where the teenager said the car was parked, we'd found the blood. Because of the fog and the gathering darkness, the boy hadn't gotten a license number.

I'd stayed on the scene until eleven-thirty, then left Canelli in charge. His responsibility hadn't ended until everyone in the neighborhood had been interrogated and every foot of the house and grounds searched.

Thursday night, thinking about Ann, I'd gotten less than five hours' sleep. Last night, thinking about the Booker murder, I hadn't done much better.

Now, at eight-thirty Saturday morning, I dialed Parrington, in the lab. My muscles ached with fatigue. My eyes felt hot and dry.

"Do you have anything?" I asked.

"Yessir," he answered promptly. "I don't have it written up yet. But I can tell you about it."

"Fine."

"Everything we found more or less confirms what you thought, Lieutenant. The blood inside the garage was two different types, for instance. And the blood beside the service door matched the blood on the sidewalk. We got some real good prints off that cigarette package, too—just like you thought. I calibrated the prints and put them into the computer about an hour ago. With luck, Identification could have something for you before too long."

"Good."

"I also found some clothing fibers caught under the victim's fingernails. The fabric was brown polyester, and it didn't match anything the victim was wearing or anything in the house. Which makes me think that he ripped open one of his attacker's pockets. That would account for the stuff spilled on the floor—all of which, incidentally, had latent prints that matched the prints on the cigarette wrapper."

"Did that 'Twospot' note have the same prints too?"

"Yessir."

"What about the gun and bullets? Anything conclusive?"

"It's a Beretta .32 caliber. I just called Sacramento for an ownership printout on it, but I haven't heard anything yet. The victim's prints were on the gun, but no other prints. They were on the bullets, too. If the magazine was fully loaded, and there wasn't a cartridge in the chamber, then he fired two shots. Which also adds up, assuming he shot his attacker. We found one bullet in the wall of the garage."

At that moment, I heard a quick double knock on my office door. I knew that knock. It was Pete Friedman, my senior co-lieutenant. I called for Friedman to come in, and thanked Parrington for his work. Either he'd been up most of the night, or he'd started working at six-thirty this morning. Or both.

I watched Friedman enter my office and sink down into my visitor's chair with his customary grateful sigh. It was Friedman's long-standing contention that my visitor's chair was the only one in the Department that could comfortably accommodate his considerable bulk. Therefore, according to Friedman, it was only in my visitor's chair that he could properly formulate the ideas we needed to solve the city's homicides.

"Even for a Monday-through-Friday day," Friedman said, "you're up early. Not to mention that it's a Saturday."

"You're up early, too."

Ruefully, he nodded. "I'm up early because, about midnight, I got a call from his eminence Chief Dwyer."

"What about?"

"About taking over security for Castro's visit, if you can believe it. Which I couldn't—especially at midnight. And especially when

Dwyer told me that Castro's coming to town the day after tomorrow. Christ, I thought it was a *week* from Monday."

"What happened to Captain Duncan? I thought he was in charge of security."

Friedman sighed, at the same time unwrapping a cigar and rummaging through his pockets for a match. "Captain Duncan had a gall bladder attack. He'll be all right. But not in time to throw himself between Fidel and an assassin's bullet."

Sympathetically shaking my head, I pushed my ashtray across the desk toward Friedman. His cigar ash almost never found the ashtray, but I continued to hope.

"What's this Booker thing?" Friedman asked. "Give me the rundown. Not that I'll be able to help until after Monday."

It took almost fifteen minutes to describe the case, during which time Friedman complacently smoked his cigar—spilling ashes at random on the floor, my desk and his vest. While I talked, he regarded me with his typically lazy-lidded stare. Occasionally he grunted, signifying either surprise or puzzlement—or both. When I finished, he sat silently for a moment, thoughtfully regarding the tip of his cigar. Finally:

"That 'Twospot' note is a nice touch," he said dryly. "A little theatrical, maybe but still nice. It suggests some sinister presence. A mastermind, maybe. Or maybe an inspired red herring." He nodded approvingly. "Either way, I like it."

"I thought you would."

"I'm also intrigued by the sock-and-sand weapon," he continued. "To me, that smacks of professionalism—or, at the very least, premeditation."

"Right."

"Also," Friedman said, "the sock and the sand might smack of conspiracy *not* to commit murder, but merely to stun. Ever think of that?"

"To be honest," I answered, "I haven't got around to theorizing. I'm still trying to put the pieces together."

Friedman nodded ponderous approval. Then, speaking slowly and thoughtfully, he said, "There's something about the whole situation that doesn't add up."

"How do you mean?"

"I mean that Thursday night Alex gets his skull cracked. The next night, Jason Booker gets *his* skull cracked—fatally. Why? What's the connection?"

I shrugged. "Apparently Alex suspected that Booker was running some kind of a con on his mother. But maybe Booker was trying more than just a con. Maybe he was involved in something really heavy. And maybe Booker thought Alex knew more than he really knew. So Booker tried to kill Alex. Don't forget that Bill didn't actually see Alex's assailant, up at the winery. It could have been Booker."

Friedman nodded judiciously. "That much, I can buy. But I don't buy the part about how maybe Alex talks his way out of the hospital and comes down to the city and asks a private eye to meet him at the site of Booker's proposed murder—which happens to be the family home away from home. It just doesn't figure. It also doesn't figure that Alex would need a note reminding him of the address of his family's town house."

"Then why did Alex run?"

Friedman spread his hands. "Maybe he didn't run, ever consider that? Maybe he was killed too. And hauled away."

"Who hauled him away?"

"How should I know? It's your case. I'm just trying to stretch your mind."

"Our witness didn't see anyone hauled away."

"I shouldn't have to tell you," he said, "that single witnesses are about as reliable as weather reports. Until you've got two witnesses who saw the same thing at the same time, you don't have crap."

"Well, there's one way to tell whether Alex was shot in that garage." I pulled my notepad toward me and wrote "Alex's blood type?" on the top sheet. At that moment, my phone rang.

"This is Fenster, Lieutenant Hastings. Identification."

From his voice, I knew that he had a positive make for me. I turned to the notepad's second sheet. "What've you got, Fenster?"

"It's the prints on that cigarette wrapper. Relating to the Booker homicide."

"Yes."

"They're listed as identifying one Malcolm Howard, of this city."

"Did you pull his jacket"

"Yessir."

"Give me the rundown."

"Caucasian male. Age thirty-four. Last known address, 469

Eddy Street, apartment 670. Previous convictions—" He paused. "Do you want them all, Lieutenant?"

"Yes."

"1961, grand theft auto, this city. Suspended sentence. 1964, receiving stolen goods. Sentenced five to fifteen years. Served— let's see, about four years, I guess. Maybe a little less. Released on parole. In 1968, he was indicated for possession of a firearm and for attmpted murder. Tried, and acquitted. In 1970, in Florida, he was indicated for illegal possession of machine guns and possession of illegal explosive devices. Gun-running, in other words. Tried, and convicted. That's all his indictments and convictions."

"How long has he been back in San Francisco?"

"About a year. He was arrested six months ago in a sweep of gay bars, out on Castro Street. He wasn't booked. He's a homosexual, I guess."

"Are there any current intelligence reports on him?"

"Yessir—" I heard papers rattling. Then: "He's apparently trying to get into pornography. Male pornography. He bought a rundown movie house on Eighteenth Street, and he's showing dirty movies. He may be making some porno films, too. All gay."

"He came back from Florida with some money, then."

"It looks like it. From the gun-running, probably."

"Have you got a current picture?"

"Yessir."

"All right. Inspector Canelli will be down to pick up the jacket. Wait for him. And thanks."

"Yes, sir. Thank *you.*"

I turned to Friedman. "Ever heard of Malcolm Howard?"

Friedman nodded. "I arrested him once."

"Is he a murderer?"

"Not when I knew him, he wasn't. But he was certainly going in that direction. He's a smart, vicious punk with very kinky sexual preferences and a very strong profit motive. Mal will do anything for money. That's what his friends call him. Mal."

"Excuse me." I called Canelli, and ordered him to organize a search for Mal Howard. "When they find him," I finished, "they're to put him under close surveillance, and call me. Don't apprehend."

"Yessir. Do you want me to take charge in the field?"

"No," I answered. "I want you here. Lieutenant Friedman is

going to be busy with security for Fidel Castro. That leaves you and me to hold down the fort."

"Oh. Well. Jeeze." Canelli was plainly flustered. A combination of Castro's visit and a Saturday morning's skeleton crew in Homicide had suddenly elevated him to command status. It was the first time it had happened. "Well, okay, Lieutenant. Sure. And thanks."

"You can get some extra men from General Works, if you need them—on my authority. Let's use three teams—six men, altogether. Get the best you can."

"Yessir. Six men. Is that all? I mean, is that all you wanted?"

"No. When you've got the search for Howard organized, I want you to see how many people involved with the Cappellanis are in San Francisco. You got the names from Bill, last night. Right?"

"Yessir. Right. I was just typing up my report on his statement, as a matter of fact."

"Okay. When you get the names, set up an interrogation schedule for you and me. Beginning in, say, an hour. Clear?"

"Yessir, that's— *Oh*. Say. I forgot."

I sighed. "Forgot what?"

"Mrs. Rosa Cappellani and a guy named Paul Rosten just came in. He's the foreman up at the Cappellani Winery, according to that private detective. I was just going to call you, when you called me. You want to see them?"

"Yes," I answered. "Bring them in."

Canelli tapped on my door, opened it and ushered Rosa Cappellani and Paul Rosten into my office. After making his awkward introductions, Canelli moved his blue-stubbled chin toward the interior of my office, silently asking whether he should stay. Surreptitiously, I shook my head. I wanted Mal Howard found.

Friedman remained long enough to covertly form his own impression of the woman and man, then excused himself, mumbling something about "Fidel" under his breath.

Wearing a mink coat over a dark woolen dress, with her hair coiled regally on her head, Rosa Cappellani was plainly a woman accustomed to center stage. She moved with calm, concise assurance. Still in her fifties, slim and full-breasted, she held her head high and proud. Her face was aristocratically lean, with a prominent nose, high cheekbones and a decisive mouth. On appearance, she was a woman who set her own style. Her simply cut dress must have been made especially for her. She wore no visible makeup; her hair was untinted, strikingly gray-streaked. The effect was elegant indifference to fashion—and to the pandering to opinion. Her gray eyes moved quickly and shrewdly, compelling attention.

"Have you found out who killed Jason?" she asked abruptly.

"It's too early to say for sure, Mrs. Cappellani. But I can tell you that we've got a prime suspect."

"Who?"

"A man named Malcolm Howard." As I said it, I glanced quickly at both Rosa and Rosten, looking for a reaction. I saw them exchange a puzzled look, nothing more.

"You don't know him," I said. "Is that right?"

"That's right," Rosa answered impatiently. "Who is he? Is he the one who tried to kill Alex, Thursday night?"

I countered with a question: "We have reason to believe that the murderer had the address of your own house on his person when he struggled with Booker. A slip of paper was found with the address of your house and the word 'Twospot' typed on it. Does 'Twospot' mean anything to either of you?"

Again, the two exchanged a glance—with the same negative result.

"Who is this Malcolm Howard?" the woman asked.

"He's a professional criminal, Mrs. Cappellani—a man with a long arrest record that includes attempted murder." Letting her think about it, I watched her closely. Her eyes wandered thoughtfully past mine as she asked, "Do you think Howard came to rob the house, and killed Jason in the process? Is that what you suspect?"

I shook my head. "No, Mrs. Cappellani, that's not what I think. Howard isn't a petty hoodlum. He isn't a burglar, either."

"Then why was he there? Why did he kill Jason?"

"He was probably there," I answered, "because someone hired him to be there. If he killed Jason Booker, he probably did it for money. Plenty of money."

"Why do you say 'plenty of money'?" The question came quickly, shrewdly.

"Because," I answered, "Howard apparently has some money already. So he wouldn't come cheap."

"I don't understand this," she said. "I don't understand any of it." She spoke angrily. Her eyes snapped impatiently; her head moved with restless exasperation. Faced with frustration or uncertainty, it was her nature to strike back.

Still watching her closely, I said, "I think that the attempt on Alex's life and the murder of Jason Booker might be connected."

"Connected?"

I nodded.

"Why? How?"

"I have no idea. However, on two successive nights, they were both attacked. They could have been attacked by the same person. Or else—" I let it go unfinished.

"Or else what?" she asked. As she spoke, her eyes narrowed.

I decided not to answer. I wanted her to think about the other possibility: that, directly or indirectly, Alex was responsible for the attack on Booker.

Rosa Cappellani drew a slow, measured breath. "I'm here for two reasons, Lieutenant," she said, speaking with deliberate emphasis. "I'm here because Jason and I were friends. Good friends." As she said it, I saw Paul Rosten stiffen almost imperceptibly. He hadn't liked Booker.

"But more important," Rosa continued, "I'm here because of Alex. Where is he? What's happened to him?"

As concisely as I could, I told her everything I knew about Alex Cappellani's movements, finishing with the stark, brutal statement that Booker, while probably intending to meet Alex at the Cappellanis' town house, had been murdered. After the murder, I continued, Alex had apparently run—or else been taken away. As I spoke, Rosa Cappellani's eyes burned into mine with an intensity so fierce that I dropped my own gaze to the desk.

Her voice was low and tight as she said, "You're telling me that my son might be either a murderer or a murder victim, Lieutenant." It sounded like a warning—or a threat.

"No, Mrs. Cappellani, that's not what I'm telling you. I'm simply giving you the facts. I'm hoping you can tell me what they mean."

"They mean that Alex is trouble—that you've got to help him, not hunt him for a murderer."

"I've got to find him before I can help him, Mrs. Cappellani. And that's why I'm questioning you. Because I want to find him." I let a beat pass before I added, quietly, "I'd hoped you could help me."

Silently, remorselessly, her eyes continued to challenge me.

Then I saw the firm, uncompromising line of her mouth weaken. For the first time, her eyes shifted uncertainly.

"How can I help you?" she asked finally.

"By telling me everything you can about your son. About your family life. Everything. Because that's where this whole thing seems to have started—with your family.

She looked at me for a last long, speculative moment, making up her mind. Then, speaking slowly and steadily, she began:

"Until my husband died, thirteen years ago, Alex was always happy—always smiling. He was never very serious, not like his brother Leo. Alex took life as he found it. Leo was like his father —always trying to change things. And often succeeding, too."

"Did it bother Alex? That Leo succeeded?"

"I don't think it bothered him. But, to be honest, I don't really know." Under the mink, her shoulders lifted. Slowly, she shook her head. It was a regretful gesture, an admission of parental helplessness. "After my husband died, I had my hands full, running the winery and handling my husband's—" Momentarily, she hesitated. Then: "My husband's other affairs."

"What 'other affairs' do you mean?"

"He was very active in politics."

"How about you?" I asked. "Were you active in politics, too?"

"Not to the extent my husband was involved. I had only the interest. He had the conviction—the fire." As she said it, she exchanged a quick, meaningful look with the man beside her. "In any case," she continued, "the fact is that I was never able to get close to either of the boys after my husband's death. Leo, of course, was already in his twenties. He didn't need me. Alex, though—" Again, she shook her head. "Alex had his problems. I knew it, and tried to help. But I had my problems too."

"The boys grew up well," Rosten said, speaking for the first time since he'd introduced himself. "Differently, but well."

"I suppose so." But, plainly, she didn't believe it—didn't choose to delude herself. "Actually, after only a few years, Leo took over a lot of the winery management. I made the major decisions, but Leo handled day-to-day matters—and very well, too."

"What about Alex? What was he doing during that time?"

Lips compressed, she hesitated before saying, "Alex tried— different things. From the first, it was obvious that he and Leo couldn't work together—not as equals, anyhow. So, for several years, Alex drifted. First there was college. Or rather—" She shook her head, remembering. "Rather, a succession of colleges. Then he lived in the East for a while. But then, a few years ago, he came back to California."

"And now he's working under Leo's direction. Is that right?"

She nodded. "That's right." There was a note of finality in her voice. The subject of the two brothers and their rivalry was closed.

So I said: "Alex was very concerned about your-friendship with Jason Booker. That's apparently how all this started." I decided to say nothing more. She knew why I'd said it. Either she would respond, or she wouldn't.

A long, uncomfortable moment passed while she studied me. Then, having made her decision, she spoke calmly and concisely.

"Jason began working for us about six months ago. We became —friendly. From the first, Alex didn't like Jason. I knew it, but there was nothing I could do about it. I—" Again, the glance at Rosten. "I've always lived my own life, especially since my husband died. I don't interfere with my sons' lives. I don't expect them to interfere with mine."

"It's my understanding that you and Jason Booker were more than just 'friendly.'" I hesitated. Then: "You were close friends. *Very* close friends. Is that right?"

She lifted her chin and stared at me with scornful defiance before she finally spoke. "Yes, Lieutenant. If it's any concern to your investigation—yes, we *were* very close friends."

Disconcerted by her obvious scorn for my policeman's grubby duties, I self-defensively asked, "Did you know that Alex retained a private investigator to look into Booker's past?"

She stared at me coldly for a moment before she said, "I don't believe you."

"It's true, though."

For the second time, Rosten spoke. "The man at the winery, Thursday night," he said. "The one who found Alex—who was wrestling with Shelly, out in the vineyards. It must be him."

Rosa questioned me with a single haughty look. Silently, I nodded.

"He might have saved Alex's life," Rosa said. She spoke quietly, thoughtfully.

"Your son trusted him," I said. I waited, hoping she'd say something more.

Instead, Rosten spoke again. His brown, weather-seamed face

was impassive as he said, "This private detective—he seems to know a lot about us. About the winery, and the family. Everything."

"Alex gave him a rundown, I'm sure."

"He shouldn't have done it," Rosten said. "It was wrong, hiring someone to spy on his own mother."

Thoughfully, I turned my full attention to this strangely implacable man, who didn't hesitate to criticize Alex Cappellani, even to his mother.

"Do you have any ideas, Mr. Rosten?" I asked quietly. "Do you know why Alex might have been attacked, or Booker murdered?"

For a long, silent moment he held my gaze. Then, slowly, he shook his head. "Those are things for Rosa to tell you," he said. "Not me."

Rosa, he'd said. Not *Mrs. Cappellani.*

At that moment my phone rang. Impatiently, I lifted receiver. At the same moment, Rosa rose decisively to her feet, motioning for Rosten to do the same.

"Just a minute," I said into the phone. And to Rosa: "Where can I get in touch with you, if anything develops?"

"At the winery. In St. Helena."

I passed her one of my cards, asking to her to call me if Alex contacted her. "Will you do that?" I asked.

"Yes," she answered gravely. "Yes, I'll do that."

"By the way, do you happen to know Alex's blood type?"

Half turned toward the door, she turned back, staring at me. "Blood type?"

"For the record."

"It's the same as mine," she said. "O positive. For the record." She spoke in a low, bitterly mocking voice. I hadn't fooled her.

I waited for them to leave the office, then spoke into the phone: "Yes. Sorry."

"It's Canelli, Lieutenant. Did I interrupt you?"

"It's all right. What is it?"

"I just wanted to tell you that the only ones I could find are Logan Dockstetter, who's the Cappellanis' sales manager, and Leo Cappellani and Shelly Jackson. They work at the winery's offices in the city here, as I understand it. Mr. Cappellani wasn't very anxious to see us, but I finally, ah, insisted. So he said we could see him about two o'clock, at his office. And the Jackson woman, too."

"What about Dockstetter?"

"He's going to have lunch at the San Francisco Yacht Club. He said he'd meet us there, at noon."

"All right. Fine."

"I've never been inside that yacht club," he said. "I hear it's pretty fancy."

"It is."

9

Canelli pulled into a parking place, switched off the engine and sat for a moment staring out over the yacht harbor.

"Jeeze, Lieutenant, did you ever stop to think how much money there is in San Francisco? I mean, every once in a while when I'm downtown, I can't believe how many Cadillacs I see. Not to mention Lincolns, and Mercedes, and all. And then this—" He gestured to the long rows of pleasure boats moored side by side to wharves ranked endlessly along the shore. The Yacht Club was built on a stone breakwater that protected the harbor. The largest, most expensive yachts were moored closest to the club. The smaller craft, mostly sailboats, lost definition in the distance: a constantly criss-crossing tangle of masts and rigging lines, gently shifting with the swell.

For a moment we sat staring out across the harbor. Last night's fog had burned off; sunlight sparkled on the water. To our left, a small sailboat, bright white, was just clearing the breakwater, heading out into the bay.

Marveling, Canelli shook his head. "It's another world, you know that, Lieutenant? It's a whole other world."

Instead of replying, I glanced at my watch. The time was exactly noon. I reached for our microphone and pressed the "transmit" button.

"This is Inspectors Eleven," I said. "Lieutenant Hastings."

"Yessir, Lieutenant." It was Halliday, my favorite communications man.

"We'll be in the San Francisco Yacht Club for thirty or forty minutes. Any messages?"

"No, sir."

"Any developments on either Mal Howard or Alex Cappellani?"

"No, sir."

I sighed. In addition to the six men looking for Howard, I'd detailed two men to watch the Cappellani house and another two men to watch the Cappellani offices. Including Canelli and myself, twelve men were assigned to the case. For a "routine homicide," I'd reached the departmental manpower limit.

I signed off and got out of the car. As we walked across the parking lot I asked, "Is there anything yet on those blood types?"

Canelli exhaled loudly, irked with himself. "I forgot to tell you. Booker's type is AB negative, which was most of it. The blood, I mean. The type at the garage door and on the sidewalk outside is O positive."

"Alex's type." I pushed open the huge front door of the Yacht Club, gesturing for Canelli to precede me.

"Right," he answered. "Except that I couldn't find out about Howard's type. And O positive is the most common. So I guess there's a better than even chance that it could be Howard's type, too. At least, that's what I—" His voice trailed off. A middle-aged man who looked like a successful investment banker stepped forward to greet us, subtly blocking our progress into the club's elegantly paneled interior hallway. The man was deliberately assessing Canelli, head to toe. Plainly, the verdict wasn't favorable.

"We're meeting Mr. Logan Dockstetter," I said, stepping forward. "We're expected."

The man's gaze transferred itself to me. Resignation clouded his voice as he asked for our names.

Dockstetter was sitting at a corner table facing the huge plate-glass windows that looked out on San Francisco Bay. Following his gaze, I was startled to see the long, slate-colored shape of an atomic submarine passing under the Golden Gate Bridge, slipping out to sea. Above the submarine, in front and behind, two outriding Navy helicopters hovered like giant dragonflies.

"They're sinister looking, those submarines," Dockstetter said. "They always remind me of crocodiles."

"Because they only show their snouts, you mean."

He nodded, and gestured us to seats across from him. When we declined his perfunctory offer of drinks, he was visibly relieved. Like the man who'd greeted us at the door, Logan Dockstetter was obviously pained at our presence in this high-ceilinged, richly carpeted, antique-furnished citadel of privilege.

I settled back in my chair and took a moment to survey the bar room. Red-jacketed waiters moved discreetly from table to table. Expensive glassware tinkled and sparkled. Conversation was slow and melodious. Laughter was muted. Seeing it all, I secretly winced. During the year I'd played professional football, I'd been married to an heiress. Early in our marriage, some of our best moments had been shared in places like this. At the end of our marriage, after football had ruined my knees and a "public relations" job in my father-in-law's executive suite had robbed me of my self-respect, most of my worst moments had been spent in the same places.

"I'm afraid I don't have much time," Dockstetter said, consulting a wafer-thin gold wristwatch.

"We won't need much time, Mr. Dockstetter." As I spoke, I placed my notebook on the table between us. "I just wanted to get a few facts straight." I flicked my ballpoint pen. At the sound, Dockstetter seemed to start. He was a slightly built man of about forty. Height, average. Weight, not more than a hundred fifty pounds. His face was pale and narrow, drawn into prim lines of permanent disapproval. His mouth was pursed, his washed-out eyes distant and disdainful. He looked like an overbred English aristocrat. Canelli had told me that Dockstetter was the winery's sales manager. It was hard to imagine this pale, fastidious man cajoling a customer.

Canelli had also said that Dockstetter was probably gay. That, I decided, was a good guess.

"You were present at the Cappellani winery on Thursday night, when Alex was attacked. Is that right?"

Sipping something that looked like a gin and tonic, he inclined his beautifully barbered head. "That's right."

"Who do you think was responsible for that attack, Mr. Dockstetter?"

Plainly, the question startled him. Frowning, he placed his glass on the table before him. "I—I'm not sure I know what you mean," he said carefully.

"It's very simple." As I spoke, I put a faint edge of patronizing contempt on my voice. If I could ruffle Dockstetter's carefully preened feathers, I might learn something extra from him. "I'm asking you to tell me who you think tried to kill Alex."

"But I—" He blinked. "I don't know. How could I know?"

"Guess, then. I want input."

"But that would be—slander, if I guessed."

I shook my head. "Wrong. I'm a police officer, and I'm asking you a question in connection with a murder investigation. I want an answer to the question. In this case, I want you to make a guess. There's a witness present—" I nodded to Canelli. "Technically, if you don't do as I ask, you could be obstructing justice."

"But I—I never heard of anything like that." He stared at me for a moment, then dropped his eyes. His fingers tightened on the gin and tonic glass. I noticed that he wore two small golden rings, one on each of his little fingers.

I looked at my own watch. "I'm waiting, Mr. Dockstetter."

"Well, I—ah—" His tongue tip circled pale lips. "I—ah—I'd have to guess Booker, then. Jason Booker."

Across the table, Canelli grinned. "That's a safe call, I guess, if you're worried about slander. Since he's dead, I mean."

Both Dockstetter and I stared hard at Canelli—who promptly flushed, and began to fidget.

"Did you see anything or hear anything Thursday night that made you think it was Booker?" I asked Dockstetter.

"No. Nothing. I'm just guessing." He flicked his hand in a small, petulant gesture. "That's what you wanted, I thought—a guess."

"Would you guess that Booker actually struck the blow? Or would you say he hired it done?"

"Well—ah if I had to choose, I'd say he hired it done. I mean, it's hard to imagine Booker actually trying to *kill* anyone." Again Dockstetter's hand moved, fluttering now.

I slipped Mal Howard's picture from my pocket. "Have you ever seen this man, Mr. Dockstetter?"

Annoyed, he drew a pair of horn-rimmed half-glasses from the inside pocket of his blue blazer. He glanced briefly at the picture, shook his head and quickly returned the glasses to his pocket. Obviously, reading glasses didn't fit Dockstetter's self-image.

"No, I've never seen him. Who is he?"

"The man who may have killed Booker," I answered, staring him straight in the eye. "His name is Malcolm Howard. Mal, for short. His fingerprints were discovered at the murder scene."

Peevishly, he blinked at the picture. I felt that he wanted to look at it again, now that he knew its significance. But he didn't want to put on the glasses again.

"Some people figure," Canelli said, "that Alex thought Jason Booker was trying to run some kind of a con on Rosa Cappellani, to maybe get some of her money. Maybe all of her money. So then, some people think, maybe Booker hired Mal Howard to get to Alex. Like, to warn him off, maybe, with a lump on the head. How does that sound, Mr. Dockstetter? For guessing, I mean?"

As Canelli had been talking Dockstetter had drained the last of his drink in two long, noisy gulps.

"But—" He gestured to the picture, still lying on the table. "But you said that he—Howard—killed Booker."

Canelli raised his beefy shoulders, shrugging. "Maybe Booker didn't pay Howard for the job Thursday night. Maybe that's why they were going to meet yesterday, at the Cappellani house—so Booker could make the payoff. But maybe he didn't make it, or couldn't. So there was a fight. And Howard won."

I looked thoughtfully at Canelli. Except for the fact that it didn't account for Alex's presence at the town house, it was a good, sound theory. I wondered whether it had just occured to him. If not, I wondered why I hadn't heard about it.

"Do you think Booker was doing something illegal, Mr. Dockstetter?" I asked. "Something that might have been calculated to defraud Mrs. Cappellani?"

Dockstetter's pale eyes narrowed. "Is this another guess you're asking for?"

"Yes."

"Then I'd say that, definitely, Booker was up to no good, as the saying goes. Rosa—Mrs. Cappellani—is very—" He paused, searching for the word. "She's very susceptible," he said finally. "She's very vain. And according to the rumors, she's very—" Again he hesitated. Finally: "She's very hot-blooded." Saying it, he registered disdainful disapproval.

"Sexually, you mean."

He nodded primly. "That's her business, of course. However, when her, ah, appetites affect the welfare of the winery, then others become involved. And that's what's happening."

"Is the winery in trouble?"

"Not serious trouble. Not yet. But it could happen. Both Rosa and Leo have had other things on their minds, lately. And it's beginning to show. Cappellani wines used to have a reputation for quality. That's no longer true."

I thought about what he'd told me, then decided to say, "Rosa came to see me this morning, along with with Paul Rosten. She said that Leo has taken over the management of the winery—and is doing a good job."

He sniffed. "Leo *was* doing a good job, up until a year or so ago. Then he began to get involved in politics, just like his father. It's the same pattern, all over again. As soon as the old man got a little power—a little money—he immediately began to think of himself as a kingmaker. The same thing is happening with Leo. If it weren't so—so ludicrous, it would be funny. Basically, they're nothing but grape growers who got lucky. In the fifties, the old man was constantly flying off to Texas, or New York, or God knows where, instead of tending to business. The *real* kingmakers must have laughed at him—and used him, too."

Obviously, the thought gave Dockstetter a certain malicious pleasure. He was a man who enjoyed minimizing the achievements of others. I saw him raise a finger to a passing waiter, point to his empty glass. He didn't ask whether Canelli or I would join him.

"Paul Rosten is another—" Dockstetter hesitated, searching for the word. "He's another strange one," he finished lamely.

"How do you mean?"

"I mean—" Again, he hesitated, this time while the red-jacketed waiter took away his glass. "I mean that as a winemaker, he's impossible. He simply has no feeling for the job. But Rosa would never think of firing him."

"Why not?"

Dockstetter looked at me shrewdly. I thought I knew why. He was about to pass on more gossip—gratuitously, for his own self-serving purpose.

"Rosten was very close to the old man—birds of a feather. That's one theory. There's also a theory that Rosten and Rosa were lovers after the old man died. Or maybe—" He permitted himself a small, self-satisfied smirk. "Or maybe before, others, say."

At my belt, a small electronic pager buzzed. I pressed the button and heard Halliday requesting that I phone Communications, code two.

"I used to have one of those," Docksetter said, pointing to the pager. "But I eventually decided it was a terrible nuisance. Simply terrible."

I rose to my feet. "That's negative thinking, Dockstetter," I said. "You should've thought of it as a status symbol."

He didn't return my departing smile.

I'd seen a phone outside the Yacht Club, at dockside. As we walked toward the phone, Canelli said, "That Dockstetter's sure a pris."

"A what?"

"A pris. You know—for prissy."

"Have you got a dime?" I asked.

"How's two nickels?"

"Fine. Thanks." I dialed Communications and asked for Halliday.

"I hope I didn't disturb you, Lieutenant," he said. "But Lieutenant Friedman is out, and Canelli is with you, I gather. And I've got a couple of things that I thought you should know about, on the Booker homicide."

"It's all right, Halliday. What've you got?"

"First," he said, "a black and white car spotted Alex Cappellani's car. It's on upper Grant Avenue, near Greenwich. They're keeping it under survelliance. I thought I'd better notify you."

"I'm glad you did. Are you in contact with the team watching the Cappellani offices?"

"Yessir, I am."

"All right. On my authority, tell them to proceed to Alex's car and relieve the uniformed officers. Tell them to stay well back, out of sight. Clear?"

"Yessir, that's clear."

"What else've you got?"

"The team that's looking for Mal Howard drew a couple of blanks, but now they're sure they've located his present address.

They found someone who got burned by Howard on a dirty movie transaction, and he's willing to cop, out of spite. It looks pretty solid. I thought I should tell you."

I took out my ballpoint pen. "What's the address?"

"1976 Scott Street. Near Pine."

"I'll send Canelli to take charge. Have a sector car pick him up at the Yacht Club, outside. I'm going to the Cappellani offices. I shouldn't be there for more than an hour. Then, if nothing else develops, I'll go downtown."

"Right."

"You're doing a good job, Halliday. Are you going to be on duty for a while today?"

"I'll stay as long as you want me, Lieutenant, if that's the question."

"That's the question, Halliday. Thanks."

10

The receptionist's face was expressionless as she examined my badge. She was a pale, fussy woman of about thirty, with a narrow head and a scrawny body. A bright red mouth accented the unhealthy pallor of her face. A tight sweater clung to a torso that was barely pubescent. Dark eyeshadow enlarged eyes that were already protuberant.

"Is Mr. Cappellani expecting you?"

"He's expecting me at two. I'm early, but I hope he'll see me. I'm having a—busy day."

Plainly displeased, she lifted her phone and spoke in a hushed voice. She handled the phone as if it were covered with germs.

"He'll see you, Lieutenant." Disapprovingly, she gestured to a tall walnut door with brushed chrome fittings. A matching chrome nameplate was inscribed L. CAPPELLANI. The effect was understated elegance.

"Go right in, please."

The Cappellani offices occupied a suite on the third floor of one of the huge brick warehouses that had been built close to the waterfront at the turn of the century. As shipping declined, the fortresslike warehouses had fallen vacant. Then, during the last decade, developers had profitably restored the old buildings, remodeling them to accent worn wooden beams and the timeless texture of natural brick. Leo Cappellani had a corner office. On two sides, big plate-glass windows set into the massive exposed-brick walls offered a magnificent view of San Francisco Bay.

Leo Cappellani sat behind an oversized rosewood desk. As I entered the office he rose to his feet and gestured me to an armchair placed about five feet from the desk. As I sat down, I realized that my chair was several inches lower than Leo's. He didn't offer to shake hands.

"I hope this won't take long, Lieutenant. I don't mind telling you that I'm having a hell of a day." He ran his fingers impatiently through dark, curly hair as he threw himself back into his elegant black leather swivel chair. "First, there's Alex—and then Booker. And then, in addition to everything else, we just had a goddamn shipment of wine hijacked, if you can believe that. And, as if *that* weren't enough, my secretary phoned in sick."

"You had a wine shipment hijacked?" I asked incredulously.

He nodded angrily. "I've just got off the phone with the FBI. They think the shipment was hijacked by mistake." He shook his head disgustedly, as if someone had played a bad joke on him. "It seems that the hijackers were looking for a shipment of pocket calculators, for God's sake. And they—" His phone buzzer sounded. Grimacing, he picked up the receiver. "Miss Farwell," he said acidly, "I thought I told you to hold my calls." He listened for a moment. "My wife?" As he listened again, frowning, I had a chance to assess him. He had his mother's large, high-bridged nose and dark, restless eyes. His face was squared off, with a strong jaw, prominent cheekbones and heavy ridges above dark, full eyebrows. It was a willful, powerful face. Wearing a helmet and breastplate, he could have been a Roman centurion.

He had apparently agreed to talk to his wife. He listened impatiently for a moment, still frowning. I saw him clench his right hand hard into a fist, and begin rhythmically striking the desk— suffering her silently. The gesture revealed a strong, dominant man who bore frustration badly. Even from across the desk, I could hear a strident, metallic voice on the phone. Finally Leo interrupted.

"Listen, Angela, I simply don't have time for this. Now, I've already told you to stay out of it. Rosa doesn't need your help, and I don't *want* your help. You'll just—what?"

The frown became a furious scowl. The fist was white-knuckled now. On the phone, the metallic voice continued its shrill protestations. Again, he roughly interrupted her.

"What you're doing, Angela, is trying to make a big production number out of this. But the facts—the simple, unvarnished facts —are that Booker got himself killed, which was good riddance, and Alex's got himself in yet another scrape, which was inevitable. Now, if it'll make you feel less left out, you can go downtown and buy yourself a black dress, just in case Alex is dead, too. But in the meantime, please—please—get off my back. And—" Suddenly he stopped speaking. He took the phone away from his ear, glared at it for a moment, then banged it down. His wife had hung up on him.

Immediately, the phone buzzed again.

"Goddamn son of a bitch." He lifted the phone. Speaking in a low, dangerous voice, he said, "Miss Farwell, for the last time—" He paused, blinked, then sat for a moment in irresolute silence. Finally he said shortly, "All right. Tell her to wait for me. It'll just be a few minutes." As he hung up, he glanced quickly at me, as if to assess how much I'd heard—and guessed. Now he swiveled in his chair to face me squarely. He allowed a moment of silence to pass as he eyed me speculatively, taking my measure. As he stared, his hand strayed to his expensive silk tie, absently adjusting the knot. Finally:

"What can I do for you, Lieutenant?" His voice was clipped, his eyes cold. He could have been speaking to an employee—or a servant.

I matched his manner. "I'm looking for your brother. His car's been located on Grant Avenue, near Telegraph Hill. Does he know anyone in the area?"

"Not so far as I can remember." The answer came so quickly that he couldn't have given it an instant's thought. Before I'd asked the question, he'd decided on a negative reply.

I pointed to the phone. "I gather that you don't keep very close track of your brother's life."

"What's *that* supposed to mean?" he asked truculently.

"It means that you don't exactly play the role of the devoted brother."

"I don't have time for role playing, Lieutenant. I'd rather just tell the truth. I've found that it saves a lot of time and energy. And the truth is that I've never really liked Alex very much. And he's never liked me much, either. We're two different people."

88

"He could be dead, Mr. Cappellani. Or in danger. Aren't you concerned?"

"Of course I'm concerned. But I'm not going to let his mistakes dominate my life. I learned that little trick a long time ago."

As I rose slowly to my feet, I decided I didn't like Leo Cappellani. I looked at him for a moment in silence before I asked quietly, "Do you know anyone named Mal Howard?"

"No."

"Does the word 'Twospot' mean anything to you?"

"No."

"Do you think that Jason Booker intended to marry your mother?"

He drew a deep breath. "I think he intended to *try* and marry her. But he never would have succeeded. I can assure you that my mother would never have been taken in by Booker."

I nodded. "I think you're probably right." I laid my card on the corner of his desk. "If you hear from your brother—or about your brother—I'd like you to call me."

He didn't reply. Realizing that I could expect nothing from Leo Cappellani, I turned and left the office. In the reception room outside, on a leather sofa, I saw a handsome young woman seated with her legs crossed, leafing through a copy of *Time*. She was wearing beige wool slacks, a Levi-styled jacket made of the same material and a brown turtleneck sweater. The close-fitting jacket modeled round, high breasts and a trim, exciting torso. When I opened the door, she lifted her head to look at me over the magazine. Her face was a classic oval, with a firm mouth, a straight nose and calm, level brows. She was a small, slim woman, almost petite. But the squared-off set of her shoulders and the arch of her neck suggested vitality, determination and strength. Her hair was dark auburn, cropped close. Her gray-green eyes were coolly appraising. Under my scrutiny, she lifted her chin a disdainful half inch. She held herself as if she was accustomed to having men look at her.

From Bill's description, I could guess her identity.

"Are you Shelly Jackson?" I asked, at the same time slipping my shield case from my pocket. Watching my gesture, she raised her hand. "You don't have to show me your badge. I know who you are." She put the magazine aside, recrossed her legs and turned on the couch to face me fully. "I understand you want to talk to me."

"I understand you want to talk to me."

"Not especially. We want to talk to everyone who was at the winery Thursday sight. And I understand that you—" I hesitated, searching for the right phrase. "I understand that you participated."

It was an awkward, ineffectual opening—a mistake. I should have begun with a question, putting her on the defensive. It was a basic police tactic, based on the premise that every interrogation is a contest.

Questioning desirable women, I always made the same mistake.

As if she sensed my momentary dissatisfaction with myself, her mouth moved in a small, condescending smile. The green eyes regarded me calmly, with an aloof, supercilious tolerance. Suddenly I knew how Canelli must feel, trying to cope with a constant succession of citizens who caused him to blush, or perspire, or otherwise surrender to confusion.

"How do you mean that, exactly?" she asked.

"I mean that you were apparently very helpful." As I sat beside her on the sofa, I saw the inefficient Miss Farwell enter Leo Cappellani's office. Shelly Jackson and I were alone in the reception room.

This time maintaining eye contact, I pitched my voice to a crisp, official note as I said, "I understand that you gave statements to the Napa County Sheriff's office indicating that, except for the private detective, you didn't see anyone in the vineyards Thursday night after the attack on Alex. Is that right?"

"That's right."

"Is there anything you can add to what you told them?"

She raised her shoulders, shrugging. Her eyes were steady, never leaving my face. Her hands were clasped easily in her lap, relaxed. Innocent or not, most witnesses betray nervousness during questioning. Not Shelly Jackson. She was a cool customer.

"I probably can't add anything to what you already know," she answered. "You're apparently pretty well informed about what happened."

"You work for the Cappellanis, I gather."

"Yes. I'm in their marketing division."

"You know Logan Docksetter, then."

"Of course."

"What d'you think of him?"

"As a man, or a sales manager?"

"As a man."

"I don't think he's much of a man." She let a deliberate moment pass before she added, "You can take that any way you like—and you'd probably be right."

"How long have you worked for the Cappellanis?"

"Just a few months."

"What'd you do before that?"

Again she shrugged. The slow movement of her shoulders suggested a self-confident sensuality. I found myself thinking that she would be a bold, exciting lover.

"I was in marketing. I'm pretty good at it, as a matter of fact.

"Did you work here in San Francisco?"

"No," she answered shortly. "In Florida. My—" For the first time, she hesitated. Then: "My marriage broke up. So I came west." As she said it, she challenged me with her eyes, putting the subject of her broken marriage off-limits.

"I wouldn't think there'd be much wine marketed in Florida. They don't grow grapes, do they?"

The comment seemed to amuse her. "As a matter of fact," she said, "I was in nuts, as they say. Pecans. But marketing is marketing, Lieutenant." Her eyes still held mine, coolly waiting.

"You're an intelligent woman, Miss Jackson. I'd like you to tell me how the Cappellanis strike you—as a family, I mean."

She looked at me for a moment, obviously deciding how much to say—how far she could trust me. Finally she said, "Alex is a lightweight and Leo is a light-heavy. The mother, Rosa, is the only one who knows who she is and what she's doing. But she apparently can't do without a man, so that's a weakness, I guess. Anyhow, Booker could get her giggling like a schoolgirl, sometimes."

"You didn't like Booker."

She shook her head.

"How about Paul Rosten?"

"I don't know him very well. He never talks. At least, not to me."

I was trying to decide whether to ask if she thought Rosa and Rosten had been lovers when, suddenly, the paging device at my belt buzzed. It was Halliday again, asking me to phone him. I crossed the office, punched an outside line and dialed Communications. In spite of himself, Halliday was exicted as he said:

"Inspector Canelli just called to say that he thinks he has Mal

Howard pinned down at 1976 Scott Street. He wants instructions."

"What does he mean by 'pinned down'?"

"I'm not sure, sir."

"Tell him I'll be there in ten minutes. Tell him not to take any action until I get there. He's to keep the place buttoned up, nothing more. Clear?"

"Yessir."

11

I drove past the Scott Street address twice before I spotted Canelli. He was across the street from the house, crouched down behind a laurel hedge. Whenever I saw Canelli concealing himself behind a tree or bush, I thought of an amiable hippo bulging out on all sides of a small hummock.

I surreptitiously nodded to him, drove around the corner and parked out of sight. Moments later, he slipped into my car.

"What's the situation?" I asked.

"Well," Canelli said, "what happened is that they been back-tracking on Howard all day, the way I get it—going from one old address to another. You know. So anyhow, at one of the addresses, Marsten ran across this guy he'd busted a couple of months ago, when he was in Vice. So Marsten thought, what the hell, he'd give the guy a toss, for old time's sake. So he finds the guy carrying some cocaine—which makes the guy think about making a deal, of course. And, besides, the guy had a beef with Howard, about some dirty movies, and was pretty pissed off, the way I get it. So anyhow, the guy cops. We've been here for about an hour and a half, showing Howard's picture around. And it sure seems like he's in there, all right. I mean, people saw him go in, but nobody saw him come out."

"Have you got the back covered?"

"Sure, Lieutenant." Canelli's soft brown eyes reproached me for asking the question.

"How many men have you got?"

"Six, including me. I figured I should pull the whole detail in."

I nodded agreement. From where I sat, I could see the building. It had once been a large, elegant two-story Victorian town house, built on a double lot. One side of the house was attached to its neighbor. An alleyway five feet wide ran along the other side of the house. The alleyway was secured by an iron gate. The gate was more than six feet high. The house itself was in fair repair—not completely restored, but not beyond hope, either. It wasn't the kind of place I'd expect to find a hoodlum. Like the house, the neighborhood had been down as far as it would go, and was starting up on the other side. Most of the homes in the area had been built before 1900: spacious, ornate Victorian buildings, elaborately constructed for some of the city's best families. In recent years, a city-sponsored Victorian restoration program had started the process of reclamation, reversing the slide toward decay. Private enterprise was finishing the job.

"Does he live by himself?" As I asked the question I studied Mal Howard's picture: a thin, drawn face, sparse sandy hair, small eyes set deep over unusually high cheekbones, a flattened streetfighter's nose and a tight, sullen mouth. Howard would be easy to identify.

"No," Canelli answered. "It turns out that Howard's gay—at least, if you want to believe the guy with the cocaine, he's gay. And apparently there's three or four of them living together, there. They're all gay. The gays like those old Victorians, you know. They fix them up, and everything. You know—artistically."

"Are Howard's friends hoods, too?"

Canelli nodded. "According to the guy with the cocaine, they're all hoods. And pretty heavy types, too, Marsten says."

"How many of them are in there now?"

"I don't know, Lieutenant. I didn't want to ask around the neighborhood too much, in case some wise guy should call them up, and warn them. That happened to me a few months ago. Remember?"

I remembered. The shootout had sounded like a war.

"How are your men dispersed?"

"Did you see that blue van with the white letters parked across the street from the house? It says General Alarms on the side."

"No."

"Well, it's there. A friend of mine has a burglar alarm business. His name's Pat Harvey, and he's one of those eccentric geniuses, I guess you'd say. When I was an electrician, I used to work with him. So I borrowed the van from Pat. I put three of our guys in the van with a walkie-talkie and two shotguns. Then I sent Marsten and a guy from General Works to cover the back of the house. I forget the G. W. guy's name. But they got a walkie-talkie." As he spoke, Canelli withdrew his own walkie-talkie, and offered it to me. "You want to check out the positions?"

"You do it. Designate the van position one. Marsten is position two."

He spoke briefly to Marsten and the men in the van, then left the walkie-talkie on the seat between us, switched on. Neither of the positions reported any movement, either inside or outside the house.

By the book, I should order the surveillance continued until Mal Howard was identified either entering the house or leaving it.

But, during the ten-minute drive from the Cappellani offices, I'd received a report of another homicide: a housewife in Noe Valley had followed her husband to another woman's house, and killed them both in the woman's bedroom. The housewife's father had once served on the city's board of supervisors, and the woman in bed was the daughter of a four-star general. Already, the reporters were hot on the scent. Friedman was handling the case until I could take over, but he was still muttering about Castro. And, on a Saturday afternoon, half our detectives were unavailable to us, except in an emergency.

"Things are piling up downtown," I said. "Maybe we should go in. You and me. Want to give it a try?"

Canelli knew what the book said, too. He knew that I wasn't giving an order. I was asking for a volunteer.

"Well—sure." He shrugged. "Why not? Should I—" He cleared his throat. "Should I get a shotgun, or what?"

"No. Let's do it slow and easy."

"Yeah. Okay, Lieutenant. Slow and easy."

"Where's the burglar alarm van in relation to the house? How far away?"

"About two, three houses away. It's on the opposite side of the street, though."

"I'm going to order them to wait until we ring the doorbell. Then I'll tell them to approach the house slowly. When we get inside—if we do—they can double-park directly in front of the house, ready to come in behind us. Is that all right with you?"

"Well, sure, Lieutenant. Anything you say."

I gave the orders, handed Canelli the walkie-talkie and swung the car door open.

As we mounted the four steps to the porch, I took my last chance to scan the windows. In an upstairs window, a curtain moved.

"Did you see that?" Canelli whispered.

"Yes." Under cover of the porch now, I unbuttoned my jacket and loosened my revolver in its holster. I gestured for Canelli to stand to my right, slightly behind.

"Ready?"

"Yeah."

The old-fashioned door was heavily built, with a pane of beveled Victorian frosted glass set in the upper half. Gently, I tried the knob. The door was locked. As I pressed the bell button, I glanced over my shoulder. The van was inching out of the parking place. Inside the house, chimes were melodiously ringing.

"Pretty fancy," Canelli muttered. "Chimes."

A half minute passed. I rang the bell again, and waited another half minute. Now I could hear a soft scuffling on the other side of the door. I glanced at Canelli. He'd heard it, too.

As the door came open on a chain, I had my shield case in my left hand. My right hand was inside my coat, gripping the butt of my revolver. In the crack of the door I saw a spectacled eye, a large pimply nose and a dark, ragged mustache.

"Police," I said. "Lieutenant Hastings and Inspector Canelli. We want to talk with Mal Howard. Open the door."

"You got a warrant?" The voice was deep and rough.

"We aren't searching the premises. And we aren't making an arrest," I lied. "Mal Howard is a material witness in a homicide investigation. He's also a felon on parole. Which means that we don't need a warrant. Now open the goddamn door."

"Homicide investigation?"

"That's what I said. Open it."

"He's not here."

"Open the door, asshole. *Now.*" As I said it, I heard Canelli's walkie-talkie come alive. To hear it better, Canelli drew back the flap of his jacket.

". . . someone coming out on the roof in back," a metallic voice was saying.

At the same moment, the door began to close. Quickly I stepped back, extended my arms straight in front of me and hit the door with the heels of both hands. The door flew open. I was inside, standing over the man with the dark mustache. He sat splay-legged on the polished parquet floor. With one lens broken, his aviator glasses were cocked askew on his forehead. His nose was bleeding heavily. He was slowly shaking his head. His eyes were blank.

"Sorry," I said. "But you should have opened it." Through the open door I called for two detectives to come inside, and one to stay in the van, with the radio. The van's front doors came open; two detectives dressed in coveralls climbed the four stairs, fast. The first man carried a shotgun. At a gesture from me, he pointed the shotgun at the fallen man's head. Eyes wide, the man began scrabbling across the floor. The gun barrel followed him, the muzzle inches from his eyes. His mouth was open, but he couldn't speak. His hands came up before his face, fingers delicately touching the muzzle, as if to gently push it away. Suddenly he closed his eyes tight. Tears streaked his stubbled chin. He thought he was going to die.

"Where's Mal Howard?" I asked.

He began to shake his head. "H—h—h—"

I kicked him in the thigh, hard. "He's on the roof, isn't he?" I kicked him again. *"Isn't he?"*

"No. I swear to God, no. He—h—h—"

"Hold on to him," I ordered the two detectives. "And shut that door." I took the walkie-talkie from Canelli and called position two.

"Is he still there, Marsten? On the roof?"

"Yessir."

"What's the access to the roof? How'd he get out?"

"There's a window at the back of the building that opens on the roof. It's a flat roof, shed-style. The window's wide open."

"What's his exact position?"

"He's standing to the right—my right—of the window. Your left. Repeat, your left."

"Our left. Roger. We're coming up and try to collar him."

"Roger, Lieutenant. Watch it, though. He's got a gun. An automatic. Repeat, he's got a gun. Do you read me?"

"I read you. Out."

With Canelli close behind me, I turned to the stairway. Holding my revolver in my right hand, I went slowly up the staircase, one cautious step at a time. As my head came even with the floor of the upstairs hallway, I saw curtains billowing out from the open window at the end of the hall. I pointed to the window, and Canelli nodded—just as his walkie-talkie crackled to life.

"This is position two. Can you read me?" Marsten was speaking softly. His voice was static-blurred.

Crouching against the wall of the staircase, Canelli spoke cautiously into his own walkie-talkie. "I read you, Marsten. What is it?"

"He just tried to get off the roof. He went to the edge, and tried to jump off the roof, into a big redwood tree, back here. But he couldn't make it. So he's coming back toward the window. Do you read me?"

"I read you," Canelli repeated.

Motioning for Canelli to keep his position on the staircase, I quickly ran back down the stairs, holstering my revolver. I gestured for the detective to give me his shotgun.

"Is there a round in the chamber?" I whispered.

"Yessir."

I checked the safety catch as I went back up the stairs. Exposing only his head, Canelli was watching the open window.

"Anything?" I whispered.

"No. Marsten says he's still just to the right—Marsten's right—of the window, flattened against the side of the building. He's got a big automatic, Marsten says. Maybe a Colt .45, for God's sake. And he's just standing there. Waiting, maybe."

"Christ." I was suddenly aware that my shirt and jacket were sweat-soaked. Perspiration covered my forehead, ran into my eyes. Cautiously, I surrendered my grip on the shotgun's forestock, drew the arm of my jacket across my forehead, then gripped the forestock again. The open window was about twenty-five feet from our position—perfect range for buckshot.

"We going to wait him out?" Canelli whispered.

"Do you want to get a shotgun?"

"No, that's all right." Under pressure, Canelli was good with a handgun.

"Let's get closer," I said. I pointed to an open bedroom door, ten feet from the window. "You get in that doorway. I'll cover you. Then I'll put myself beside the window, against the wall, on the left side. Our left side. If he comes through the window, you challenge him. That'll distract him. Then I'll try to take him. Clear?"

"That's clear."

"If it comes to shooting, I'll shoot first. I don't want you shooting toward me."

"Right."

Moving on delicately tiptoeing feet that looked ludicrously small for his outsize body, Canelli scampered up the stairs, down the hallway and into the safety of the doorway. I was flexing my legs, ready to follow him, when my paging device suddenly buzzed. Swearing, I switched the box off. Then, drawing a deep breath and mopping my streaming forehead one last time, I slipped off the shotgun's safety. A dozen strides took me up the last of the three steps and down the hallway to the window. I was breathing heavily—from fear.

At short range, only a shotgun does more damage than a .45.

I looked toward the bedroom door and saw Canelli peeking around the doorjamb, exposing half his broad, swarthy face. Canelli was sweating, too. I nodded. He nodded in return. We were ready.

I heard Marsten's voice on Canelli's walkie-talkie, but couldn't make out the words. Softly answering, Canelli momentarily drew back his head.

At that moment, the big square barrel of a .45 automatic came slowly through the window, poking against the billowing curtains. Next came a hand, gripping the gun. Deliberately, inexorably, a forearm followed.

I set the shotgun's safety, raised the barrel and brought it crashing down on the forearm. Bone snapped. The .45 roared, leaped from the disembodied hand, fell to the floor. The hand disappeared.

"Oh—*shit*."

Without exposing myself, I ripped the curtains free of the window. With my breath coming in short, ragged gulps, with sweat still in my eyes, I forced myself to wait a long, deliberate moment, listening. I heard a ragged shuffling of feet, moving away from the window. I placed the shotgun on the floor, drew my revolver and cautiously looked through the window. I saw a man crouched on the edge of the flat roof, facing away from me.

"Hold it," I yelled. "Hold it right there."

He gathered himself and leaped toward a huge redwood that grew close beside the roof. I saw him disappear, heard a crash.

I climbed out on the roof. As I cautiously approached the edge, I heard Marsten calling, "It's okay. We've got him. It's all right."

I looked over the edge. With Marsten and another detective standing over him, surrounded by broken branches, he lay on his back, staring up at me. His hair was dark, worn medium long. His face was almost as swarthy as Canelli's, with a broad jaw and thick, full lips.

Not Mal Howard.

"Where the hell is Howard?" I shouted down at him. "Tell me, or it's your ass." I heard my voice shrilling, then cracking ineffectually. It was the hysterical backlash of tension and fear. "It's his ass, Marsten," I shouted. "Tell him. Tell the son of a bitch."

Still lying flat on his back, the swarthy man called, "Howard's gone. He's been gone for an hour, pig. And he ain't coming back."

I recognized the truth in his voice, saw truth in his face. Furious, I holstered my revolver. "Search him and cuff him," I called down to the men on the ground. "We'll call for an ambulance."

"Is it him?" Holding the shotgun, Canelli was framed in the open window behind me.

"No, goddammit." I climbed back through the window. "Is there a phone?"

"I saw one in the bedroom."

I dialed Communications. After a delay of almost a minute, Halliday came on the line.

"Sorry, Lieutenant. I was talking to the phone company. I didn't think I'd gotten through on the buzzer, and I was getting the phone number of 1976 Scott Street."

"What is it, Halliday?" Wearily, I sank down on the bed, closing my eyes. I was thinking that, with every year that passed, it became harder for me to face a gun.

"We just got a call from Alex Cappellani," Halliday was saying. "He asked for the officer in charge of the Booker investigation.

He's in an apartment on Telegraph Hill. It's 2851 Greenwich, a rear apartment. It's a half block down from upper Grant, near Coit Tower. He wants you to go see him."

"How's he sound?"

"He sounds nervous."

"Did he give you a phone number?"

"No. He gave me the message, made sure I had it, then hung up. There's a phone in the apartment, though. I checked."

"I'm on my way." I hung up the phone.

"What's happening, Lieutenant?" Canelli was standing beside me.

"Alex Cappellani called in. He's on Telegraph Hill."

"You want me to go with you?"

I stood up. "No," I answered. "I want you to stay here, and finish up. I want you to take both these characters downtown. But before you do that, I want you to get the story on Mal Howard from them. I want to know everything about Howard. I don't care how you do it—the hard way or the easy way, it's all the same to me. Just find out about Howard."

"You want me to lean on them, you mean? Really lean on them?"

"I want the information, Canelli. If you have to bend the rules to get it, I'll back you up. I don't have to tell you that we're short-handed. Which is why I'm leaving it to you. Understand?"

He frowned, thinking it over. "You want me to make a deal? Like that? Let these guys off, if they cop?"

"Goddammit, Canelli, I'm telling you what I want. How you do it, that's up to you. I want Mal Howard. I don't care what you do with these two. They're nothing. I want *Howard*. Is that so hard to understand?"

I knew I'd hurt his feelings, but I didn't have time to worry about it—or to apologize.

"Tell Marsten to follow me to 2851 Greenwich," I said shortly. "Tell him to bring a walkie-talkie, tuned to channel ten." I was already walking down the hallway to the stairs. "I'll meet him in front of 2851 Greenwich. Got it?"

"2851 Greenwich. Channel ten." Looking at me with reproachful brown eyes, he nodded. "Got it," he sighed.

12

With Marsten a half block behind me, I drove slowly past 2851 Greenwich. During the fifteen-minute drive from Scott Street, I'd ordered Halliday to contact both Leo and Rosa Cappellani, asking whether the Greenwich Street address was known to the family. It wasn't, apparently.

Like the Cappellani town house, 2851 Greenwich was an example of choice six-figure San Francisco real estate. It was a "low-rise" apartment building, built to the city's code that protects an owner's right to a view. The building was new: a stark, squared-off stucco box, architecturally undistinguished. But it was located on the north slope of Telegraph Hill. From the rear of the building, floor-to-ceiling windows would command a vista of San Francisco Bay and the Golden Gate Bridge, with the low green hills of Marin County for a background and Alcatraz and Angel Island in the foreground. Full-width balconies would allow affluent tenants to drink martinis and barbecue steaks while they admired the view.

Two entrances fronted on Greenwich, designating two large flats, numbered 2847 and 2849. The number 2851 was fixed to a gate on the uphill side of the building, and marked a garden apartment with a rear entrance and access through the gate. The front windows of the two flats showed no signs of life. Circulars littered the two entrances, and the mailboxes were full. The gate on the uphill side was closed—but not littered with the same circulars.

The building was only two blocks from Alex's car, still parked on Grant Avenue. He'd probably borrowed the apartment from a friend, to hide. He'd parked his car close enough to get it in a hurry—but not close enough to betray his hiding place.

Just ahead, Greenwich Street began a tight uphill curve that ended in the tourist parking circle that served Coit Tower, on the crest of Telegraph Hill. The circle was less than two blocks from 2851. Following a green Porsche, I drove to the crest and made a circuit of the parking area, finally pulling into a red zone. Using my walkie-talkie, I told Marsten to pull in beside me. I rolled down my window.

"I'll leave my car here, and walk back. You follow me in your car, a half block behind. If it looks all right, I'll go in by myself. There's a gate beside the house that leads back to the apartment. When I go through the gate, I'll leave it open. You take up your position opposite the gate. Stay in your car. Clear?"

"Yessir."

"I don't think there'll be a problem. He's scared, probably, and wants to talk. He might talk to one man, rather than two."

"Right," Marsten said shortly. Displeasure was plain in his voice. He'd been hoping for action. Marsten was still in his thirties—a hard-working, ambitious, savvy cop. But he was hot-tempered. He'd grown up a tough kid, and hadn't changed. Working on the vice squad, his street sense had helped him second-guess the hoods and the whores and the hustlers. In Homicide, though, his temper worked against him. He was too quick with his fists—and his gun, too. As a partner, Marsten was a calculated risk.

I raised my walkie-talkie. "We'll stay on channel ten."

"Right."

I locked my car, slipped the walkie-talkie into my inside pocket and began walking back the way I'd come. It was a clear, warm Saturday afternoon, and the observation circle was crowded with tourists. But, despite the balmy weather, most of the tourists remained in their cars, staring at the sights through their windshields. A few of them—children, mostly—clung to the big coin-operated telescopes, focusing on Alcatraz, or the Golden Gate Bridge, or the ships sailing into San Francisco Bay. Some of the tourists emerged from their cars long enough to take a snapshot or pose for one. Then they quickly returned to their cars.

As I walked down Greenwich Street, I glanced to my right, down the steepest slope of Telegraph Hill. The rock slope was overgrown with wind-stunted laurel and juniper, as impenetrable as a forest thicket. Yet, despite the steepness of the terrain and the denseness of the undergrowth, I could see tunnels burrowed through the tangled branches. The small, twisting tunnels could have been made by animals—but weren't. They were made by children, playing. I'd grown up in San Francisco. I could remember playing on this same wild slope during a time when tourists were a novelty, not a nuisance. One of the tall rock outcroppings had been my Indian fortress. I'd been a cowboy, stalking the enemy, attacking with shrilly shouted "bangs" and "pows," followed by equally shrill arguments and arbitrations.

Thirty-five years later, I was still stalking the enemy.

I paused at the side gate of 2851 Greenwich, and casually looked up and down the street. On both sides, the sidewalks were deserted. From my right, a station wagon filled with squirming children came up the hill. From my left, Marsten's car was coasting down toward me.

The gate was made of thick redwood planks, secured by a simple black iron latch. I tripped the latch and pushed the heavy gate slowly open. A flight of cement steps led down to a redwood deck. The stairs were about three feet wide. On my right was a high wooden fence. The stucco side of the house rose on my left, a sheer wall with only two small, high windows. Pine and laurel grew across the top of the redwood fence, touching the stucco of the house. Even though the time was only three-thirty, the fence and the overhanging foliage and the high stucco wall cut off much of the afternoon light.

I tried to leave the gate open, but it was spring loaded. I looked for a hook to latch it back, but couldn't find one. As Marsten drew to a stop at the curb, I let the gate swing free, shrugged and raised my walkie-talkie, signaling for him to listen.

"It won't stay open," I said. "So listen for me. Okay?"

"Okay."

I slipped the walkie-talkie into my pocket and began descending the cement steps. I saw a door leading from the redwood deck to the garden apartment. Beginning on the far side of the deck, a flight of wooden stairs ran down the hill to a tall privet hedge that probably marked the lower boundary of the lot. Except for a single huge pine tree, nothing grew on the property. The ground was covered with thick-growing ivy. A small wooden gate was set into the privet hedge.

The deck was about fifteen feet below street level. Before I stepped on the first of the deck's redwood planks, I stopped to look—and listen. I didn't like the silence—didn't like the feeling of the place. I was confined by a fence on one side and a stucco wall on the other. I was isolated by trees and darkening foliage and an ominous silence. I felt closed in, cut off—threatened.

Why?

Was it because there wasn't a sidewalk in front and an alley behind—because I didn't have a man beside me, and men in the rear?

Did a city cop draw his strength and his courage from the pavements—from cars and radios and, most of all, from other cops close at hand?

I was on the deck now, walking lightly toward the door, moving one slow, cautious step at a time. I'd unbuttoned my jacket. My revolver was loose in its holster.

The door was half glass, but curtained. Beside the door was a narrow window, also curtained. The door opened inward. A small brass knocker was mounted on the door-frame to the right of the door. With my left hand I reached across my body for the knocker, so my right arm would be free. Another step, and . . .

The door flew open. An arm held a black iron poker raised against me. I threw myself back, pivoting away. My left shoulder struck a concrete bulkhead, hard. In the dim light, the figure of a man filled the doorway—a big man, still with the poker raised. My gun was in my hand as I dropped to a crouch.

Ready to kill him.

"Jesus, Frank!"

The private detective—Bill.

"What the hell—" Wrathfully, I holstered my revolver. "Where the—" I realized that I was sputtering. I straightened, brushing leaves and dirt from my left shoulder.

A big man spoke urgently. "A guy just tried to get to Alex—tried to get in the basement window. He's about thirty, thin face, sandy hair, fighter's nose." He pointed down the hill, toward the small gate set into the privet hedge. "He came up from down there. He was carrying a handgun. He went back the way he came —through that wooden gate."

It was Mal Howard. The description fitted perfectly.

"Is Alex all right?" I asked.

"Yes."

"All right, get back inside." Through the door, I'd seen a telephone in the entryway. I stepped inside and switched on my walkie-talkie. Bill closed the door behind us.

"Marsten?"

"Yessir."

"Come down here. Bring your walkie-talkie and a shotgun."

"Yessir."

I went to the telephone and called Halliday, ordering him to dispatch two black and white units to the scene. The officers were to remain in their cars until I contacted them on channel ten—or until they heard shooting.

I saw Bill pull the door open. Carrying a shotgun across his chest, Marsten stood in the doorway. I explained the situation to him, then turned to Bill. "Stay with Alex," I ordered. "Don't let him take off again. And lock the door behind us."

A moment later Marsten and I were cautiously descending the steep wooden steps that led down from the deck to the gate below. Taking the lead, I constantly scanned the base of the privet hedge. If Mal Howard was waiting for us, lying flat on the ground and shooting through the hedge, we'd be easy targets.

"Did you order reinforcements?" Marsten asked.

"Yes. But I told them to stay in their cars until they get orders. I don't want them behind us, shooting."

Speaking in whispers, we were standing in front of the gate.

"Ready?"

Marsten nodded calmly. He looked ready.

I slowly pushed open the gate, standing to the left as the gate swung wide to the right.

The terrain beyond the gate was similar to that higher on the hill: a wild, twisted tangle of low-growing underbrush and stunted trees. In the heart of San Francisco, I was facing a wilderness. To my right, a ragged line of tall pines ran down the hill, ending abruptly at a man-made cliff that had been blasted away to allow construction of the street below. To my left, the sheer concrete wall of an elegant high-rise apartment building rose fifty feet from the ground. The wall extended almost to the cliffside, with a cy-

clone fence running to the very edge—and even extending beyond, protection against prowlers. Two sides, then, were secure.
He couldn't climb the wall, wouldn't have gone over the cliff. The
third side, marked by tall pines, was bounded by another high
wire-mesh fence. The fourth side—the uphill side where I stood—
was bordered by three private pieces of property. One of the lots
ended in the privet hedge. The second lot was bounded by a brick
wall. A wooden fence secured the third piece of property. The
enclosed tract of overgrown land measured about two hundred
feet square.

"If he's in there," Marsten said, "we've got him. He can't get
out. But the cover's so thick, you should order a helicopter."

The remark was typical of Marsten. He was always suggesting,
always pushing. Always bucking. I turned deliberately away from
him and moved a few paces down the steep slope and into the
cover of the first small, twisted trees. For a moment I stood alone,
eyeing the wooden fence that adjoined the brick wall. The fence
was no more than five feet high.

Howard could have escaped over the fence, the weakest point.

If he'd escaped, and I ordered a 'copter, I'd look like a fool.
Once every three months, the departmental comptroller called
each unit commander into his office for a "cost of operations" re-
view. For all of us, it was a dreaded moment of truth.

And a helicopter was charged out at three hundred dollars an
hour.

I drew a deep breath. "All right, Howard," I called. "Come on
out. Bring the gun with you. Throw it on the ground when we tell
you to do it. You've got one minute."

Except for a woman's head thrust out of a nearby window,
there was no response. I called again, louder. Nothing.

By now, I knew, two black and white units were standing by,
parked on Greenwich Street. I switched on my walkie-talkie and
ordered the uniformed men to come down the stairs—with their
units' shotguns. And flack vests and helmets, if they had them.

Less than a minute later, with all of us crouched like jungle sol-
diers among the low-growing trees, I was explaining the problem
to the four uniformed men, two of whom I knew by name, two by
sight.

I pointed to the uphill perimeter: toward the hedge, the brick
wall and the wooden fence. "Two of you guard that line," I ordered, indicating the two men I didn't know by name. "If he's

going to break out, he'll probably try to go over one of those fences, or else through the hedge, maybe." The two men were young and nervous. Both wore khaki-colored Army flack vests and big white helmets with S.F.P.D. stenciled in front. The bulky vests made their arms look frail and spindly. The helmets made their necks look scrawny. Both swallowed hard—then nodded in unison. They looked like boys playing war, dressed in their fathers' combat gear.

"The rest of us will spread out," I said. "We'll work our way downhill to the cliff, through the trees. Each of you will carry a shotgun. Marsten, you take the far side—" I pointed uphill, toward the pines and the cyclone fence. "I'll take the left. Let's try and keep a line. And let's not shoot each other."

The two young patrolmen tried to smile—but couldn't make it. Holding his shotgun high, Marsten began forcing his way through the underbrush. Watching the decisive, bull-shouldered way he moved, I realized that Marsten hoped to find Howard first—and kill him.

I drew my revolver and moved to my left, toward the towering concrete wall of the apartment building. The wall was blank, with only a series of vent holes, probably marking bathrooms on each floor. I counted eight balconies overhanging the cliff, one for each floor. On four of the balconies, figures had come to the railing, watching the show below. Sirens and flashing lights and screams and drawn guns attracted them: the rubberneckers, the impassive ghouls. They assembled silently, coming from nowhere—and everywhere. When it was over, when the sirens finally faded away and the blood was drying on the pavement, they silently disappeared.

I turned to my right, looking along the line. Three men with shotguns were working through the tangled trees. Two men with drawn pistols guarded the upper line of fences and walls and hedges.

"This is your last chance, Howard," I called. "It's the hard way or the easy way—your choice."

Nothing.

The silence threatened a fiasco—an assault team assembled against an enemy long gone. Thank God I hadn't called for the helicopter.

"All right," I called out, "let's get him out of there—slow and easy."

In unison, the four of us entered the underbrush. Immediately I was surrounded by foliage. Here there were no tunnels burrowed by playing children. There were only bramble branches, tearing at my clothing. That morning, realizing that I would be interrogating the affluent Cappellanis, I'd have chosen one of my best suits. Now I was sorry. I should have—

A flicker of movement came from my right. Crouching low, I brought my revolver up—and saw the blue of a police uniform over my sights. I lowered the gun just as I heard a shout from my left, above.

"*Policeman. Hey.*" It was a high-pitched voice. A child's voice, from high above me. From one of the high-rise balconies. Looking up, I saw two small arms waving.

"Policeman. *Hey.* I see him. By the fence, there. Right down there. Right down below me, there."

And ahead something moved—something brown, not blue. Through close-growing tree limbs I saw a trouser leg—a shoe—a hand.

And a flash of metal, bright among the branches.

"Over here," I shouted. "To your left. *Here.* He's . . ."

A shot cracked—and another shot. I flinched, then plunged ahead. I couldn't see him now—so he couldn't see me, either. So he couldn't hit me if he shot again.

"Policeman. *Hey.* He's climbing over the fence. *Hey.*"

Arms flailing, legs pumping, feet slipping and sliding, I fought free of the foliage, staggering into a cleared strip of rocky ground that paralleled the building.

He was climbing up the eight-foot wire mesh fence that ran from the apartment building to the edge of the cliff. Incredibly, he'd almost reached the top.

"Howard—" I raised my revolver, shot in the air—then lowered the gun, aiming at the desperately climbing figure. A part of my mind registered the image of a frenzied ape, trapped in his chain-link cage. The distance between us was less than thirty feet. If I squeezed the trigger, I couldn't miss.

He threw his right arm over the top of the fence—then his right leg.

"Howard." I took careful aim at the dangling left leg, and fired.

And missed.

With his left hand he reached for his waistband. The hand disappeared inside his jacket—then reappeared, holding a revolver.

"Howard. Drop it."

Still hanging grotesquely on the fence, clinging to the top by an arm and a leg, he swung the big revolver toward me.

And fired. Once. Twice.

Close behind me, branches snapped, bullets whined.

I raised my revolver, steadied the sights squarely on his chest, and squeezed the trigger. I watched his body convulse, heard him sigh—

—and saw him slowly surrender his ape's grip on the wire, then suddenly fall. The ground was rocky where he fell. He landed flat on his back, spread-eagled. His neck snapped; his head struck the rocks with terrible force. For a moment he lay motionless, staring straight up into the sky. Then, when his eyes began to glaze, his arms and legs began to twitch.

"Policeman. *Hey.* You got him."

PART THREE

The Private Detective

13

When the shooting started in the woods down behind the apartment building, Alex Cappellani jerked and twitched on the settee as if he were imagining the bullets thudding into his own body. His eyes were dark and frightened; his face had a grayish pallor. He had been edgy when I got here an hour ago, but the sandy-haired guy with the gun had completely unnerved him. He had that ostrich look—like he wanted to crawl into a hole somewhere and hide himself from the world.

I said to him, "I'm going to have a look back there. You stay here, don't move."

He gave me a convulsive nod.

Still carrying the fireplace poker, I left him and went into the dining area that was part of the L-shaped living room. The rear windows looked out over the woods, and in the distance over the Bay and the Bay Bridge and the hills of Oakland and Berkeley; I peered through them, but I could not see any sign of Hastings or his partner or the sandy-haired guy—just a uniformed cop with his service revolver drawn, running through the gate in the privet hedge below. There was the sound of distant shouting, and two more echoing shots; then the shooting stopped altogether and there was nothing to hear but the shouts.

I turned away from the windows and hurried back into the living room proper. Alex was up on his feet, one hand pressed against the bandage that encircled his head, his mouth pulled into a painful grimace. He said shakily, "What's happening? Is it over?"

"I couldn't see much," I told him. "But it's over, all right, one way or another."

He sat down again and clasped his hands between his knees. "God," he said. "God."

It got very quiet in there for a couple of minutes. I replaced the fireplace poker and paced around on the balls of my feet, looking over at the front entranceway. Nothing happened. My stomach was knotted up and I wanted a cigarette in the worst way; the craving was sometimes intense in moments of stress.

Another minute crept away. Then there was the sound of heavy footfalls on the stairs outside, and seconds after that somebody pounded on the door. Alex's head jerked up, but I gestured for him to stay seated; I went over into the entryway, up to the door.

"Who is it?"

"Hastings."

I let out a breath and unlocked the door and opened it. Hastings was alone out on the landing. His big athletic body was tight-drawn and his squarish face was grim, damp with sweat. He gave me a brief nod and came inside past me. I shut the door again after him.

"You get him, Frank?"

"Yeah," he said, "we got him."

"Alive?"

"Barely. I had to shoot him. I don't think he's going to last long enough to answer questions."

"Christ. Do you know who he is?"

"His name is Mal Howard. Strong-arm hoodlum, gun-runner, you name it." Hastings looked past me to where Alex was visible in the living room, watching us with his frightened eyes. "That Alex Cappellani?"

"That's him."

He nodded. "Let's have your story first, before I talk to him. What're you doing here?"

"Alex called me at home a little after two," I said. "Out of the blue. He said he's been holed up here since Friday night. The apartment belongs to a girlfriend of his; she's a model, in New

York now on some sort of magazine assignment. He's had her key
for months, apparently."

"Go on."

"He swore to me he hadn't killed Booker—that he found the
body at the Cappellani house, lost his head because he was afraid
he'd be blamed, and came here. But he's not the fugitive type, and
he said he's been having second thoughts. He wanted my advice
about what to do."

"Why you?"

"I suppose because I was working for him and because I had
something to do with saving his life the other night," I said. "Anyhow, I told him to turn himself in, but he wasn't ready to do that,
not without talking to me in person. He sounded sincere and I decided to give him the benefit of the doubt."

"So you agreed to come over here."

"Right. It seemed the best way to handle it."

"And you convinced him to give himself up?"

"Yeah. He balked at letting me escort him down to the Hall,
but I talked him into calling your office. While we were waiting
for you to come the sandy-haired guy—Howard—showed up and
tried to get inside. Only he made too much noise doing it and we
heard him. I armed myself with that poker, ran into the kitchen,
locked the cellar door, and made a lot of noise about having a
gun. I thought it was him coming up to the front door when I
heard you on the stairs."

Hastings inclined his head again, slowly, digesting all of that.
Satisfied, he said at length, "Okay. Now I want—"

Outside, on the stairs, there had been more running footfalls,
and now somebody else began pounding on the door. Hastings
turned and opened it. Past him I saw the other plainclothesman,
the one I didn't know, and a uniformed officer farther back on the
landing, standing against the redwood fence. With the door open I
could hear the excited babble of rubberneckers up on Greenwich
Street, the pulsing wail of approaching sirens.

Hastings and the plainclothesman held a hurried conference.
What they were saying was none of my business; I went back to
where Alex was sitting. He looked up at me in a plaintive way, so
I let him have a small, reassuring nod. The tension had gone out
of me, if not out of Alex, and I felt limp and tired—the way Hastings looked. You don't go up against somebody armed with a gun,

whether directly or indirectly, without a drained physical reaction setting in.

When Hastings finished talking to the plainclothesman he shut the door and came in to where we were and stood in front of Alex. For several seconds he gave him a long, probing look; then he dragged up one of the free-form chairs—the apartment was furnished in somebody's idea of ultra-modernism, all black and white and chrome, with huge impressionistic paintings that took up most of the wall space—and sat down. I sat down too, on the opposite end of the settee from Alex.

Hastings introduced himself. And immediately took a Miranda card from the inside pocket of his suit coat and read Alex his rights. "You understand all of that, Mr. Cappellani?" he said then.

Alex looked at him in a numb way. "Yes."

"Would you like an attorney present?"

"No. No, that's not necessary. I want to cooperate with you."

"Fine. All right, to start with I want to know everything you've done since Thursday night."

In a low, nervous voice Alex told him essentially the same story he had told me on the phone and after I arrived here. It still sounded reasonable and sincere. And foolish. Leo Cappellani had been one hundred percent right about his brother: Alex, it seemed, more often than not acted without good judgment.

When Alex was done speaking, Hastings said, "Let's go over a couple of things. Booker was already dead when you found him?"

"Yes."

"How did you get inside the garage?"

"Through the side door," Alex said. "It was open. I saw it as I pulled into the driveway behind Booker's wagon."

"Did you see anyone else in the vicinity?"

"No. No one."

"Did you touch anything in the garage?"

"No."

"Did you go inside the house?"

"No. I just . . . ran. I was confused and afraid; all I could think to do was to get away from there."

"Do you have any idea who would want him dead?"

Alex shook his head.

"Or why he was murdered?"

"No. No."

"Do you know a man named Mal Howard?"

"Howard? No, I've never heard that name."

"You're sure?"

"Positive. Is he the man who tried to break in here?"

"Yes. Have you left this apartment since Friday?"

"No."

"Not even for a newspaper or groceries?"

"Not at all. I didn't eat much and I listened to the news on television."

"Did you call anybody at all?"

Alex looked at me again. "Just him."

"So no one knew you were here."

"That's right. No one."

"Mal Howard knew it," Hastings said.

That got him a couple of blinks and another bewildered headshake. "I don't know how he could have . . ."

"The woman who lives here—what's her name?"

"Virginia Davis."

"How long have you been seeing her?"

"About six months."

"Is your relationship an open one?"

"Open one?"

"Do other people know about the two of you? Friends of yours, relatives. Or have you kept it a secret for some reason?"

"Oh, I see," Alex said. "No, we haven't kept it a secret. I haven't taken Virginia to meet my family or anything like that; it's just a casual thing—you know, a sex thing. But I've mentioned her to people."

"Would you also have mentioned where she lives?"

"I might have. I don't remember."

"If you did, it would indicate someone you know fairly well has it in for you, wouldn't it?"

"I guess so. But it doesn't make sense. I don't know *why* anybody would want me dead. Except Booker, and now he's dead himself."

"Whoever it is must want you out of the way pretty badly," Hastings said. "What happened here this afternoon makes two attempts on your life in three days."

"I don't know," Alex said again, and there was desperation in his voice now. "I just don't know."

Hastings ran a hand through his thick brown hair. "Do you have any idea what the word 'Twospot' means, Mr. Cappellani?"

That was another one out of left field for Alex, apparently, because the police had not released anything about the Twospot note to the media. He just sat there looking blank. "Twospot?"

"That's right."

"Is that a name or what?"

"We're trying to find out. There was a piece of paper on the floor beside Booker's body, with the address of your Russian Hill house and the word Twospot typed on it."

"Twospot," Alex repeated, and the blank look transformed into a frown. "You know, it does sound vaguely familiar."

"In what way?"

"I'm not sure. I may have heard it once—but I don't know where."

"Think about it, Mr. Cappellani."

Alex thought about it. And came up empty. He spread his hands in a helpless gesture.

On the stairs outside there were more sounds—thudding footfalls, the clatter of something bumping down the steps, a voice grumbling a warning to somebody else to watch out for his end of the stretcher. Which meant that the city ambulance had arrived. I listened to the sounds recede down the stairs to the privet hedge, and then shifted my gaze to Hastings.

"Frank," I said, "do you think Howard might be the man who attacked Alex at the winery?"

"It's possible," he answered. "There's no way of knowing for sure now."

Alex said abruptly, "Maybe this Howard is the one who killed Booker too. Maybe somebody hired him to do it."

"Howard killed Booker, all right. There's not much doubt of that."

I leaned forward. "How do you know, Frank?"

"We found his fingerprints inside the Cappellani house," Hastings said. "And he had a gunshot wound under a bandage on his left shoulder; I checked that before I came up here. It explains the different types of blood on the floor of the garage and what happened to the missing bullet from Booker's gun."

Relief had slackened the muscles in Alex's face. "Christ," he said, "why didn't you tell me all of that before? I've been half out of my head sitting here, worrying that you still suspected me—"

"You're not off the hook yet, Mr. Cappellani," Hastings said quietly. "Running from the scene of a murder, hiding out the way you did, doesn't make you look particularly innocent."

"But I told you—"

"What you told me seems plausible enough, but it doesn't clear you of complicity in Booker's death. Not yet."

Alex's eyes turned plaintive again. "Are you going to arrest me?"

"Not exactly. I am going to take you in as a material witness, for further questioning. You can call your attorney from the Hall of Justice if you've changed your mind about wanting one present."

Alex had nothing to say to that. He stared down at his hands, and the ostrich look came back onto his gray face.

I said to Hastings, "Do you want me to come down to the Hall, too?"

"I don't think so. I'll let you know later if we need you to sign a statement."

So the three of us got on our feet and went out of there, Hastings locking the front door after us with a key Alex gave him. When we climbed up to Greenwich Street there were twenty or thirty people milling around, gawking, and half a dozen reporters and mobile camera crews from the local television stations. Alex covered his face with one arm as Hastings led him away to a parked police car. Most of the media people followed them, chattering questions and working their cameras, but a couple of them decided to come after me. I managed to get to my car before they reached me and locked myself inside. I started the engine, pulled away immediately through the crowd.

And damned if one of the cameramen didn't stand in the middle of the street and film me all the way down to the corner and around it out of sight.

14

I drove straight home to my flat.

On the way the attempted break-in by Mal Howard, Howard's apparent death, the things Alex Cappellani had told me, and then Hastings, kept replaying in my head. Along with the string of questions centering on this whole business: Who wanted Alex dead, and why? Why hadn't his attacker killed him outright at the winery on Thursday night, instead of knocking him unconscious and trying to drag him off somewhere else? Why had Booker been killed? How and why had Howard been recruited as triggerman? What did Twospot mean? Was the Cappellani Winery a factor, or did the motive or motives behind the murder of Booker and the two attempts on Alex have to do with something else entirely?

Too many questions, no answers at all that I could see. Well, Hastings was in the best position now to get to the bottom of it, either through a break in further questioning of Alex and the others involved, or through police technology and legwork. And when the break came I'd have my answers. Meanwhile, there was not much point in brooding about the case. Now, finally, I was out of it, wasn't I?

Sure I was.

It was after six when I keyed open my front door; the day was pretty well shot. I had called Shelly Jackson last night and again this morning, with the intention of inviting her out for dinner tonight, but she hadn't been home on either occasion; I had planned to try her again after I got home from the meeting with Alex. Only the events on Greenwich Street had robbed me of all enthusiasm for a Saturday night out on the town, and now I did not feel like doing much of anything except vegetating—curling up on my comfortable old couch with a beer and a stack of pulp magazines.

So I got a can of Schlitz out of the refrigerator and half a dozen issues of *Black Mask* and *Dime Detective* off the shelves, and did that. I read one of the 1931 *Back Masks* straight through from cover to cover—great stuff by Raoul Whitfield, Horace McCoy, Frederick Nebel, and old Cap Shaw himself. Then I had a sandwich and another beer, and came back and sampled stories from the other issues. Two reporters called on the phone, but I put them off with "no comment"; nobody came to see me. By midnight my eyes were a little strained but I was feeling considerably better than I had earlier. You can lose yourself in the melodrama and the machine-gun prose of the pulps, and sometimes when you come back to reality again you find you've left things that were bothering you with the ops and dicks and newshawks in those brittle pages. They're not just fictional crime-solvers for me; they're birds of my feather, and watching them shoulder the burden of their work helps to ease the burden of mine.

I went into the bathroom and changed the bandage on Shelly's teethmarks; the wound was healing all right now. Then I got into bed and drifted off immediately. A long time later I dreamed I was a pulp detective who joined forces with Jerry Frost and Jo Gar and Captain Steve McBride to clean up a gang of Prohibition rum-runners. It was a good dream and I was enjoying it—except that the damned phone kept ringing while we were trying to interrogate the boss rum-runner. McBride answered it, but it kept on ringing anyway. Race Williams came in out of nowhere and blew it to pieces with one of his .44s, and it kept on ringing, and the dream got confused and mixed up with reality, and I woke up.

There was daylight in the room: morning, early Sunday morning. Seven A.M., for Christ's sake, by the clock on my nightstand. Beside the clock, the phone kept on jangling. I scraped mucus out of my eyes, pinched the bridge of my nose until I was awake enough to be coherent, and finally caught up the receiver and said hello.

A woman's voice made a question out of my name. When I said

yes, it was, she said, "This is Rosa Cappellani. I apologize if I've gotten you out of bed but it couldn't be helped."

God, I thought, now what? I threw the covers off and swung up into a sitting position with my feet on the cold hardwood floor. Outside the bedroom window tracers of broken fog chased each other across the roofs of the neighboring buildings. Which told me that in another couple of hours the fog would have blown inland and burned off and the day would be clear and windy.

I said, "What can I do for you, Mrs. Cappellani?"

"I'd like to see you this morning, as soon as possible."

"About what?"

"I'd rather not discuss it on the telephone."

"If it has to do with Alex and what happened yesterday, I can't tell you anything more than you already know by now."

"I don't want you to tell my anything," she said. "I want you to do something for me—something for which you'll be well paid."

The imperiousness was there in her voice, but it was muted somehow; I thought she sounded tired and worried. I ran my tongue over the sleep film on my teeth, thinking about it.

"Well?" she said.

Well. "Where are you?"

"At the winery."

Another hundred-and-fifty-mile drive, round trip. But I was curious, and if she was willing to pay for my time I was willing to drive up to the Napa Valley again. I said, "Okay, Mrs. Cappellani. I should be able to get there by ten."

"Fine," she said, and she sounded relieved. "I'll expect you then."

She rang off before I could say anything else; I had wanted to ask her about Alex, if he was still in police custody or if the family lawyers had gotten him released. I sat there and looked at the silent handset for a couple of seconds, realized what a stupid thing that was to be doing, and put it down on its hook. Telephones. Every time one had rung the past few days, I seemed to get myself more deeply involved in the trials and tribulations of the Cappellani family.

Maybe Race Williams had the right idea, I thought. And got up and went into the bathroom to shower and shave.

In the glare of the morning sun the winery buildings had a dusty, ancient look that made them and the surrounding vineyards seem even more turn-of-the-century Italy or France. A few sun-hatted grape pickers were spots of color here and there in the curving rows of vines, working with lug boxes; a group of men was doing something with one of the gondolas on the north side of the main cellar. Only the trucks and cars parked or moving in the area spoiled the illusion of things past and far away.

I drove down to where the gated lane branched off the road and led up to the old stone manorhouse. The gate was open; I passed through and pulled my car onto a cleared section beneath several of the shading oaks. There were two other cars parked there—a new silver Lincoln Continental and a Porsche a couple of years old.

A warm, vine-scented breeze fanned over me when I stepped out; you could not smell the fermenting wine at this distance from the cellars. I went up a stone pathway, past an old-fashioned bas-ket wine press set on a kind of stone pedestal, with rose bushes and a dozen or so smaller, unfamiliar plants growing around it in a circle. There was nothing else in the way of decoration or gar-den, nothing at all except for the heavy old oaks.

I climbed two steps onto a sort of narrow, galleried porch, found a bell-push beside the black-painted door, and pushed it. The walls must have been a foot thick; I did not hear any bells or chimes ring inside, but the door opened after ten seconds and an elderly Chicano woman looked out at me with grave black eyes.

I told her who I was, and she nodded wordlessly and widened the door so I could come inside. The interior was cool and smelled faintly musty, like the inside of an old cedar chest. But there was not anything gloomy about the place, at least not in the foyer or the rooms off it that I could see into. Unshaded windows let in plenty of morning sunlight, and although the walls and ceil-ings were paneled in heavy dark wood and the floors were of stone, a number of cheerful-looking paintings—Napa Valley land-scapes, mostly—and Indian-style rugs and upholstered furniture in whites and blues added a good deal of color.

The Chicano woman led me down a hallway, pointed to a closed door, and went away toward the rear of the house. I won-dered pointlessly if she was a mute. Then I shrugged the thought away and knocked on the door, calling out my name.

Rosa Cappellani's voice told me to come in. When I opened the door and stepped through, I found myself in a den or office filled with books and file cabinets and old furniture and a lot of military-type decoration: sabers cross-mounted on one wall, a glass case jammed with handguns and bayonets, old cavalry and World War II photographs. An American flag in a floor stand flanked one side of a battered oak desk that appeared as if it had been wounded in action on a number of different occasions. It was a man's office, obviously, not unlike the one in the San Francisco town house; Mrs. Cappellani had no doubt inherited it from her late husband.

She was standing in front of the American flag, wearing a mannish gray suit and a stoic expression. And she wasn't alone.

I shut the door and crossed to the desk. From where he was sitting sprawled on a creased leather sofa, Alex Cappellani watched me with dullish eyes. He looked as if he had been thrown there—legs splayed out, arms propped up at loose angles on the sofa's armrest and back. Raggedy Andy. If he had slept much last night, his face belied the fact; the grayish pallor and the ostrich look were worse than they had been yesterday.

Mrs. Cappellani said, "Thank you for coming," without inflection and without moving.

"Sure." I looked over at Alex. "When did the police let you go?"

"Late last night," he said. His voice was as dull as his eyes. "That lieutenant, Hastings, gave me permission to come up here."

"Have they found out anything new?"

"From me? God, I told you and I told Hastings everything I know yesterday at Virginia's place."

"So you still haven't remembered where you heard the word Twospot before?"

He shook his head loosely.

"And the police haven't learned anything on their own about Howard or who hired him?"

"No. Howard died in the ambulance on the way to the hospital."

Mrs. Cappellani came forward a couple of steps and said to me, "How efficient is this man Hastings?"

"Pretty efficient," I said.

"Then you feel he and his people will find out who is behind Jason's murder and the attempts on Alex's life."

"Eventually, yes."

"Eventually," she said. "And in the meantime?"

"Pardon?"

"Someone clearly wants my son dead, for whatever incredible reason. He doesn't know; I've spoken to him at length and I'm convinced of that." She was talking as if we were the only two people in the room, as if Alex were somewhere else. "That someone has tried twice to kill him or have him killed; it's reasonable to assume that there will be a third attempt."

"Maybe," I said. "And maybe not. Two failures might have scared off whoever it is."

She was silent. But her eyes said she was worried about a third attempt and she did not want any hollow reassurances from me to the contrary. I glanced at Alex. He was plenty worried about it too, you could see that plainly enough. Fear glistened like pinpoints of light in his pupils.

"Look, Mrs. Cappellani," I said, "I can understand and I can sympathize with your concern. But if you asked me up here as an investigator, I'm going to have to turn you down. There's nothing I can do. Even if the San Francisco police would sanction my involvement in a murder case, which they wouldn't, I don't have any facilities for—"

She cut me off with an impatient slicing gesture. "I'm well aware of that," she said, "and I did not bring you here to undertake a private investigation. Nor do I particularly want advice from you."

"Then why *am* I here, Mrs. Cappellani?"

"I want to hire you to act as Alex's bodyguard."

"Bodyguard," I said. But sure, it figured.

"I want you to go everywhere he goes, live with him, stay at his side twenty-four hours a day."

"Uh-huh. For how long?"

"Until the person behind this madness is caught."

"That might be a long time," I said, and thought but didn't add: And it might be never.

"I realize that."

"It could also cost you a substantial amount of money."

"I do not give a damn," she said stiffly, "how much it costs. This is my son's life we're discussing here."

"I wasn't trying to be insensitive, Mrs. Cappellani; I was only stating a fact." I shifted my gaze to Alex again. "How do you feel about this?"

"I don't like it much," he said. "But I'm scared and I don't mind admitting it. Good and scared."

I nodded and said nothing else. The two of them watched me, Alex expectantly, Mrs. Cappellani calculatingly. I swung away from them and walked across to the nearest of the bookshelves and scanned the titles while I did some thinking. Military history, political history, wines and winemaking; no fiction of any kind. There had not been much romanticism in Frank Cappellani's soul, apparently; the same kind of no-nonsense practicality that his wife exhibited.

Behind me she said, "We're waiting."

I turned and came back to them. "I don't carry a gun," I said. "I don't even own one. I don't like them much."

"I see. Which means you refuse to carry one even under special circumstances."

"I'm afraid so."

"Then perhaps we should find someone else who will."

Before I could say anything to that, Alex said, "No," and got abruptly to his feet and came over to me. "Listen, will you take the job if you don't have to carry a gun?"

I hesitated. The truth was, I did not care for personal bodyguard work. The responsibility was too great; if something happened in spite of my efforts, I would have to shoulder the blame— it would be on my conscience. Still, I was already mixed up in this business, I knew most of the people involved, I was curious about what lay behind it all, and I needed the damned money.

Mrs. Cappellani's mouth had puckered up as if she were tasting lemons. "He isn't interested," she said to Alex, and there was disdain in her voice; now it was me she was talking around. "There's no point in wasting any more time with him."

Alex ignored her. To me he said. "I trust you. Christ knows, I need somebody to trust right now. And I watched you in the apartment yesterday, when that Howard character tried to break in. You know how to handle yourself in a tight situation, and you don't need a gun to do it. Take the job, will you? For God's sake."

I let out a breath. He was like a frightened puppy, and how do you turn your back on a frightened puppy? I said, "I'll have to make a telephone call first."

"To whom?" From Mrs. Cappellani, acknowledging my presence again. She wanted me as badly as Alex did, I realized— either because he had convinced her earlier that I was the only man for the job, or for reasons of her own.

"You can listen in if you like. May I use your phone? It's a long-distance call."

"Of course."

The thing was anchored on one side of the desk; I went over to it and picked up the handset. One of the two buttons marked "Open Line" was already depressed. I dialed the 415 area code for San Francisco and then the number of the Hall of Justice. Frank Hastings turned out to be in his office, despite the fact that it was Sunday, and he came on the line right away.

I told him where I was and why I was here and what I had been asked to do. "I wanted to check with you before I take the job," I said. "If you have any objections I'll back off."

He thought it over for a couple of seconds. "Just bodyguard work, nothing else?"

"Right. If anything should come up that you'd be interested in, you'll hear about it right away."

"Go ahead, then." He paused. "Just take it easy out in those vineyards this time. No more nighttime wrestling matches."

I smiled a little. "Not if I can help it. Thanks, Frank."

"Keep in touch," he said.

I rang off and turned to look at Alex and Mrs. Cappellani. They were both staring at me, standing side by side.

"All right," I said. "You've hired yourselves a bodyguard."

15

Twenty minutes later, with money matters settled, Alex took me up to my room on the second floor rear, adjacent to his room. It was spacious but cluttered with the sort of old dark mismatched furniture that people replace individually with more modern fixtures, can't bear to get rid of for sentimental reasons, and tuck away in guest rooms like this one. The windows overlooked the cellars and the pond and the green-and-brown vineyards beyond. There wasn't a connecting door between the two rooms, but there was a connecting bathroom that amounted to the same thing.

I was only going to be staying here tonight, since Alex had told me he was planning to return to San Francisco in the morning; otherwise Mrs. Cappellani would have had to send somebody down to my flat for toiletries and changes of clothes, or I would have had to go down there myself with Alex for company. He had not sounded happy about returning to San Francisco; he still wanted to crawl into a hole for the duration, and the one that looked best to him was right here. But he had obviously decided —no doubt with his mother's help—that it was best for him to keep his mind occupied by keeping up a pretense of normal activity. I could just hear the old dragon telling him that there was no shame in being afraid, only in letting others see just how frightened you really were.

After I had looked the room over I said, "What about today, Alex? You have any plans?"

"I'd like to get shit-faced drunk," he said.

"That won't help any."

"I know that." He smiled in an ironic, humorless way. "There's a fest this afternoon; we're all supposed to go."

"Fest?"

"Wine fest. There are a lot of them in the Valley around this time, after the crush. This one's being put on by the Simontaccis; they own one of the big vineyards a few miles up the Silverado Trail, and we buy most of their grapes."

"Do you want to go?"

"Christ no. Music, dancing, picnic lunches—it makes me cold just thinking about it. But I've got to go anyway. The Simontaccis have been having these things for twenty years and the Cappellanis always attend in full force. It's tradition, good PR."

"Under the circumstances, I'd think you could bow out gracefully."

"Tell that to Rosa. She's going, and so are Leo and Rosten and Shelly and the rest of the people from here and from the office. She thinks I ought to go too. So I'm going—and you're going."

"Uh-huh."

"Don't look at me like that. I'm not a mama's boy, despite appearances. It's just that she's one hell of a tough woman and I've learned the hard way that it's easier to let her call the shots."

"Does Leo feel that way too?"

"He wouldn't admit it but he listens to her as much as I do."

"Is he already here?"

"Yeah. He came up last night."

"Does he know about this bodyguard idea?"

"No. Not yet. Nobody knows but you and me and Rosa."

"They'll all have to know eventually."

"So they'll know," he said, and it was obvious by his tone and his expression that he did not care for the idea. Pride, probably—the Cappellani pride that Leo had alluded to and that was obvious in Rosa. *Don't let anyone know how frightened you really are.* "Look, the fest doesn't start until one o'clock and I don't feel like being cooped up in here until then. You know anything about winemaking?"

"Not much, no," I said.

"Then let's go down to the cellar. I'll show you around."

So we went downstairs again and out into the sunlit morning. On the way I didn't see any sign of Mrs. Cappellani, who was probably still in her late husband's office, or of the silent maid. Or of anyone else. But when we walked down the lane and turned onto the road, I saw Leo and Paul Rosten come out from the direction of the nearest small cellar and start toward us.

Beside me Alex said softly, "Here we go."

I said, "I'll handle the explanations if you want."

"Yeah."

When the four of us came together on the road, Rosten was wearing a grave expression and Leo no expression at all. Neither of them seemed surprised to see me—maybe because too many surprising things had happened in the past few days.

"You do get around, don't you," Leo said to me. But there was no irony in the words; it was just a statement. He appeared cool and imperturbable, and the image was enhanced by his country-squire-casual outfit: a tailored white short-sleeved bush jacket and the kind of faded denims that cost upward of forty dollars.

"Your mother asked me to come up, Mr. Cappellani."

"Oh?"

"She's concerned that there might be another attempt on Alex's life," I said. "She thought it would be a good idea to have me around for a few days."

"I see."

Abruptly Alex said, with some challenge, "You don't mind, do you, Leo?"

"What sort of question is that? Why should I mind?"

"You didn't like the idea of my hiring a private detective in the first place. You've made that plain enough."

"That's an entirely different matter; you were meddling in Rosa's private affairs. Now that Booker has been killed and your life is in jeopardy, we need all the help we can get."

"Thanks for your concern."

"Is that sarcasm, Alex?"

Alex just looked at him.

Around the cold nub of a Toscana cigar, Rosten asked me, "Are you going to be investigating what's happened?"

"Private detectives aren't allowed to work on murder cases," I said.

"Well, the police don't seem to be getting anywhere."

"They will. They just need time."

Leo said, "Have you had bodyguarding experience?"

"Enough."

"Good. Then I'll feel better about things with you watching over my brother."

Alex did not like that. "The hell with this crap," he said, and pushed between Leo and Rosten and started down the road again in short choppy strides.

I nodded to Leo, to Rosten, and went after Alex. When I caught up with him I said, "Take it easy. You won't do yourself any good if you let things get to you."

"Yeah," he said.

"You don't get along with your brother, is that it?"

"He's a bastard. He's just like my mother—thinks he's superior, thinks I'm a weakling and a fool."

He had nothing more to say after that, and we crossed the gravel yard and entered the cellar in silence.

For the next hour he showed me the grape crushers and the French continuous action wine presses and the testing laboratory and the bottling plant; he told me how grapes were vinified, how varietals were made, how samples were taken from dozens of different grapes and vines so that the total sugars and total acids could be measured for the best balance. It was all a little like being with a programmed automaton: a steady stream of facts and figures, with no interest or enthusiasm whatsoever. There was nothing I could do to bring him out of his funk, nothing I could say to reassure him; I just let him drone on, asking polite questions now and then to keep him going.

It was past noon when we came out of the bottling plant, and he had turned restless and sullen by then. He said, "We might as well go back to the house. It's almost time for the goddamn fest."

So we went back to the house. And a little while after that we filed out again with Rosa and Leo and got into the Lincoln Continental—it belonged to Leo—and drove off through the vineyards in an atmosphere of grim silence. Like people on their way to a funeral instead of a fest.

There were at least a hundred people at the Simontacci place, considerably more than I had expected, and the party was already in full swing. Picnic benches had been set out under oak and pepper trees in the side garden of a rambling old brick house—the house and its two outbuildings sat in the middle of several hundred acres of foothill vineyards—and a couple of guys in peasant costume strolled among them, playing Italian polka music on a pair of accordions. Woman in brightly colored skirts and dresses and men in crisp white shirts danced together or talked among themselves; a dozen or so children ran around playing games the way kids do. Two small wine casks sat on chocks to one side, tended by a jovial mustached man, and beyond there were a long brick-sided barbecue pit and two tables overflowing with salads and a dozen different kinds of antipasto. The air was pungent with the smoky aroma of barbecuing chicken.

An elderly type in Neapolitan country garb greeted the Cappellanis; I gathered that he was the head of the Simontacci family. Other people joined them, and there was a lot of handshaking and vocal gaiety that struck me as being a little forced: everyone was aware of the recent events and trying to pretend that they weren't. Nobody paid any attention to me.

I drifted over to one of the pepper trees and stood watching Alex. He had the sort of half-panicked look on his face a person gets when he wants desperately to be alone somewhere and finds himself instead in the middle of a crowd. In less than a minute he broke away from the group, hurried over to where the wine casks were, and got a large glass of red wine from the bartender. Then he went to one of the empty picnic benches and sat down and worked on the wine, not looking at anybody, withdrawing into himself. It was obvious he did not want company; I stayed where I was under the pepper tree.

More people arrived, among them Paul Rosten and Logan Dockstetter. Dockstetter was alone—I did not see any sign of Philip Brand—and his pinched face was gaunt-eyed and troubled. Lovers' quarrel? Or was there something else on his mind? He spent a couple of minutes saying hello to Rosa and Leo and a few of the others, and then, like Alex, made for the bartender and the wine casks.

Time passed, and the party got louder and gayer. I did not enjoy it much. I wasn't here for festive reasons, that was one thing; and another was that these people were all strangers—even the Cappellanis—and I did not belong to their way of life, pleasant as it might have been. It gave me an uncomfortable feeling, as if I were an interloper.

Alex had two more large glasses of wine and his face took on color, and he began to come out of himself a little; he spoke to some of the others, circulated in a hesitant way. But it was the kind of loosening that is sometimes double-edged: you need more and more alcohol to maintain it, and the more you drink the more likely your mood will eventually shift back into an even deeper depression. If he gets drunk, I thought, then what? Do I step in and handle him myself, like a keeper? Or do I let his mother take care of—

A voice at my elbow said, "Well—look who's here."

I blinked and turned my head, and it was Shelly.

She was dressed in a flared Mexican skirt and an opennecked white blouse with puffy sleeves, and she had her head cocked to one side, smiling at me in that bold way of hers. Dapples of sunlight made her auburn hair shine with red-gold highlights. Looking at her, I felt a faint stirring of sexual need; my attraction to Shelly Jackson seemed to be sharpening a little more each time I saw her.

She said, "I had a feeling you might be around, after that business with Alex in San Francisco yesterday."

I smiled back at her. "You know about that, huh?"

"Word gets around. So do you—for somebody who isn't working for the Cappellanis."

"You might as well know," I said. "I'm working for them now."

"As a bodyguard, maybe?"

"Is that a lucky guess?"

"Educated guess." She glanced over the crowd and settled her gaze on the wine casks. Alex was there again, waiting for a refill. His face had a damp, glazed look now that had nothing at all to do with the warmth of the afternoon. "Poor Alex," she said. "He really doesn't know how to cope with a crisis, does he."

"It isn't easy for anybody to cope with two attempts on his life."

"No, I suppose it isn't. Her eyes turned sober. "Do the police have any clues yet?"

"I don't know."

"Are you going to watch over Alex for the duration?"

"Maybe; that's up to him and Mrs. Cappellani."

"Well, it'll be nice to have you around for a while."

"Will it?"

"I think so." The bold look again. "Weren't you supposed to call me? It seems to me you said something about that at lunch the other day."

"I did call you, as a matter of fact," I said. "Friday night and yesterday morning."

"I came up here Friday night. What did you have in mind?"

"Dinner, a show. Something like that."

"Something like that," she said. "Well, right now you can buy me a glass of wine."

We walked over to the casks. Aelx had drifted away again, but Dockstetter was there for a refill of his own. As we approached, Rosten came up from the opposite direction and jostled Dockstetter's arm and made him spill some of his wine over the sleeve of his cashmere jacket; it looked like an accident, but Dockstetter wheeled around and gave him a withering glare.

"What do you think you're doing?" he snapped.

"Sorry," Rosten said. "It was an accident."

"Oh—was it?"

Rosten's eyes narrowed. "You calling me a liar?"

For a moment there was the kind of belligerence in Dockstetter's face that a man gets when he's spoiling for a fight. Maybe Rosten was a specific target, or maybe it was something and somebody else bothering Dockstetter and the winemaker was a handy outlet. But then the belligerence faded, and his mouth turned petulant; he held up his stained coat sleeve.

"You've ruined this jacket," he said. "Red wine won't come out of material like this."

"That's too bad," Rosten said.

"I ought to make you buy me a new one."

"Yeah, sure." Rosten turned away to the bartender.

Dockstetter glared at his back for a couple of seconds and then spun the other way, toward where Shelly and I were. He gave Shelly a passing glance, me a slightly longer one, but said nothing to either of us. He disappeared behind us into the crowd.

I said to Shelly, "What's his problem?"

"Who knows? He had a fight with his boyfriend at the office Friday afternoon, God knows about what, and Brand hasn't shown up here; maybe that's it." She shrugged. "You know how these fags are."

No, I thought, I don't. But I said only, "Has there been trouble between Rosten and Dockstetter in the past?"

"Not that I know of. But Brand and Rosten have had words."

"What about?"

"Winery matters. Brand thinks Rosten is incompetent."

"Is he?"

"Not according to Leo and Mrs. Cappellani."

"Does Alex get along with Dockstetter and Brand?"

"He tolerates them and vice versa. You're not thinking that it could be one of them who's trying to kill him?"

"I'm not being paid to think anything," I said, but that was a half-truth. I was thinking about the possibility, all right—not that it got me anywhere. It could be Dockstetter or Brand or both of them, but it could also be Rosten, or Leo, or Shelly herself, or anyone else Alex was acquainted with. Without positive evidence of some kind, it was nothing but a damned lottery.

We got glasses of white wine—Grey Riesling, Shelly said it was —and took them to one of the picnic benches. We talked for a time about nothing much, and I looked around periodically to keep tabs on Alex. He was still belting wine. When I saw him go back to the casks for yet another refill I excused myself from Shelly and went over to him.

"You'd better take it easy with that stuff," I said.

There was a bleariness in his eyes that made the whites seem curdled. "Why?" he said. "What difference does it make?"

"I thought you decided getting drunk wouldn't solve anything."

"Neither will staying sober."

"I told you earlier that I don't like bodyguard work much," I said. "I don't like it at all if it means looking out for a drunk."

"All right," he said, and waved a hand loosely, and the expression on his face became self-pitying. "All right, have it your way." He banged his empty glass down on the table, left it there, and moved off a little unsteadily.

I rejoined Shelly, and she asked me if I knew how to polka, and I said it had been a long time and I wasn't much good at it anyway; dancing was the last thing I felt like doing at the moment. We sat talking some more instead, listening to the accordion music. From time to time she touched my hand or my arm, and finally she moved close to me and I could feel the warmth of her hip and thigh against mine. I wondered if she was feeling the same sexual stirrings I was.

At three o'clock the elder Simontacci called lunch. We sat with the Cappellanis and Rosten and ate antipasto and barbecued chicken and garbanzo bean salad and homemade French bread. I had not had anything all day, so I wolfed my portion; Shelly ate with the same gusto. But nobody else seemed to be hungry, and there was little conversation. Leo appeared more interested in the passage of attractive women than in any of us—I wondered briefly where his wife was—and Rosa gave most of her attention to Alex. She did not look at Rosten and Rosten did not look at her; I thought that if Brand had been right in his comment at The Boar's Head and they had or had had some sort of sexual relationship, it was completely private and secretive. Alex picked listlessly at his food and semed to be getting more and more restless. And half-way through the meal he got up abruptly, without saying anything, and went off toward the Simontacci house.

He was gone for fifteen minutes. When he came back I knew right away that he had gone after more alcohol in spite of my warning; the color was high in his face and he was walking in that slow, measured pace drunks affect when they don't want you to know they've been drinking: it doesn't fool anyone but themselves. Well, *damn* it. I gave him a sharp look as he sat down, but he avoided my eyes.

Beside him Leo said distastefully, "My God, you smell like a fermentation vat. How much have you had to drink?"

"None of your business," Alex muttered.

"It's my business if you make a spectacle of yourself."

"Sure, that's right. Somebody's trying to make me dead and all you think about is your public image."

Rosa said, "Alex, be quiet," in her imperious voice.

He ignored her. "How'd you feel if you were a target instead of me?" he said to Leo. "Huh? How'd you feel?"

"I wouldn't get drunk in public," Leo said.

"You'd be nice and calm and rational, right?"

"Yes."

"Oh sure," Alex said. "Big man, big business executive—a god-damn iceberg, that's what you are. No feelings at all. You don't give a shit about anything except profit-and-loss statements and Monday-noon projects; you don't care about anybody except yourself."

We were all staring at him now, Leo with his face drawn tight and cold. Rosa said in a flat, mother-to-recalcitrant-children tone, "That's enough, both of you. You're only making matters worse."

"Screw it," Alex said. He shoved away from the bench again, stood up; he seemed to be having trouble keeping his eyes focused.

"Where are you going?"

He did not answer her, but then he didn't have to: he went off in an unsteady gait toward the wine casks.

The rest of us exchanged glances. I said to Mrs. Cappellani, "Unless you've got an important reason to stay on here, I think we ought to get him home."

She nodded. "Yes, you're right."

"Do you want me to tell him?"

"No. I will."

"You can also tell him that if he keeps on drinking, I won't go on working for him. I mean that, Mrs. Cappellani; I'm no good with drunks."

That broke things up. She gave me a long unreadable look but no argument; another nod, short and stiff, and we all stood from the bench. Shelly took my arm, and when Mrs. Cappellani and Leo and Rosten were out of earshot she said, "One big happy family. You're going to have your hands full if you stay on."

"Yeah," I said.

Two accordion players started up with a traditional tune, and the people at the benches began clapping their hands in time to the music. There was laughter, spontaneous singing.

Some fest, I thought wryly. Some celebration.

16

It was after four when we got back to the Cappellani Winery. I rode in the back seat with Alex; Leo did the driving and Mrs. Cappellani sat like a block of granite beside him. None of us had much to say. Alex was sullen and fidgety, and you could see the beginnings of withdrawal sickness in his eyes and in the blotchy pigmentation of his skin.

When Leo parked the Lincoln in front of the house, Alex got out immediately without saying anything to any of us and went inside in quick jerky strides: a man on his way either to his bed or to his toilet to do some vomiting. The rest of us got out and stood looking after him. As soon as he was gone, Rosa turned to me.

"He won't drink any more today," she said. "He'll probably just sleep."

I nodded.

Leo said, "He never could hold his liquor very well."

She fixed him with a stony gaze. "Must you always make disparaging comments about Alex?" She said. "He's not as strong as you, Leo, we all know that—and he knows it as well as any of us."

Leo seemed about to argue with her, changed his mind, and

said instead, "Yes, I guess he does. Maybe you're right, Rosa. Maybe I have been a little rough on him."

You said it, brother, I thought.

The two of them went into the house. I stayed out there in the warm sunshine, for no particular reason except that I did not want to shut myself up in any of those musty rooms. It was quiet in the vineyards and around the winery buildings; all of the grape pickers and the cellar workers had evidently gone home for the day. Shelly and Rosten—and Dockstetter too, I supposed—were still at the fest. Shelly had said, just before we left, that she would see me later tonight; I may have read promise in that where none was intended, but I found myself thinking now, again, about going to bed with her.

I killed five minutes doing nothing, decided that was hardly what I was getting paid for, and finally went inside. Neither Leo nor Mrs. Cappellani was around; the house had a hushed aura to go with its mustiness, like something out of a Gothic novel. Or maybe that was just my imagination.

Upstairs, I went through my room and into the adjoining bathroom and stood listening at the closed door to Alex's room. Silence, except for a faint breathy sound that might have been snoring. I opened the door and looked in, and Alex was sprawled out face down on his bed, clothes on, shoes on, breathing heavy sour odors through his nose. I went in there and took his shoes off and opened his shirt and covered him with a blanket. He did not move through any of that; he was going to be out for a while.

Back in my room, I pulled off my jacket and my own shoes and lay down on the bed. I thought about reading, but I had not brought any pulps with me and the only books I had seen downstairs were those on military history and winemaking. So I closed my eyes, just to rest—but the day had already been a long one: I was pretty tired. I fell asleep within minutes.

Nothing happened to disturb me, and it was dark when I woke up. My watch read seven forty-five. I got up and put my jacket on —the air in there had turned a little chilly and a little dank; I did not like the feel of it in my lungs—and went to look in on Alex again. He was still sleeping, lying on his back now, the bedclothes rumpled around him.

That damned musty dankness drove me out of my room and downstairs. People can learn to like living in different places, different environments, but the Cappellanis could have this place and welcome to it.

When I stepped down into the foyer I saw somebody sitting in the big family room across from the stairs. Shelly. I detoured over there and went inside, and she smiled when she saw me and got to her feet. There was nobody else in the room.

"Sitting here all alone?" I said.

"Not until a couple of minutes ago. I was having a drink with Leo, but he's gone into a business conference with Mrs. Cappellani. He's leaving for San Francisco tonight."

"When did you get back from the fest?"

"A little after five. It was pretty dull after you left. How's Alex?"

"Still sleeping it off."

"Looks like you've been sleeping yourself. Your hair's mussed."

Which told me I had forgotten to run a comb through it before leaving the bathroom. Old age or chronic slob, take your pick. I got the comb out and worked with it briefly and put it away again. "Better?"

"I liked it more the other way. Want a drink?"

"I don't think so. I was going out for some air. How about joining me?"

"I'd love to—as they say in the old movies."

We went outside and wandered down the lane and then down the road past the cellar. There were drifting clouds in the sky now, obscuring what there was of a moon, and the air had an autumn crispness that cleared my lungs immediately. We were the only two people out and around that I could see. The winery buildings and the rolling vineyards were dark shadows against the dark sky; the nightlights on the main cellar had a remote look.

Shelly took my arm and held it so that I could feel the swell of her breast, intentionally or otherwise. I began to think again about getting laid. She was thinking about it too, because when we got down beneath the black oak near the pond she stopped abruptly and turned to face me, and a couple of seconds after that we went into a clinch. As they say in the old movies.

The intensity of her kiss surprised me: there was a kind of violence in it. Violence, too, in the way she wrapped both hands not around my neck but in the material of my shirt, as if she wanted to tear it off me, and in the hard thrusts of her body against mine. It went on that way for twenty or thirty seconds before I stopped it; one of her clutching hands had dug into the wound where she'd bitten me on Thursday night.

"Hey," I said, "take it easy. I'm an old man."

"Sure you are." Up close this way, her face had a kind of fixed intensity of its own. Even in the darkness I could see that her eyes were bright and excited. "Let's go somewhere."

"Where? Your cottage?"

"No. Come on."

She let go of my shirt, reached down for one of my hands, and pulled me along the shore of the pond. But there was nothing where she was heading except the curving rows of grape vines. I said something to her about that, but she didn't give me an answer; she just kept moving forward, hurrying, holding tightly to my hand. I had known eager women in the past, and I had been eager myself a few times—I was eager enough right now—yet there seemed to be something just a little odd about the way she was acting.

She led me straight up into the vineyard, between two rows of tall old vines where the ground was hard and clodded. Then she stopped and pivoted to me, kissed me again—quick, hard—and tugged on my jacket and my arm so violently that we both went down to our knees. She leaned in against me, breathing rapidly now, and began banging the side of my neck with a bunched fist. Not gently; with enough force to hurt.

Confusion and the pain from her blows made me grab both her wrists, hold her away from me. "Christ, Shelly," I said, "what're you doing?"

"Come on," she said, and there was a kind of animal wildness in her face. "Come on, come on."

"Here?"

"Right here, right now. Just like the other night."

"What?"

"Rough, rough. Make me fight you, hurt me a little."

I got it then, and it was like having cold water splashed on the back of my neck. I said, "Jesus."

"What are you waiting for? Come on!"

Just like the other night, I thought. Out here in the vineyards. That was the big attraction for her, that was what all those looks had meant on Thursday and at The Boar's Head on Friday and this afternoon at the fest. *Make me fight you, hurt me a little.* All the eagerness and all the desire went out of me; I released her wrists and pushed up onto my feet.

I said, "No. No way."

She sat on her knees on the hard ground and stared up at me; the wildness faded out of her expression, the intensity faded, and what was left was bewilderment. Thickly she said, "What's the matter with you?"

"I'm not into rough stuff. If that's the impression you got of me the other night you couldn't be more wrong."

Silence at first while she came to terms with what I was telling her. Then things happened in her face, giving it a bunched, masklike appearance for an instant, and she called me something obscene that I was not and never would be. I thought I was going to have to deal with savage outrage—only she surprised me on that score too. As soon as the one word was out of her mouth, her features smoothed and her lips quirked upward at one corner in a wry smile. She got slowly to her feet.

"You like your sex all cozy and cuddly in bed, is that it?" she said. "Strictly missionary position, right?"

"Not exactly. But you've got the idea."

"Then that's your tough luck, big man. I stopped liking it cozy and cuddly the first time my ex-husband raped me."

"I'm sorry."

"For me? Bullshit. Different strokes for different folks."

"If you like it that way, why did you fight me the other night when you thought I was a rapist?"

"You were a stranger then," she said, as if that explained it.

The other night. Out here in the vineyards.

The thought made me frown because it kept replaying at the back of my mind. Out here in the vineyards; just like the other night. Then something else jarred in my memory, and all at once I was hearing Frank Hastings's voice on the telephone this afternoon, saying to me at the tag end of our conversation, "Just take it easy out in those vineyards this time. No more nighttime wrestling matches."

But how had Hastings known about what happened between Shelly and me on Thursday night? I hadn't told him; I had not told anyone.

I said abruptly, "Shelly, did you tell anybody about the other night? About us, about what happened with us?"

The sudden shift of the questions made her blink. And then she misread my reason for asking them. Her smile curled up at the other corner of her mouth: contempt mixed with the wryness. "Worried about your reputation?"

"No. Listen, *did* you tell anybody?"

"No, I didn't tell anybody."

So how did Hastings know?

Unless—

Sure. The only other person who could have known, who could have seen me wrestling with Shelly, was the man I had been chasing—the man who had attacked Alex. And if that man had accidentally let a comment slip to Hastings at some time during his investigation, and Hastings could remember who it was . . .

I looked at Shelly for a moment. I did not condemn her for her sexual preferences; I had no right to judge her morality. But she was judging me, all right—hating me a little with her eyes as she had that other time in the vineyards. We had come full circle: we had no more relationship now than we'd had before I mistook her for Alex's assailant.

So there was nothing to say to her except good night; I said that and then turned and made my way back between the rows of vines. She had one last thing to say, though, and she said it to my back. "Big man," she said, but with different meaning and different inflection than any of the times before.

In my room at the house I picked up the extension phone, punched an "Open Line" button, and dialed the number of San Francisco's Hall of Justice. I did not expect Hastings to be there at this hour on a Sunday night, and he wasn't. The guy I spoke to on the Homicide Squad said he wasn't at liberty to give out home telephone numbers or information on where officers could be reached to anyone under any circumstances. I got the switchboard back and asked for my friend Eberhardt, but he was not at the Hall either.

Telephones, I thought. I was getting pretty damned sick of them.

I rang up Eberhardt's house, found him in, and got him to part with Hastings's home number. When I tried that number, a woman's voice answered and wanted to know who was calling and then went away with my name; half a minute after that I heard Hastings's voice.

"What's up?" he asked.

"I'm not sure yet," I said. "Maybe something useful. Do you remember the last thing you said to me this morning—about not having any more nighttime wrestling matches in the vineyards?"

"Vaguely. Why?"

I explained it to him.

"I see what you mean," he said. "But even if you're right, it's hardly conclusive evidence."

"No, but it's something worth pursuing. Can you recall who told you about it, Frank?"

"Not offhand. I've talked to dozens of people in the past few days. Give me a minute to think."

I waited. It seemed even danker in the room than before; I could feel my chest tightening up again. I carried the phone over to the window and raised the sash several inches to let in some fresh air.

Hastings said at length, "I think I've got it. But when I give you the name, what're you planning to do?"

"That's up to you. It's your baby."

"Not exactly. The man we're talking about is probably up there at the winery with you, and the particular attack in question is the jurisdiction of the Napa County Sheriff's people."

"We could call them in and let them handle it."

"We could, but it's a pretty tenuous thread for any cop to make headway with. At least at this stage."

"Well, I could talk to the guy myself. He cracked my head too that night, and I'm the one who chased him; I might be able to spook him a little, get him to admit something incriminating. And then I could go to the local police with a little more substantive information."

He thought that over. "You wouldn't push it hard enough to get yourself in trouble?"

"No. I know my limits and my obligations."

"All right then, go ahead. But keep me posted."

"I will. Who is he, Frank?"

"The winemaker up there," Hastings said. "Paul Rosten."

17

From the top of the hill where the dirt-and-gravel secondary road crested through the line of eucalyptus trees, I had my first look at what was in the shallow valley beyond. Six small cottage-type buildings, set well apart from each other in random arrangement, all but two of them showing light. More rolling acres of vineyards silhouetted against the cloudy black sky. A continuation of the road I was on, winding past the cottages and out of sight across the brow of another hill.

There was nobody on the road as I took my car down it toward the cottages. There had not been anybody in the vineyards on the other side either, or out around the winery buildings. I wondered if Shelly had gone back to her guest quarters here. Even though Paul Rosten was uppermost in my mind, I had not quite forgotten about her and what had happened a little while ago. The incident had left me with a vague undercurrent of depression, but I did not know if that was because of the discovery we lived in two separate worlds with no common ground, or simply because I had not gotten laid. Genuine regret or wounded male ego?

The hell with it. I concentrated on Rosten.

He could have been the man I had chased on Thursday, all right. He had come to the cellar later, with the Cappellanis and

Brand and Dockstetter, but he could have doubled back to the house through the eucalyptus and through the vineyards; there had been enough time for him to do that and to catch his breath while I was struggling with Shelly. But what motive could he have for bashing Alex over the head? The two of them seemed to get along well enough, and I had not heard anything about bad blood between them. There evidently *had* been bad blood between Rosten and Jason Booker, if what I had overheard Brand say in The Boar's Head was factual, which made it possible that Rosten had been the one to hire Mal Howard to dispose of Booker. But then if Rosten had bludgeoned Alex, why hadn't he taken care of Booker himself? Another thing: Rosten did not strike me as the type of man to go around hiring hardcases like Howard; he was a follower, it seemed to me, not a leader. So was somebody else behind it all—somebody who gave orders to both Howard *and* Rosten and who, for whatever melodramatic reason, was known as "Twospot"?

I gave it up; I just did not know enough facts to begin fitting things together into a coherent pattern.

When I got down to the nearest of the cottages my headlights picked up the figure of a heavy-set man sitting on the porch steps, smoking a cigarette. I recognized him as the assistant winemaker, a guy named Boylan; Alex had introduced me to him earlier, during our tour of the winery. I had no idea which of the cottages belonged to Rosten, so I parked near Boylan's place and went over to him to find out.

He was listening to pop music on a portable radio, and he shut down the volume long enough to answer my question. Rosten's cottage, he said, was the last one on the east, the one with the oak growing in the front yard. I thanked him and moved along in that direction—and I could feel myself starting to tense up as I went.

Maybe bearding Rosten this way was a good idea, and maybe it wasn't. It might have been better if I stayed where I could keep a close eye on Alex tonight and then had my confrontation with Rosten in the morning. But if Rosten *was* a threat, I wanted to know it as soon as possible. And I had checked Alex again before I left the house: he'd still been asleep. If anything else was going to happen to him, I could not believe it would happen while he was in his own bed.

So all right, I thought. I'm here, let's see what goes down.

Rosten's place was somewhat larger and set farther back than the rest; it was porchless, built of framewood anchored on a two-foot stone foundation. A dented, dark-colored Ford pick-up sat off to one side, and on the other side was what looked to be a small vegetable garden dominated by tomato vines. The oak tree was big and leafy and threw heavy shadows over the packed-dirt walk that led up in front. Light glowed behind a shaded window to the left of the door; the window was open a foot or so.

I came up to the door without making any noise: because I had learned to walk softly while I was on the cops and because of the packed ground, rather than with any conscious intent at silence. The night was quiet too, hushed except for the faint droning of insects and the distant rise and fall of music from Boylan's radio. Both of those things—my silent approach, the night's stillness—kept Rosten from hearing me and at the same time let me hear him when his voice said suddenly from inside, muted but distinct, "This is Paul. I've been trying to get you for the past five minutes."

I came to a standstill two feet from the door. My first thought was that he had company, but then I realized he must have just called someone on the telephone—the bloody telephone again. Unlike the pulp detectives, I don't make a habit of eavesdropping; but this was a special case. I stayed where I was and listened.

"Do you still want me to go ahead?" Rosten's voice said.

Pause.

"I just don't like it, that's all. What if something else goes wrong?"

Pause.

"I know that. Don't you think I know that?"

Pause.

"When?"

Pause.

"What about that private detective?"

Pause.

"All right. Yes—I understand."

There was another moment of silence and then a banging, ringing noise, the kind a phone handset makes when it's slammed down into its cradle. As soon as I heard that I made a half-turn and eased backward and at an angle through the deeper shadows of the oak, putting its thick trunk between me and the cottage.

The muscles in my chest and stomach were knotted up: apprehension, urgency. There was little enough doubt in my mind now that Rosten was Thursday night's attacker. What I had just listened to did not have to mean anything ominous, but that was the way I had read it; instinct told me Rosten and whoever had been on the other end of the line were talking about another attempt on Alex's life—and soon, maybe tonight. So there was nothing to be gained in my confronting him now; he would only deny guilt—or maybe even make a try for me, too, when my back was turned. There was no way of telling how dangerous he was, how desperate the motives were behind all of this. My obligation was to Alex; I had to alert him, convince him to leave here as quickly as possible, stash him somewhere safe, and then take my suspicions to the police and let them worry about breaking the truth out of Rosten.

I stepped out of the yard, still in shadow, and broke into a run toward the road, onto it. The front door to Rosten's cottage remained closed. I ran up to where I had left my car, started the engine, swung into a U-turn, and headed back up the hill. There was still nothing to see behind me when I cleared the crest and started through the trees.

When I drove past the deserted cellar buildings to where the house lane intersected the road, a car was just coming out: Leo's Lincoln Continental, with Leo alone at the wheel. He raised a hand to me as he made the turn, heading toward the Silverado Trail. I let him go; with his supercilious attitude, there was nothing I could expect him to do except get in the way.

I left the car half on the parking area and half on the road and hurried inside the house. Cold silence greeted me; you could have heard insects crawling in there. I went up the stairs two at a time, bypassed my room, caught the knob on Alex's door, and pushed inside.

And came to an abrupt stop because the bed was empty, the room was empty.

Alex was gone.

The first thing I did was to run down the upstairs hall, knocking on doors and throwing them open. But the rooms were all dark, unoccupied. Then I came pounding downstairs again and looked into the family room, the dining room, a parlor. Empty, all of them. I was on my way to the office when the Chicano maid came out of another doorway and peered at me with wide eyes.

I said, "Where's Alex? Have you seen him?"

She shook her head.

"Mrs. Cappellani?"

One hand came up and pointed at the office door. I ran to there, shoved it open, and went inside by a couple of steps. Rosa was sitting behind the desk with a big ledger book in front of her and a pencil upraised in one hand like a sceptre. And she was alone.

Her expression fluctuated between annoyance at my sudden entrance and concern at what she must have seen in my face. The concern won out when I said sharply, "Have you seen Alex?"

"Isn't he in his room?"

"He's not in the house at all."

"You're upset. What is it, what's wrong?"

"I don't have time to explain now."

I wheeled around, nearly collided with the maid beyond the doorway, brushed past her, and hustled up to the foyer again. Where the hell was he? And why had he left his room, left the house? A walk to clear his head, maybe—or, Jesus, maybe Rosten had called him and arranged a meeting somewhere on some sort of pretext; I had not even considered that possibility.

There was a cold sweat on my body when I lumbered outside again; I could feet it trickling down from my armpits. My responsibility, goddamn it. If anything happened to Alex tonight, it was my fault, I was supposed to be his goddamn bodyguard . . .

I ran past my car without even realizing it was there. Where? I was thinking. Down at the cellar? At one of the other buildings? Out in the vineyards? *Where?* Then I thought about the car, taking the car, but I was already out through the gate and onto the road. I hesitated, took a step back toward the lane—and saw the pick-up truck down in the yard before the nightlit cellar.

The same Ford pick-up I had seen parked alongside Rosten's cottage.

A sensation like the touch of a cold hand settled on my neck and between my shoulders. The pick-up was backed up near the cellar's entrance, and its headlights were on, laying an elongation of light across the gravel and across the road beyond; I could just hear the steady rumble of its engine. Nothing moved down there —there was just the truck and the frozen beams of light.

I started to run again.

But I had not gone more than ten yards, into heavy shadow

from the bordering oaks, when the shapes of two men appeared through the big brassbound doors, crowded close together, one pushing the other toward the pick-up. I pulled up again, on reflex In the pale shine of the nightlights I could identify both of them, all right—not clearly but clearly enough. I could not identify the object Rosten was holding in one hand, but I knew what that was too. The sensation of coldness deepened and spread; I tasted bile mixed with the brassiness of fear.

I did not know what to do. Neither Rosten nor Alex was looking in my direction, could not have seen me in the shadows if they had been; they were at the passenger door of the pick-up, and Rosten had it open and was pushing Alex inside to the wheel. I couldn't get to where they were before they were ready to drive off—and if I tried it anyway, or if I yelled to let them know I saw them, Rosten might panic and start shooting. *Do something, for Christ's sake!* I backed up, got off the road and into a thicker pocket of blackness. Rosten was inside the pick-up too, now; I heard the engine sound magnify, saw the truck jerk forward and the lights swing around in a left-hand quadrant. They were not coming this way. They were heading back to the east, onto the secondary road that led through the vineyards to the cottages.

I was already moving by then. I raced back to the lane, and just as I got to it Mrs. Cappellani appeared in front of me: she must have followed me down from the house. For the first time she seemed to have lost some of her imperious composure; her face was a white frightened oval in the darkness.

"Call the police," I yelled at her, "tell them Alex has been kidnapped—tell them it's Paul Rosten."

She gaped at me. "Kidnapped? *Paul?*"

"Do what I told you, call the police!"

I shoved past her and made it to where my car was. My breath had a clogged feel in my chest; sweat fused my shirt to my skin, made the palms of my hands slick. I dragged the door open, slid inside. And kicked the engine to life, jammed the transmission lever into reverse, threw my right arm over the seat back, and laid into the accelerator.

The car bucked backward, picked up speed and began to yaw; I had a death grip on the wheel with my left hand. Through the rear window I saw Mrs. Cappellani scurry out of the way, waving one arm up and down in a gesture that seemed to have no meaning.

Then I was past her and through the gate, onto the road in a sliding right-angle turn.

I hit the brakes and got the wheel straightened out and the transmission into Drive. The tires spun in place, smoking, before they caught traction and sent me lurching ahead. I left the headlights off; the last thing I wanted was for Rosten to know right away that I was coming.

When I was abreast of the cellar, still driving too fast and too recklessly, I could see up the secondary road to the line of eucalyptus trees. Empty. No sign of the pick-up.

Where was he taking Alex? His cottage, possibly—but that made no sense; you don't for God's sake bring somebody to your house to kill him. For that matter, why hadn't Rosten just finished him off in the cellar? Questions, questions. And one more, the most important one: what was I going to do to help Alex when I caught up with them?

Cross that bridge when you come to it, I told myself grimly. Find them first, take it one step at a time.

I made a skidding turn onto the secondary road, and I had no choice then but to slow down. The car jounced on the rutted dirt-and-gravel surface, its old springs shrieking in protest; there was the danger of a tire blowing, of losing control. And the night's heavy blackness shrouded the vineyards, moonless and starless because of the running mass of clouds, so that I could not see more than two hundred feet ahead of me with any clarity.

Working the brakes, I cut my speed to thirty as I climbed to the top of the hill. Once I got into the eucalyptus trees I had to chop it all the way down to ten miles per hour: I could barely make out the roadbed in the dark and almost missed negotiating the curve there as it was. On the far side, where I had a clear look down to the cottages, I gave her more gas and hunched forward to scan the area.

There was no activity around any of the cottages, no automobile lights anywhere in the valley; the road was empty all the way to the next hill. But beyond there I could see a suggestion of light against the inky sky. I had no idea what lay in that direction, where the road went or how far it went—but that was where they were.

The slope on the far side of the second hill turned out to be gradual and to blend into a long rumpled terrain full of little hillocks, all of them coated with grape vines. The road curled away to the left and skirted a narrow but longish section ribbed with outcroppings of limestone. I thought I saw the blood-colored flicker of a taillight over there, just as I topped the hill, but then it was gone; the long rocky section hid the path of the road beyond.

I resisted the impulse for more speed—I was not going to do Alex any good at all if I pushed myself into an accident. The tension had tightened up my chest again, making my breath come in short coughing pants. I sleeved sweat out of my eyes, worked saliva through my dry mouth and into the back of my throat.

It took me a full minute to get to where I could see past the wall of outcroppings. The vineyards ended over there and the land was dry, brown, uncultivated, patterned with bunches of trees growing on hillocks and scattered boulders and rock formations. The road dipped down into a hollow, dipped back up again, and went across another rise. Behind the rise light shimmered again, the kind of up-and-down shimmering that an automobile's headlamps make on badly eroded road surfaces. The light kept on dancing that way until I cleared the hollow and started up the slope; but then the wavering lessened, became steadier, became just a reflected glow.

The pick-up had slowed and come to a stop.

Instinctively I took my foot off the accelerator and let it rest on the brake pedal. A muscle on my right cheekbone began to jump; I took one hand off the wheel and wiped it dry on my pantleg, did the same with the other hand. Twenty yards to the top of the rise. I realized I was trying to hold my breath and let it out noisily between locked teeth. Fifteen yards, ten—and I was onto the crown, looking down the far side.

At the foot of a hundred yards of gradual slope, the road leveled off for twenty yards and then came to a dead end in front of a sheer, thirty-foot-high limestone bluff. To the left there was a small stream, flowing north to south, and where it passed along the base of the bluff it filled a kind of geological bowl and became a pool. The pool and the bluff were ringed on three sides by madrone and oak and pine, creating one of those backhill spots that families use for picnics and kids use for gameplaying and beer busts. The pick-up was parked twenty feet from the edge of the pool, and its lights reflected off the wrinkled surface of the limestone formation, giving it an eerie look of frozen, rust-colored water.

I saw all of that in the time it took me to bring the car across the short flat top of the rise, nose it down the other side—three or four seconds. And I saw, too, that neither Rosten nor Alex had yet gotten out of the truck. I had a brief mental image of Alex down there inside, arguing, pleading for explanations, begging for his life, and that kept me from hesitating, wasting time. There was no way I could stop the car and get to them on foot; I had no weapon to use anyway against Rosten's gun. My only option, my only chance, was to use the one thing in my favor: the element of surprise.

I braced myself, held tight to the wheel, and came down hard on the accelerator.

The uneven, chuckholed roadbed made the car bounce crazily up and down as it gathered speed. Through the windshield I watched the pick-up seem to expand in size, watched the doors on both sides because when they heard me coming their first reaction would be to get out of there. When less than thirty yards remained to the bottom of the slope I took my left hand off the wheel long enough to pull the headlight knob. An instant after the lights came on and began throwing weird patterns across the landscape, the passenger door burst open and Rosten started to scramble out with the gun in his hand. The light-glare seemed to blind him; he lost his balance and threw his free hand out to the door to keep himself from falling.

I stood on the brakes.

The car sailed across the bottom of the slope, bounced onto and across the short level stretch. Rosten was just starting to shove away from the passenger door, and Alex had the driver's door halfway open, when I skidded into the back of the pick-up.

Even though I was braced for it, the impact slammed me forward into the wheel and sent daggers of pain through both arms, through my chest. Metal crumpled with an explosive crunching noise, both headlights shattered, the pick-up's rear glass shattered; the force of the collision drove the truck forward to the edge of the pool, rocking it like a hobby horse. I had a confused impression of Rosten down on his hands and knees to one side, where the impact must have thrown him, and of Alex's head and arm thrust through the pick-up's open side window. Then the fusion of twisted metal separated on the right side, and the Ford's rear end slewed around to the right and the rear end of my car came around to the left—the same effect as when you snap a stick in the middle. The truck tilted up on two wheels at the edge of the pool, but the rocks there kept it from falling all the way over into the water. The left front tire on my car jolted up against those same rocks; the engine rattled and died.

I had my left hand on the door handle, and soon as the car came to a shuddering rest I threw the door open and staggered out. Alex was struggling free of the pick-up; I heard him yell something at me. But I was already turned and looking across the hood, looking for and then at Rosten.

He was still down on all fours, crawling a little, trying to stand up and not making it, and then crawling again. He did not have the gun anymore, but in the darkness I couldn't tell where it was or if it was what Rosten was heading after. I swung around the front fender of my car, trying not to stumble on the rocks. Alex shouted something else, and in response I yelled over my shoulder, "Find the gun, get the gun!"

Rosten heard that and heard me coming; his head jerked around and he made another effort to gain his feet, clawing uselessly at the branches of a huckleberry bush for leverage. His left leg would not support his weight: he must have broken a bone or sprained something. He fell back onto his right knee against the bush, with his left leg bent out to the side and one arm coming up to defend himself—but it was too late then, I was on him.

I kicked his left leg just above the ankle, and he made a bleating agonized sound and lunged at me, and I sidestepped that and threw myself down on top of him shoulder first, like a football defender spearing a ball carrier. The breath went out of him; his body jerked wildly beneath my pinning weight. I got him wedged against the base of the huckleberry bush, levered up and managed to set myself for a looping right-hand swing at his head. The blow went past one of his upthrust arms and landed flush on his left temple, snapped his head back and to the right. He made a sighing sound and his body stopped thrashing around under me; I felt him go limp.

And just that quickly, it was over.

I got up in slow, painful movements—stood over him trying to drag air back into my constricted lungs. My chest felt numb, hot; the thin dry cough started up. I ran a hand over my face, took the hand down and peered at it. Steady.

When I looked for Alex I saw him in a flat-footed stance alongside my car, staring over at me; he was holding the gun laxly in one hand. I started toward him, after another couple of seconds, and he moved at the same time—jerkily, as somebody will after a full release of tension. His face was stark and frightened, and his eyes seemed glazed. He looked as sick as a man can look and still be on his feet. I took the gun out of his hand, saw that it was a big plow-handled .357 Magnum, and put it away in my jacket pocket.

"He was going to kill me," Alex said. The sickness was in his voice too. "He was going to shoot me with that gun."

"Yeah," I said.

"He's the one—it must've been Rosten all along. My God. My God, I've known him all my life."

I did not answer him because right then, suddenly, reaction set in—just as I knew it would, just as it always does. The detachment with which I had functioned for the past few minutes vanished, and my hands started to tremble and there was a liquidy feeling in both legs that made me think I was going to fall down. I leaned back against the car and sweated and kept on sweating.

"Why?" Alex was saying. "Why would he want to kill me? *Why?*"

He was talking to himself as much as to me, and I had no answers for him anyway. I looked at Rosten; he had not moved. Then I looked at my hands and waited for them to quit shaking.

18

It was a good two minutes before the reaction faded and I was all right again. When the sweating stopped and my hands were still I went around to the front of the car to look at the damage. Both fenders and the grill were pretty mangled; the bumper had been torn loose on one side and was hanging at a wobbly angle. The tires were okay. The left fender was buckled down to within an inch of that tire, but the clearance was enough so that it would not scrape against the tread when the car was rolling.

Pain lanced through my chest as I straightened up, made me wince until it went away. I felt my ribs and my breastbone, but there seemed to be no damage beyond a couple of bruises; I could breathe almost normally now, without coughing. I walked to the driver's door and slid in under the wheel. Alex started to get in on the passenger side, but I waved him away. We were not going anywhere yet —and maybe not for a while if the engine failed to start.

The first three times I turned the key in the ignition, nothing happened except a grinding stutter. The fourth time, though, it caught and held and seemed to sound healthy enough. I put the transmission into reverse and eased backward away from the pool. The car was drivable, all right, if only for the distance between here and the winery.

I shut off the engine, got out and went around to where Alex was. He seemed to be coming out of it a little now; there was animation in his face and his eyes had lost their glazed look. He said, "Where did you come from? How did you know we were here?"

"I saw Rosten take you out of the cellar and I followed you."

"God, I thought I was dead. You saved my life again."

"That's what you're paying me for," I said bitterly. "Listen, did Rosten tell you anything, give you any explanations?"

"No. He didn't say a word the whole time—not a word."

"What happened at the cellar?"

"He just came in and pointed that gun at me and shoved me outside. I've known him all my life, but he was like a stranger, a crazy man. I was . . . Jesus, I was petrified."

I said nothing. I was thinking that we could wait here for the sheriff's people to show up, but it might take an hour or better for them to come and find us and I did not care much for the idea of sitting here with Rosten and Alex for that length of time. Which meant transporting Rosten back to the winery. Alex was in no condition to drive or to hold a man at bay with a gun; the only safe way to do it, I decided, was to put Rosten in the trunk.

I got the key out of the ignition, took it around to the rear, and unlocked the trunk and raised the lid. Just as I did that Alex shouted, "He's moving over there!"

Quickly I stepped out to where I could see Rosten. But he was not moving much—just twitches and spasms of his limbs. "Take it easy," I said to Alex, "he's not going to give us any more trouble."

I took the Magnum out of my pocket, held it down along my right leg, and walked over to Rosten. The twitches and spasms were giving way to more normal movements, a sign of returning consciousness. I stopped a couple of feet from him, heard him make a groaning sound. Then his body stiffened and was still again—and that told me he was awake and functioning mentally, remembering where he was and what had happened.

"Get up on your feet, Rosten," I said.

He stayed where he was, motionless.

"Get up or I'll put a bullet in you."

That was bluff, but he did not know me nearly well enough to realize it. Another three seconds passed, and then he rolled over slowly and with evident pain and stared up at me out of cold, blank eyes. No hatred, no frustration—no emotion of any kind.

He said thickly, "I can't walk. My ankle's sprained."

"You can hobble. Get up."

He got up, putting all his weight on his right let. I heard Alex approach behind me and to my right, heard him say to Rosten, "For Christ's sake, why? Why do you want me dead?"

Rosten did not even look at him; he was watching the gun.

I told him where to go and what to do, and he went there and did it. No argument or hestitation; he just climbed into the trunk, grimacing at the pain in his leg, and curled himself into a half-fetal position around my spare tire. His eyes never left the gun; you could see him wanting it the way an alcoholic wants a drink.

I reached out and up with my left hand, caught the trunk lid— and said quickly and sharply, "Who gave you your orders on the phone tonight, Rosten? Was it Twospot?"

It was a shot out of left field, but a pretty good one. He reacted: even in the darkness I could see his head jerk, emotion ripple across his face, his eyes flick upward from the gun to meet mine. Then the mask came down again; he looked back at the gun and kept looking at it stoically until I slammed the lid to lock him in.

Alex said, "Twospot? You know what it means?"

"No, but Rosten does. And maybe you've got some idea."

He shook his head. "I told you, I can't remember where I heard it before."

"Well, try—and keep on trying. Rosten's not alone in this thing, and that means you're not out of the woods yet."

He fixed me with an alarmed stare. "Are you sure Rosten isn't the only one?"

"Sure enough. You heard what I said to him; I overheard his end of that conversation."

Alex said something sacrilegious in a nervous voice, but I did not bother to respond to it. I pushed him toward the passenger door, went around and took the wheel. And took us away from there.

I had to drive slowly with the lights broken and the front end in the shape it was; the car made a lot of noise but showed no signs of wanting to quit. Alex sat over against his door with his head in his hands, doing what I had told him to do: trying to remember about Twospot. I did not hold out much hope that he would get anywhere, in his condition.

But he surprised me, and probably himself. We were back into the vineyards, on the long rumpled section of terrain, when he said abruptly, "I've got it."

I glanced over at him. "Got what?"

"Twospot. I remember now, I know where I heard it."

"All right—where?"

"A dinner party down in the city, at the town house. It was Booker who said it."

"Booker? In what context?"

"I can't remember that. It was after dinner and we were having brandy in the living room. He said something like, 'How's the big Twospot project coming? You know, the one a week from Monday at noon.' "

"Who was he talking to?"

"I think it was Leo."

"Who else was there?"

"Rosa. Brand and Dockstetter. But they didn't hear it. They were on the other side of the room."

"What was Leo's reaction?"

"I'm not sure. I was only half paying attention."

Twospot project, I thought. Monday at noon. And I remembered something myself, something from this afternoon. "Monday-noon project," I said. "So that was what you meant at the fest."

"Fest?"

"You said something to Leo about it while we were eating."

"Did I?" He shook his head numbly. "I don't remember."

I was silent for a time, thinking. Then I asked him, "Why were you down at the cellar tonight? Did Rosten call you to meet him there?"

"No," Alex said. "Leo woke me up and asked me to go down. He needed a statistical report prepared on our generic—" He stopped suddenly, as if the rest of the sentence had gotten clogged in his throat. When I glanced over at him again I saw that his face had twisted up and he looked even sicker than before. "Oh my God," he said. "You don't think *Leo* could be—?"

"I don't think anything yet," I said, but that was a lie. I was thinking Leo, all right—and something else occurred to me, a possible way to confirm my suspicions against him. It meant stopping at Rosten's cottage, and unless the county police were already on the scene I would do just that on my own.

Alex had his head in his hands again; I let him alone with his thoughts. There was a kind of grim excitement inside me now, the sort that a cop feels sometimes when a case is about to break wide open. Things were beginning to make a certain sense to me: the random bits and pieces of this affair finally starting to slot together, like in those intelligence-test puzzles where you have to put multi-shaped blocks of wood into correspondingly shaped holes.

I began to work with the pieces as I drove. Leo has some sort of big and no doubt unlawful project going for noon tomorrow; Rosten is in it with him, and maybe Mal Howard too. And Booker? No. Booker had not gotten along with either Leo or Rosten, I had testimony to that. And he was a loner, a small-time opportunist looking to marry Rosa Cappellani. Blackmail? That added up: blackmail would fit Booker's personality well enough. Figure, then, that he found out somehow about the project and put the screws to Leo. Maybe mentioned it to him in front of Alex at that dinner party to goad Leo, push him into paying off.

Only Leo isn't having any of that; the project is too important to him and maybe he doesn't trust Booker, and in any case he was the kind who would never stand still for blackmail. So he decides Booker has to die—and that Alex has to die too, because he's afraid that Alex will tip himself to the project and jeopardize it. Which made Leo a sick, coldhearted son of a bitch, plotting the death of his own brother. But there are people like that in the world, too damned many of them; and it could be, too, that his evident dislike for Alex had evolved into a homicidal hatred. Whatever his exact motivations, he marks both Booker and Alex for execution.

On Thursday night he sends Rosten after Alex at the cellar. But wait, why not Booker first? Booker would be the logical first choice because he presented the major threat to the project. Unless Booker *was* also slated to die on Thursday. Unless Rosten was supposed to literally kill two birds with one stone: knock Alex out, take him away from the cellar to a prearranged meeting with Booker, and then eliminate both of them at once, maybe make it look like an accident. That would explain why I had heard Rosten dragging Alex's body across the office floor. And why Booker had showed up in his car after the police arrived, looking agitated and perplexed: he could have been waiting for Rosten to come, could have been waiting for the promised blackmail payoff.

Okay, so far so good. Booker goes back to San Francisco after getting permission from Rosa to stay in the family town house. Figure he calls Leo and demands his payoff Friday night. So Leo sends Mal Howard to keep that appointment—not Rosten because Rosten has already fouled up once with Alex. Gives Howard the slip of paper with the address and the Twospot name typed on it. It would follow that Howard was not supposed to leave Booker's body in the town house, because of the attention it would call to the Cappellani family; it could be he was to kill Booker and then take the body elsewhere and dump it. Only Booker is on his guard by this time and he's packing a gun for protection; after a struggle during which he rips Howard's pocket, Booker manages to wound Howard before Howard can finish him with a blow from the homemade blackjack. And Howard then panics and runs, leaving Booker and the Twospot note on the garage floor.

Leo has to be beside himself by then: two bungled jobs in two nights. But because Howard's wound is superficial, Leo gives him another chance on Saturday: take care of Alex at Virginia Davis's apartment on Greenwich Street. It was logical that Leo would be aware of Alex's girlfriend and where she lived, and reason out that Alex might hole up there.

Now—today. Time is getting short; Monday noon is almost here. After *three* bungled jobs, maybe Leo doesn't want to run the risk of ordering yet another try for Alex; too many things have happened already to focus police attention on the Cappellanis, and I've been hired to act as Alex's bodyguard. But then, at the fest, Alex makes his comment about Monday-noon projects, and Leo decides he can't take the chance of Alex remembering about Twospot and endangering his project. So he orders Rosten to kill Alex tonight; Rosten doesn't like it, but for whatever reasons he goes along with it. Leo waits until he's sure I'm out of the way—heading over to Rosten's place, though he couldn't have anticipated that—and then goes into Alex's room and wakes him up and sends him down to the cellar. Which was what he told Rosten on the phone. The idea, again, is for Alex to just disappear: Rosten is supposed to take him to that backhill spot at the end of this road, shoot him, and hide the body somewhere so that there's not another immediate murder investigation to threaten tomorrow's project.

It was a pretty good scenario. Whether or not it was wholly accurate was up to the police to find out after I gave him to them.

But the primary question still had no answer: what *was* this project of Leo's? What sort of project is big enough, important enough, to trigger a mad chain of murder and secrecy? What sort of project demands a melodramatic code name like Twospot . . . ?

Light shimmered against the sky ahead of us, beyond the second hill from the cottages—another car approaching. The county police? But I did not hear sirens, and the light over there was yellow-white, not the red of dome flashers.

Alex sat forward tensely: he had noticed the lights too. I took the car up to the top of the hill, and from there I could see the outlines of the oncoming car behind the headlamp glare. It was not a sheriff's cruiser; it was just a car, too far away and too indistinct to be recognizable, traveling at a good clip.

When the driver saw us the car slowed, and I slowed, and we both pulled over to opposite sides of the road and braked alongside each other. The driver was the guy I had talked to earlier, Boylan, and Mrs. Cappellani was leaning across the seat beside him. She called something to Alex with relief in her voice, and Boylan began asking questions, and Alex chattered something about Rosten. I put an end to the confusion by saying, "There's no sense trying to talk here, follow us to Rosten's cottage," and then hitting the accelerator again.

In the rear-vision mirror I watched Boylan's car swing into an abrupt U-turn and come after us. Then I gave my attention to the road until we were over the next hill and approaching the cottages. There was still no sign of the police. If Mrs. Cappellani had alerted any others besides Boylan, they were not out and around here either; all the cottages except Boylan's were dark and the area was deserted.

I turned off the road beside Rosten's place and cut the engine and the lights, and we got out. Boylan parked behind us. I said to Alex, "You take care of the explanations. I'm going inside."

Without waiting for an answer or for Boylan and Rosa to come up, I left him and went to the cottage and tried the door. It was unlocked. I fumbled around on the wall inside, found a light switch, and flipped it.

As far as I could see in the pale glow of a ceiling globe the place had a living room, a bedroom, a bathroom, and a kitchenette. It was outfitted like a monk's cell: neat, clean, with no more than five pieces of furniture in the living room and bedroom combined. On the far wall was an open rack that held rifles, a shotgun, and four handguns on wooden mounting pegs. Near the front window was a small table empty except for a portable radio and the telephone.

I made straight for the phone and looked at the row of buttons on its base. One of those buttons was depressed, the one with the numerals 116 below it. The number Dymo-labeled across the dial —Rosten's number—was 208.

Turning, I crossed back to the doorway and stepped outside again. Alex and his mother were standing close together near my car—about as close together as they had ever been, I thought— and they were talking animatedly. Boylan was off to one side of them, looking bewildered. I caught his eye, gestured for him to come over to where I was.

When he did that I said, "The phones here—how does the intercom system work?"

He gave me a blank look. "The phones?"

"If I want to call your place from here, what do I do? Push the button with your number on it?"

"Yeah. But I don't—"

"Whose extension number is one sixteen?"

"Mr. Cappellani's," Boylan said. "Leo's. His room over at the main house . . ."

He was going to say something else, ask me questions, but I pivoted away from him and went back inside. All right, I was thinking, so that confirms it: it was Leo I overheard Rosten talking to. But it wasn't hard evidence; I had no hard evidence of any kind to give the police when they came. Unless there was something here in Rosten's effects that would point conclusively to Leo. Or something here that would give me an idea of what the Monday-noon project was.

I searched the living room first, quickly and easily because of its spartan furnishings. Nothing—no notes, no papers of any kind. Then I went into the bedroom and rummaged around in the dresser. Nothing. The only other thing in there besides the bed was a closet; I opened that up, looked through it.

And that was where I found them, in a box on the upper shelf.

Pamphlets—a dozen of them, all privately printed. Pamphlets with titles like *Castro's Rape of the World* and *The Cuban Octo-*

pus: Tentacles of Destruction and *Fidel Castro and the Communist Conspiracy.*

I stood there holding them in my hands, and the hackles began to rise on my neck. From outside, finally, I heard the first tentative wail of sirens—an eerie, unreal sound in the stillness that added to the chill forming along my back.

Castro, I thought.

The newspaper article I read last week: Castro was due to arrive in San Francisco on Monday, tomorrow, just another stop on his goodwill tour of American cities. Monday. At noon.

And Rosten had inflammatory right-wing literature in his closet. And Frank Cappellani had been a right-wing reactionary. And if Leo did not take after his mother at all, if he was his father's son . . .

Twospot and the Monday-noon project.

The sirens got louder outside. I could wait for the police, but if I did that they might want full explanations before they took action, got in touch with Hastings. Time. It was after eleven now, it was almost Monday. Hastings had to be told and he had to be told immediately. If I was right—Jesus, if I *was* right—he had less than thirteen hours to find Leo and prevent what could turn into the most devastating political assassination since the murder of John F. Kennedy.

I threw the pamphlets back into the closet and ran out of there to the phone.

PART FOUR

The Police Lieutenant

19

Softly swearing, I hung up the phone and looked at the bedside clock. The time was one-twenty A.M. I sank back on my pillow, groaned, and allowed my eyes to close. For a moment I lay motionless. Beside me, Ann stirred drowsily. I heard her murmuring, then felt her drawing close to me, snuggling up.

"Have you got to go out?" Her voice was husky, sleep-thickened. As she spoke, I felt her foot touch mine. Now her toes began a slow, sensuous movement up the calf of my leg. If I was weighing a decision, she was trying to tip the balance.

"Hmmm?" Her hand touched the top of my hip, moved slowly across my stomach, then up to my chest. My body was responding, rippling to a slow, erotic pulsing of desire. My genitals were tightening.

I groaned again. "That's not fair."

"Hmmm." Her hand was high on my chest—and now descending.

Quickly I turned to her, kissed her hard, drew the full, warm length of her body close against mine—and pushed her away.

"You're shameless, you know that?"

"Hmmm." Lasciviously.

I kissed her again with firm finality, then turned to the phone and reluctantly began dialing.

"Who're you calling?"

"Friedman. I've got to."

"Oh. Pete." As she said it, I felt her forefinger on my spine, playfully moving up—then down. Ann and Pete were friends. So she would tease me while I talked to him.

Surprisingly, Friedman answered on the first ring.

"It's Frank. Sorry."

He sighed: a long, deeply resigned exhalation. "I just walked in the house. Just this minute."

"Trouble?"

"With the Secret Service and the FBI and all the other goddamn agencies of the federal government. Not to mention the Cubans. They don't listen. They're amiable enough. But they don't listen."

"The FBI doesn't listen, either."

He snorted. Then: "What's happened?"

"I've got more trouble for you. For Castro, too, maybe."

"What're you talking about?"

Detail by detail, as concisely as possible I repeated the conversation I'd just finished with Bill. Friedman was silent for a moment. Then, softly and earnestly, he began to swear. As I listened, I rolled over on my back. Giggling, Ann began kissing my ear. Finally I heard Friedman say:

"You know these people—Leo, and the rest of them. What d'you think?"

"I think we've got to take it seriously. We've got to find Leo. Fast."

"I'm glad you said 'we,'" he answered dryly. "If that's an offer to help, I accept."

"It's an offer."

"What about Bill? Do you think he's got his facts straight?"

"You know him better than I do," I countered. "What d'you think?"

He sighed again. "I think he's probably got his facts straight."

"So what now?"

"Does Leo live in San Francisco?"

"Yes. But I don't know where. I talked to him in his office."

"Why don't you come over here? I'll find out where he lives. We can go from here."

"Right."

"Let's take that," Friedman said, pointing to a cruiser parked in his driveway.

"That's against regulations, taking a cruiser home."

"Since I've only been home for approximately forty minutes, I guess I'm clean."

I waited until he wedged his two hundred forty pounds beneath the steering wheel before I asked, "Where's Leo live?"

"Sea Cliff," Friedman grunted. "Thirty-second Avenue, north of Lake Street." He backed out of the driveway and turned north, driving smoothly, at a moderate speed. Even in hot pursuit, Friedman never seemed to hurry. But he was usually first on the scene.

I switched on the radio, turning the volume down. "Do you have a codeword for the Castro security thing?" I asked.

"Yes. Counterpunch."

"That's pretty catchy. Your idea?"

"Of course." He yawned.

"You want me to drive? At least I got two hours' sleep. You can close your eyes."

"Frankly," Friedman said, "I'd rather have no sleep than two hours' sleep. Besides, as soon as Castro leaves town—tonight, that is, at ten forty-five—I'm going to leave town, too. For three days' fun in the sun. Except that, the way I feel now, we may stay a week."

"Where're you going?"

"San Diego. Clara's aunt has a place there, on the beach. She's in Europe."

"Have you got Leo's house under surveillance?" I asked.

"Naturally."

"Did you call the FBI?"

"No."

I looked at him. "Why not?"

"Because, if Leo should happen to be home, playing the part of the innocent industrialist, one of two things might happen. One, he might have an explanation for everything, which would make us look silly, especially if we'd called the FBI, our natural enemies. Or, two, we might get lucky and foil an assassination attempt single-handed. Which would make us heroes. Plus it would also confound the FBI, our natural enemies."

"I doubt that he'll give us an explanation. More likely, he'll *refuse* to give us an explanation, and start raising hell, and call his lawyer. He'll try to run over us. That's his style."

"A real honcho, eh?"

"Yes."

We drove for a few moments in silence before Friedman ventured: "It's too bad that you had to waste Howard. If he'd fingered Leo, we'd have our case, no sweat."

Remembering the sound of Howard's head hitting the rocks, I didn't reply.

"I'm wondering how Howard fits into all of this," Friedman said.

"I think it's obvious," I answered. "He was a hired gun. He was probably hired to kill Castro. Then, when Booker uncovered the assassination plot, Howard was hired to kill Booker. Bill thinks Booker tried to blackmail Leo, threatening to blow the whistle on the plot. From what I know of Booker, I think it's a pretty good theory."

"How'd Alex get mixed up in all this?"

"Alex overheard Booker and Leo talking about it—about something Leo and Rosten are 'planning' for today. That's why Leo ordered Alex killed."

"I wonder whether Leo's had time to hire another triggerman," Friedman mused. He turned left on Twenty-fifth Avenue. In ten minutes, we would arrive at Sea Cliff.

"I don't know," I answered. "Which is precisely the reason I think you should call the FBI. They should be interrogating Rosten right this minute. He's the only real leverage we've got. We've got him dirty. He might talk. And, God knows, we need all the information we can get."

"It doesn't sound like Rosten's much of a talker," Friedman answered laconically.

"Still, we've got to *try*." I turned to him, saying heatedly, "You're just being goddamn foolish, Pete, not calling the FBI. This private feud you've got going with them is going to cost you one of these days."

"Let's see what happens at Leo's house."

"But, Christ, minutes might count."

Amused, he glanced at me aside. "The older you get, the more you're developing a talent for turning dramatic phrases, you know that? Some of them are a little trite, maybe. But, altogether, I think it's a step in the right direction. When I first knew you, I thought you were a little too taciturn."

"And the older *you* get, the more stubborn you get."

"What time does Castro get in town, anyhow?" I asked truculently.

"Eleven A.M." Grimacing now, Friedman glanced at his watch. "Exactly eight and a half hours from now."

"What's his schedule?"

"He's flying in from Dallas, on a commercial jet. He lands at eleven, like I said. He'll have a press conference in the VIP lounge, which is supposed to end at eleven-thirty. From there, he drives to City Hall."

"Will there be a parade?"

"No," Friedman answered. "Just a motorcade. He'll get off the Bayshore Freeway at Seventh Street, and travel down Bryant to the Embarcadero. He'll drive through the Embarcadero Center and the Golden Gateway, and then go south on Montgomery Street, through the financial district. He'll go west on California, then south on Polk Street. He'll drive down Polk directly to the City Hall, where his honor will be waiting on the steps. As I understand it, they'll have the blue carpet out—not the red. That's because Castro's a commie, as I get it."

"Will he have an open car?"

"No. It won't be a parade situation. He's scheduled to travel at twenty-five miles an hour, once he gets off the freeway. Beginning at Montgomery and California, the intersections will be held open for him. They don't anticipate any crowds along the streets, though. Not until he gets to the Civic Center."

"What's the rest of his day?"

"The usual. Lunch at the Commonwealth Club, followed by a speech. An appearance at the Press Club, dinner at the Bohemian Club. It's a pretty tight schedule. He hasn't even booked rooms at a hotel. At ten forty-five, he leaves for Los Angeles, where he'll spend the night." He turned right on Lake Street.

"If he's going to get killed," I said, "it'll probably be on his way from the airport, or at City Hall."

"Right." He turned left on Thirty-second Avenue. "My main concern is City Hall. The mayor will say his standard few words on the steps, and Castro will probably say several words. There'll be a crowd. Maybe an unfriendly crowd. Or, at least, there'll be protesters. Which will make a confusing situation. Which I don't like."

We passed through the two brick pillars that marked the entrance to Sea Cliff, one of the city's most pretentious subdivisions.

Built on the highlands overlooking San Francisco Bay and situated on the seaward side of the Golden Gate narrows, Sea Cliff was a part of the ocean's shoreline panorama. Here, the nights were always foggy. The fog smelled of salt and water and the pungent odor of marine life.

I pointed to a large two-story brick house, checked the address Friedman had scrawled on an envelope and said, "There it is— Leo's house."

"This isn't going to work," Friedman said, pushing the bell for the fourth time. "Either no one's home, or no one's answering."

"Push it again. Keep your finger on it."

Yawning, he leaned heavily against a porch pillar and did as I asked. A full minute passed before I saw an oblong of light fall on a hallway wall at the top of the big central stairway. A bedroom door had opened.

"Someone's coming," I said. But it was another two minutes before I saw a muff-slippered foot appear on the upstairs landing. The foot moved hesitantly beneath a richly embroidered blue dressing gown. Another foot followed the first. An angle of the upstairs wall contrived to reveal first a skirt, then a woman's torso, finally her full figure. With the dim reflected light behind her, she stood at the head of the stairs, looking down at us. I took my shield case from my pocket and held my badge against the door's single pane of glass. At the same time, Friedman rang the bell again. I saw her squint as she stared down at the badge. Finally, with one hand at her breast and one hand gathering the gown together midway down her thigh, she began descending the stairs one slow, reluctant step at a time. Underneath the embroidered blue dressing gown, her nightdress was frothy white lace. Her dark hair fell loose around her shoulders.

"Good-looking woman," Friedman said. "Leo's wife?"

"I don't know."

At the bottom of the stairs, still fifteen feet from the front door, she stopped.

"What d'you want?" she called. Clutching the robe with both hands, she evoked the classic image of the threatened female: eyes wide, mouth soft and uncertain, head held rigidly on a taut neck, bosom rapidly rising and falling. "What's happened?"

"Nothing's happened," I said. "We just want to talk to you. Let us in. I don't want to shout."

One slow step at a time, she approached the door, closely examining my badge. Even without makeup, she was a striking woman. The swell of her breasts was full and firm. Her shoulders were wide, self-confidently set. Her mouth was generous, her eyes large and luminous beneath gracefully arched brows.

But she was frightened. Badly frightened. Fear was plain in the fixity of her stare, and the pallor of her face, and the small, uncertain movements of her hands and mouth.

Friedman stepped forward. "Are you Mrs. Leo Cappellani?"

She nodded: one slow, tight inclination of her handsome head. The muscles of her neck were corded. Still clutching the robe, her hand was knuckle-white.

"Let us in, Mrs. Cappellani," Friedman ordered. "We've got to talk to your husband."

She began shaking her head in short, unnatural arcs. "Leo's not here."

"Then we want to talk to you." As he spoke, light from the house next door fell across the Cappellani porch. "Open the door," Friedman grated. *"Now."*

Her head moved sharply aside, as if he'd struck at her. The quick, spontaneous response suggested an abused wife's reaction. A moment later I heard a click and a chain rattle. As we entered the house, she retreated before us. Again she moved as if she expected us to abuse her—and was resigned to it.

"You look like you should sit down, Mrs. Cappellani." Friedman took her elbow and turned her firmly toward a darkened living room. "Let's go in here." He switched on a lamp and gestured her to a seat on the sofa. Still moving with strangely nerveless submission, as if she'd surrendered her will, she obeyed him. She sat in the exact center of a large velvet sofa. She looked like an unhappy little girl waiting for someone to come into the room and punish her.

"Where's your husband?" I asked. "He left the winery between ten and eleven. He told his mother he was coming here, to his home." I spoke in a flat, hard voice, making the question an accusation.

"He didn't come home," she answered. "He's not here." Her voice was totally uninflected: a dull, dead monotone. Her eyes, too, were dead.

"Has he phoned you tonight?"

"No, he hasn't phoned." Her embroidered robe had fallen open across her thighs, revealing a froth of white nightgown lace. She tried to close the robe with one hand and couldn't. When she used her other hand, the robe parted at the top, revealing the swell of her breasts. Defeated, she tremulously caught her breath as she struggled with the robe.

"What's the matter, Mrs. Cappellani?" Friedman asked.

Head bowed, she didn't answer. Slowly, hopelessly, she began to shake her head.

"You're very upset," Friedman said, speaking quietly and reasonably. "It's obvious. And it's got something to do with Leo, hasn't it?"

"He's in trouble. That's why you're here. Because he's in trouble." Her voice was hardly more than a whisper. Suddenly she let the robe fall away as she clasped her hands in her lap. She sat staring helplessly down at her hands.

"Leo had Jason Booker killed," I said. "You suspected that, didn't you?"

"I—I thought so. I heard him talking—saying strange things on the phone. And he—he acted strangely, too. He'd done something terrible. It was in his eyes."

"He tried to have his brother killed, too. He tried three times. Thursday, Saturday, and again tonight. He ordered Paul Rosten to kill Alex, tonight."

"Paul Rosten is—" She let her voice trail off. Still bowed over her clasped hands, she again moved her head slowly from side to side. She could have been a penitent, atoning for some terrible sin. "He's mad, I think. Paul's a little mad. I can see it deep in his eyes, sometimes. But Leo's not mad. Leo—he's fallen from grace. He's wicked and cruel. He's done terrible things, and he believes in terrible, godless laws. But he's not mad. Not like Paul."

"Do you know what Leo's planning to do in just a few hours, Mrs. Cappellani?" Friedman asked. "Has he told you?"

"Oh, no." Almost primly, she denied it. "No, he wouldn't tell me, because it's wicked. What he's planning is wicked. I know he's planning something. And I know someone's going to die. Someone very important. I—I listen to Leo, that's why. And I watch his eyes. That's how you learn about people, you know—by watching the eyes. Because the eyes are the windows of the soul. And, lately, I've seen something terrible in Leo's eyes. It looks like a—a flower of evil, blooming in his eyes." To herself, she secretly nodded. She was speaking very softly, in a small, shy, little girl's voice. She was leaving us, retreating to some safe, secret place. "At first it was just a seed," she murmured dreamily. "And then it was a bud, way down deep in his eyes. Then, one by one, the petals began to open—terrible, blood-red petals." She looked up at me and said, "Most people, you know, think flowers are beautiful. But I know better. Flowers can be poison. They can be evil and terrible—with death at the center."

I exchanged a glance with Friedman, who raised his eyes to the ceiling and silently shook his head.

"What kind of a car does your husband drive, Mrs. Cappellani?" I asked.

"He drives a Lincoln," she said. "It's a new Lincoln. Brand-new."

"What color is it?"

"It's silver. All silver, except for the top. That's black. Like leather."

Friedman heaved himself to his feet. "Where is he, Mrs. Cappellani? Do you know? Do you have any idea where he is—any idea at all? We've got to find him. And you've got to help us. You know that, don't you?"

"Yes, I know that." She raised her head, looking up at us each in turn, with wide innocent eyes. I wondered what she thought she saw in my eyes. Was it a flower? "You're good men," she said finally, nodding to me, then to Friedman. "You're good men. I can see that. I know that." As she said it, she lowered her head, staring down at her tightly clenched hands. "I know that," she whispered. "And Leo knows it, too. That's why he's running away from you. Because the evil must always flee from the good."

"Then where is he?" I urged. "Tell us."

"There's a girl. Her name is Lynda Foster. Leo doesn't know that I know about her. But I do. That's where Leo stays, sometimes. With her."

"Where does she live?"

"On Potrero Hill, I think. Close to the top. She has an apartment with a view. It costs him three hundred dollars a month. Plus utilities."

We left her on the couch, bowed over her clasped hands. Her lips were moving soundlessly. She could have been praying.

20

Friedman got out of the cruiser and looked balefully at the steep flight of stairs leading up to Lynda Foster's apartment.

"These goddamn hill dwellers," he groaned. "For a view, they kill themselves. Us, too."

Potrero Hill had always been the working man's Telegraph Hill, overlooking the warehouses and factories and switchyards of San Francisco's industrial area. Behind a confusion of railroad tracks and corrugated iron buildings towered the enormous cranes and gantries of the city's shipyards. The Bay was beyond, with the Oakland hills in the background. In recent years the real estate boom had burst over Potrero Hill. The old, tired houses had been bought by speculators, skillfully cut up into tastefully decorated apartments and rented as view property at inflated prices.

"Come on," I said, leading the way. "It's three-fifteen, for God's sake. We've got to find him."

Friedman groaned again, and began heavily climbing the stairs.

"Do you think one of us should be covering the back?" I asked over my shoulder.

"Probably," Friedman gasped, laboring behind me. "Except that I don't think there *is* a back. Not on this hill."

When I finally reached the upper landing and rang the bell, I was secretly gratified to see Friedman stopped midway up the last flight of stairs. He was holding to the railing, heavily panting and helplessly shaking his head.

"Jesus," he muttered. "Sweet Jesus."

As he said it, a light came on inside the apartment. With a peony-printed sheet wrapped around her, a girl was coming quickly toward me down a short, cluttered hallway. She moved easily, eagerly. She was expecting someone—but not the police. I watched her stop short when she saw my stranger's face, then watched her mouth come open when she saw my badge. She was a tall, slim girl with sharp features and a leggy, lithe figure under the sheet.

"Just a minute," she called through the door. "Wait a minute." She quickly retraced her steps, disappearing into a rear room. A moment later she reappeared, this time wrapped in a Japanese kimono. After a brief, noisy struggle with a nightchain and a deadbolt, she wrenched the door open.

"Miss Foster? Lynda Foster?"

"Right." She nodded decisively, tossing her hair in a loose blond whirl around her face. "What is it? What's happened?" It was a quick, avid question. She was looking for excitement.

"Nothing's happened. Are you alone?"

"Sure." Her dark, lively eyes darted between Friedman and me as she mischievously smiled. "Why?"

I decided to gamble: "But you were expecting Leo Cappellani. Weren't you?" As I asked the question, I stepped into the hallway, followed by Friedman. With the door closed, the three of us touched the walls as we stood facing each other. My foot struck something that tipped. Glancing down, I saw a shallow pan filled with kitty litter. Most of the litter had spilled on the floor.

"Sorry," I said.

"That's all right. It happens all the time," she said cheerfully. "Are you looking for Leo?"

"Why do you think we're looking for Leo?" Friedman asked.

"Because that's what you seem to be doing. Looking for Leo."

"Is he here?" I asked.

"Nope."

"Has he been here tonight?"

"Nope."

"Are you expecting him?"

She shrugged. "Who knows? What time is it, anyhow?"

"About three-thirty."

"Then I'm probably not expecting him."

"Do you mind if we look around?"

"Not if you don't mind telling me why you're looking," she answered promptly.

"I'm afraid we do mind, though," Friedman said, moving past her. "Regulations, you know."

I helped Lynda Foster clean up the kitty litter while Friedman searched the apartment. Five minutes later we climbed back inside the cruiser. I checked in with Communications while Friedman sat glumly behind the steering wheel, rubbing his eyes.

"What do you think about Lynda?" I asked.

"I think she's exactly what she seems," he answered. "She's an aging flower child who's getting smart enough to let men with money pay the rent and buy her pretty things."

"Maybe we should have interrogated her more—"

"Interrogations take time," he answered wearily. "And we don't have much. I don't think she can help us. Besides, Leo's wife convinced me."

"Convinced you of what?"

"Convinced me that he's going to try to kill Castro. It all makes sense, when you think about it. Everything adds up. Booker found out about the plan and got himself killed for his trouble. And Alex almost got himself killed for the same reason." His voice was hoarse with fatigue. Still digging his fingers into his eyes, he sat silently for a moment. Then he said, "I'm beginning to think that Leo might just be as nutty as his nutty wife. Different nutty, of course—like Hitler was nutty, say. But still nutty. And it's the nuts that do these assassinations. Like Leo and Rosten. They hire a triggerman—Mal Howard—and they're in business. Or they get someone to do it for love, like Lee Harvey Oswald." He started the engine, put the car in gear and pulled away from the curb.

"So what now?" I asked.

"So now we find Leo. That silver Lincoln with the black leather top should simplify the problem. But first, we find an all-night gas station."

"Do you have to go to the bathroom?"

"No. I've got to call the FBI. Our natural enemies."

After calling the FBI, Friedman and I stopped for ham and eggs at an all-night restaurant in the mission district. Milton Brautigan, the FBI's local agent in charge, had promised that two agents would leave within the hour, on their way to interrogate Rosten. At four A.M., Friedman and I arrived at the Hall of Justice.

"I've got to get a couple of hours' sleep," Friedman said as we rode up in the elevator to our office. "You're going to have to cover for me. I'm sorry, but I'm out of gas. Wake me up, though, if something happens."

I waved a hand. "Sleep. Either we find him, or we don't. If we don't find him, and if Rosten doesn't talk, there's not much we can do. Not until Castro arrives, anyhow."

"I think we've got to call Chief Dwyer," Friedman said. "We should do that now. And he should call the Commissioner. We can't take the whole responsibility for this."

"Is that why you're going to sleep?" I asked sourly. "So I'm the one who calls Dwyer at four in the morning?"

Friedman smiled. It was an exhausted attempt at humor. Beneath dark stubble, his face was gray with fatigue. His eyes were lusterless. In the last hour, the lines of his face had deepened.

"Go to sleep," I said, pointing to the door marked Dormitory. "Don't worry about it. I'll call him. Sleep."

At ten minutes to eight, Friedman knocked once on my office door and entered without being invited.

"For those four hours' sleep," he said, sinking into my visitor's chair, "many, many thanks."

"No problem. I slept a little myself, in fact. An hour, almost."

"I'm getting old," Friedman said. "This is the first time it's really hit me. Honest to God, for the first time in my life, tonight, I just—just ran out of gas." He shook his head. "I'm getting old," he repeated. "Too damn old for all this crap."

"You're not getting old," I said. "You're getting fat. Too damn fat. It's no wonder you get tired, carrying all that extra weight around."

"Ah—now comes the lecture. For the four hours' sleep, it turns out I got to hear a lecture." He spoke with a Yiddish patois, burlesquing the ancient resignation of the race.

"Look at the medical statistics. Look at the relationship between overweight and heart disease. Think of Clara, for God's sake."

He shrugged. "If I didn't eat so much, I wouldn't be so amiable.

And, next to Clara and my kids, you're the one who'd suffer most, if I turned into a grouch."

"I'm glad to hear you're so amiable. Does Clara know?"

"She knows." He stretched, yawned, sat up straighter in the chair. "What's happening? What'd Dwyer say?"

"He said he'd talk to the Commissioner."

"That's all? He didn't think we should change Castro's route, for instance? Or at least delay him at the airport for a half hour?"

"I don't think," I answered slowly, "that Dwyer believes anyone who's in the social register could commit murder."

Ruefully, Friedman guffawed. "You're right," he answered. "Sure as hell, you're right. Also, as always, Dwyer is covering his ass. I knew he'd do it."

"How do you mean?"

"He doesn't want to get directly involved in the anti-assassination planning. That way, if something goes wrong, he's got a patsy."

"You."

He smiled—then shrugged. "Me. Us. Take your choice."

"You."

Again, he yawned. "So what else has happened?"

"There's nothing from the FBI. And, so far, I haven't got a license number for Leo's Lincoln. It's newly registered, and apparently it's not in the computer yet. There won't be anyone in Sacramento until nine o'clock, to run a manual check for us."

"Wonderful."

"I've got four teams in the field—one at Leo's house, one at his office, one at his girlfriend's and one at the Cappellani town house. Canelli's coordinating all four teams. He's at Leo's office."

"The town house is still sealed, isn't it?"

"Yes. But Leo might not know it."

"I hope," Friedman said, "that the FBI is smart enough to question Rosa. My last waking thought, four hours ago, was that they might get more from Rosa than Rosten."

"Maybe we should—"

My phone rang. I lifted the receiver to hear, "It's Canelli, Lieutenant. Hey, you'll never guess what happened."

"Canelli. Please. No guessing games."

"Sorry, Lieutenant. I forgot you've been up all night, and everything."

"Well, what's happened?"

"Leo just arrived at his office. In his Lincoln, as advertised. He just drove up and parked in his parking place and went into the building, cool as anything. What d'you want me to do?"

"Who've you got with you?" As I spoke, I unlocked my desk drawer and took out my gun and cuffs.

"Marsten."

"Is Leo inside the building now?" I was trying to visualize the big brick building. Were there side entrances, as well as entrances in the front and back? I couldn't remember.

"He sure is, Lieutenant," Canelli said cheerfully.

"All right, you and Marsten cover the front and back, outside. Stay out of sight of Leo's office, which is on the third floor, the southeast corner. Have you got that?"

"Yessir. Third floor, southeast corner. Except that—" A pause. "Except that, I gotta tell you, he could've already eyeballed me, if that's where he is."

"It can't be helped. If he tries to leave, collar him. Otherwise, wait for orders. Clear?"

"Yessir, that's clear. Are you coming down?"

"Both of us are coming down. Right now."

As Friedman drove, I worked with Communications, trying to reach Brautigan through the FBI switchboard. Just as we were pulling into a parking place beside Leo's Lincoln, Brautigan came on the air, talking from his mobile phone.

"Don't tell him we've located Leo," Friedman hissed. "Not yet. They'll just come barging in and maybe screw everything up."

"What is it, Lieutenant?" Brautigan's static-sizzled voice was demanding. "What've you got?"

I reported that we were still looking for Leo, then asked Brautigan what his agents had learned from Rosten.

"This isn't exactly a secure line, Lieutenant." Even through the sizzling I could hear the weary condescension in Brautigan's voice.

"We need the information," I countered. "Castro's plane arrives at eleven. That's less than three hours from now. We're trying to decide whether to change the arrival schedule."

"All right. I'll check and get back to you. Where are you?" He spoke sharply: the commander, giving orders.

"We're in the field. You'll have to go through Communications."

"Tell him to interrogate Rosa," Friedman whispered.

"We're wondering whether your men questioned Rosa Cappellani," I said. "We have reason to believe that it might pay off."

"Naturally we've questioned Mrs. Cappellani, Lieutenant. We've been questioning her for two hours." Now he was the long-suffering commander, forced to endure an underling's tedious questions. I felt myself getting angry.

"Any results?" I felt asked flatly.

"I'll check that, too. Out."

"Good show," Friedman said amiably. "You really stuck it to him. You're learning, my boy."

"That supercilious bastard. I always forget how he talks."

"He's been to Yale. For only two years, though. I checked."

I snorted.

"He doesn't sound like he's exactly worried about an assassination," Friedman mused. "Whatever he's heard from the interrogation, he must not think it's damaging to Leo."

"Brautigan never sounds worried. That's not his style."

Grunting disgusted agreement, Friedman heaved himself out of the car as Canelli came to stand beside us. It was a cold, raw morning, overcast and damp. Unshaven, Canelli wore an old car coat. A brightly striped muffler was wrapped around his neck, dangling to his waist in front and back. A blue stocking cap was pulled down around his ears. He could have been going to a football game.

"What's happened?" I asked Canelli.,

"Nothing, Lieutenant."

I glanced up at Leo's office. The curtains were open, but I saw no movement inside. I turned to Friedman, asking, "Shall we have Canelli and Marsten stand by while we talk to him?"

Friedman nodded, at the same time slipping a tiny, short-range walkie-talkie from his pocket and rectifying channels with Canelli.

"Did you call off the other surveillances, Canelli?" I asked.

"No, sir."

"Do it."

"Right."

As Friedman and I walked across the parking lot toward the building's rear entrance, Friedman said, "I've never met the gentleman, but it seems to me that we should try and finesse Leo, instead of butting heads with him."

"You want to lead off? It's fine with me. You're better at finessing than I am."

As he held the door open for me, he shook his head. "You know him. You start. I was thinking, though, that we should make sure he knows he's got two lieutenants on his tail."

"Right." I walked across the small lobby that served the rear of the building and pushed the elevator button.

"Also," Friedman said, "it occurred to me that, since Rosten is in custody, Leo might not know whether Alex is alive or dead."

"You think we should try to make him think Alex is dead—and that Rosten confessed?"

"I think we should keep him guessing. If he's ready to assassinate Castro, he's going to be under pressure. And people under pressure don't like to play guessing games." Friedman stepped into the empty elevator as I pushed "3." "I also think," he said, "that time could be on our side—to a point. Let's assume that they're going to try and shoot Castro on the City Hall steps at noon. If we're still talking to him at eleven-thirty, Leo's going to start twitching."

The elevator was stopping. I reached across Friedman to depress both the "close" button and the "3" button. "Maybe we should take him downtown. We've got Alex's testimony. That's plain grounds for detention. If Leo plans to do the job himself, we solve the problem when we arrest him."

Friedman considered for a moment, thoughtfully frowning. Then: "That'd take time, though, taking him downtown. And, when we booked him, he'd call his lawyer, and then clam up. Besides, the odds are that he's found another triggerman. And that's what we need from Leo: the name of the triggerman and his location. So let's play it by ear—see what he's got to say, and see whether we can get him twitching. Are you going to start off asking him where he spent the night?"

"Yes."

"Good." He nodded to the elevator doors, still closed. "Let's see how it goes."

21

I'd expected to find Leo Cappellani a different-looking, different-acting man than I'd confronted two days earlier. I was wrong. He was just as impeccably dressed, just as clean-shaven, just as clear-eyed and alert. Wherever he'd been last night, he'd gotten some sleep.

Stressing the "lieutenant," I introduced Friedman. If Leo was disconcerted, facing two ranking officers, he gave no sign. Instead, he gestured us to chairs, smiling as he resumed his seat behind his rosewood desk. Looking at him closely, I was sure his white shirt was fresh. His sharkskin suit was unwrinkled. His tie was crisply knotted.

"I understand," he said, "that you—yourself—killed Booker's murderer, Lieutenant." As he said it, he smiled at me. It was a wide, affable smile. When he chose, Leo could be charming.

I let a long, deliberate beat pass before I asked, "Who told you that I killed him?" I wanted to throw him off balance—wanted him to wonder whether the details of Howard's death had been in the papers.

But his answer came easily, plausibly: "Alex told me Saturday night." As he spoke, Leo's dark, vivid eyes held my own, as if to encourage my questions. Today, he was on our side.

"What time did you leave the winery last night, Mr. Capellani?" I asked.

His muscular shoulders rose as he gracefully shrugged. "It was about ten-thirty, I guess. Maybe ten-fifteen." Now the smile slowly faded, replaced by a friendly, puzzled frown. If he was trying to project an innocent man's perplexity, his portrayal was flawless. "Why? Why do you want to know? Is something wrong?"

For the first time, Friedman spoke: "I gather that you haven't talked to anyone at the winery since ten-fifteen last night, then. Your mother or anyone else. Is that right?"

Leo turned to Friedman and took a long, deliberate moment to study him. Then: "That's right, Lieutenant Friedman. But my question still stands. Why're you asking?" As he spoke, his voice lowered to a deeper, more purposeful note. Resting before him on the rosewood desk, his fingers tightened into loose fists. His eyes narrowed as he studied us. The smile was gone—permanently. The message was clear: he was a busy man. He'd asked us a question. He expected an answer.

"If something's wrong," he said finally, "I want to know about it. I'd assumed that you'd come to give me a progress report on your investigation. But that's not it, is it? There's something else."

"Before I answer that," Friedman said, "I'd like you to tell us exactly what you did from the time you left the winery last night until you arrived here at this office this morning."

Instead of responding, Leo turned to look at me, as if to discover how we were trying to trick him. His eyes were hard now, studying me shrewdly. Then, deliberately, he turned again to Friedman. He'd decided how to deal with us.

"And before I answer *that,* Lieutenant, I'm afraid I'll have to know exactly why you're asking." His voice was tight, dead level. His eyes were cold and hard. Leo was in command.

"Why?" Friedman asked blandly. "I'm not trying to make this a contest. As a matter of fact, you're exactly right about the reason we've come. We're here to give you some information—some very important information, that's got nothing to do with Mal Howard. But before we can tell you about it, simply as a matter of police procedure, we've got to have an account of your movements last night." Friedman paused, then added quietly, "If you went home, for instance, all you've got to do is tell us."

"The point is," Leo said, "that I didn't go home. Which is the reason I can't tell you."

"Where'd you go?"

Slowly and deliberately, still in control, Leo shook his head. "I can't tell you. Sorry."

"You're making a mistake, Mr. Cappellani," I said. "There was another attempt made on Alex's life last night. And it looks very much like you're involved." I let a moment pass before I added, "Deeply involved."

"Another—" He looked at me, looked at Friedman, finally looked again at me. "Another 'attempt,' you say. What d'you mean, 'attempt'?" His voice rose. His dark eyes snapped. The loosely clenched fists were knotted now. "What the hell are you telling me? Is Alex dead? Hurt?"

"Before I answer that, I want you to—"

"*Goddammit.*" Suddenly he reached for the phone. Involuntarily, I moved to stop him, but Friedman quickly shook his head as Leo began dialing. I sank back, listening to Leo harshly command someone to put his mother on the line. Peremptorily, he asked her what happened last night. Listening to the faint buzz of Rosa's voice, I studied Leo's face. His expression was inscrutable. After less than a minute, he curtly thanked his mother, told her that he would call her shortly, and hung up.

For a moment, the office was perfectly silent as we stared at Leo and Leo stared straight ahead. Slowly, furiously, his face tightened.

"That son of a bitch," he said finally. "He tried to kill Alex. Rosten. He—Christ—he owes his whole life to us. Everything. And he tried to kill Alex."

Catching my eye, Friedman surreptitiously raised his chin to me. He wanted to ask the next question. I nodded. Friedman sat silent for a moment, studying Leo as he still stared straight ahead, plainly struggling to control himself. Finally Friedman cleared his throat, saying, "It didn't sound like your mother had much information for you."

Leo ignored him.

"That was probably because the FBI's still with her," Friedman said. "They're interrogating her."

Slowly—unwillingly—as if his head were being moved by some invisible, inexorable force, Leo turned to stare at Friedman.

"The FBI? Is that what you said?"

Friedman nodded cheerfully. "They're also interrogating Rosten. They've been interrogating him for two or three hours, now. Your mother, too. As I say—" Airily, Friedman waved a casual hand. "As I say, that's why she couldn't say much to you, probably. The FBI can be pretty intimidating. As you'll soon discover."

"Without realizing it," I said, "your mother gave us the key. Your father was a right-winger. You're a right-winger, too. And so is Rosten, isn't he? The two of you decided to kill Castro. And Alex found out about it."

"So you ordered Rosten to kill Alex," Friedman said. "Your own brother." He spoke softly and regretfully, as if it saddened him to say it.

"How'd you find Mal Howard, Leo?" I asked. "How much did he charge you, for agreeing to kill Castro? That was his job, wasn't it—his original job?"

"Who's Howard's replacement, Leo?" Friedman asked. "Give us a name."

"You're crazy," Leo breathed, looking at each of us in turn. "Coming in here—asking these questions, making these accusations. You must be crazy. You—Christ—you'll suffer for this. Both of you."

But now he spoke without the flare of conviction. Without force or anger.

"Who's 'Twospot,' Leo?" I asked.

"It's you, isn't it?" Friedman said. "It's your cover name." He let a beat pass before he suddenly barked, *"Isn't it?"*

Startled, Leo looked quickly at Friedman.

Picking up the remorseless tempo, I said, "Booker was murdered because he found out about the assassination plot. That was it, wasn't it? Maybe he tried a little blackmail. That'd be his style. So you ordered him killed. Mal Howard carried the address of your town house in his pocket, with 'Twospot' signed to the note. You set Booker up, didn't you—told him to meet you there, at Larkin Street. Then you sent Mal Howard to kill him."

As we hammered at him, I could see Leo's arrogant assurance slowly failing him. First he lost control of his mouth, then his hands, finally his dark, bold centurion's eyes. Now, as if it were again tugged by some invisible force, his head began to sink slowly until he sat bowed over his desk.

Friedman took up the attack. "Mal Howard didn't die instantly," Friedman said softly. "He talked before he died. That's why we're here, Leo. Because he talked."

To myself, I nodded approval. In court, the statement would

hold up. Howard had died in the ambulance—after mumbling something about a woman named Sophie.

"And Rosten's talking, too," Friedman continued. "He's talking right now, to the FBI. He's not going to fall for attempted murder. Not alone. Not when he can make a deal, and take you along with him."

"And not if he can be a hero, Leo," I said. "That's the deal the FBI's offering him, right this minute. He can be a hero. He can be on the FBI's side. You'd be surprised how attractive that is when you're in custody."

"He can blow the whistle on a plot to assassinate a visiting head of state," Friedman said smoothly. "For that, he'll get many, many brownie points—which, about now, he needs very badly. He'll be a hero, like Frank says."

Slowly, Leo's head began to shake. This time, though, the volition was Leo's, not some uncontrollable outside force. We watched him raise his head. His mouth was firmly set, his eyes defiant.

Somehow, for some reason, he'd recovered his arrogance, his self-control. For a few minutes we'd been pummeling him, seemingly scoring with ease. But, suddenly, he'd rallied.

Why?

What had changed? What mistake had we made?

Looking for the answer, I searched his face, his eyes. And then I saw it: a tiny sliver of manic light deep in his eyes—as if someone had opened a darkened door just a crack, to reveal a monstrosity behind.

"Paul won't be a hero," he said. "He's a hireling, that's all. Just a hireling."

He spoke very softly. In his eyes the telltale gleam of mad light was gone, extinguished by force of will.

The message was clear: no matter what we did, he intended that Castro should die.

22

Friedman saw it, too: the quick, secret glint of mad purpose in Leo's eyes. Saturday, Leo had played the role of the forceful, urbane executive, too busy to talk. A half hour ago, he'd played the same smooth, suave part.

Finally, though—cornered—Leo's real persona had flashed through: the zealot, the true believer. Blinded to consequences, he saw only his goal: the death of a despot.

Friedman and I exchanged a quick glance, then he looked meaningfully to the office door. We excused ourselves and stepped into the outer office, closing the door behind us. Leo's secretary was at her desk, watching us with cold eyes. We turned our backs on her, whispering together.

"The son of a bitch really is going to try it," Friedman said. "He's going to kill Castro if he can."

"I know."

"I've got to call Dwyer, and the FBI, and maybe the Commissioner, too, if Dwyer won't do it. We've got to have a change of Castro's schedule."

"It's almost nine o'clock. Two hours isn't much time."

"Still," he answered, "I've got to try. Someone's got to call the mayor, too. For one thing, I want my ass covered. If Castro's going to swallow a bullet, I'm not going to take the fall alone." He gestured to Leo's door. "You go back inside and keep working on him. He's all we've got—him and Rosten. See if you can break him down—find the goddamn triggerman. I'll get back to you as soon as I can."

"Maybe I should take him down to the Hall."

Vehemently, Friedman shook his head. "We don't have the time, Frank. We—"

"*Shhh.*" I held up my hand, moving a quick step toward Leo's door. From inside the office I heard the rapid clicking of a telephone dial. "He's trying to call someone." I opened the door and entered the office. Holding the telephone to his ear, Leo stood behind his desk. When he saw me, his dark eyes blazed.

"This is a private call, Lieutenant," he snapped. Then, to cover the flare of temper: "I'll be with you in a minute."

"Sorry," I answered. "I'm afraid you aren't going to be making any private calls for a while."

As I approached the desk I heard the phone click and an indistinct voice answer. Instantly, I lunged for the phone, to hear the voice on the other end. But Leo was too quick for me, breaking the connection. As we momentarily confronted each other, fists clenched, breathing hard, I once more saw the zealot's gleam flicker deep in his eyes.

"Who were you talking to?"

He cradled the phone and sat down behind the desk. Now his eyes were veiled. For a long moment he simply stared at me. His expression was quizzical, almost genial. It was as if we were playing some delightful game, and he'd just scored a difficult point.

But why, then, had he tried so desperately to phone someone?

"Sorry," he murmured. "I was talking to a lady. The same lady I was with last night. And the lady's not my wife. So—" He raised both hands from the desk, palms up.

"You're lying. You were trying to talk to your goddamn triggerman—trying to give him instructions."

Still the easy, sardonic smile mocked me as he said, "Have it your way, Lieutenant."

"We know you're going to make a try for Castro, Cappellani. You might've thought you covered your trail. But you didn't. You're nothing but a goddamn amateur."

Staring at me thoughtfully, he slightly inclined his head. It was a condescending nod, as if to indicate that he admired my spirit, but not my technique. With the clock running, he would pursue our delightful little game.

"I've been thinking," he said reflectively, "that you're really trying to run a bluff on me. I've been thinking that if you really had evidence linking me with Booker's murder, or the attempts on Alex's life, or—as it turns out now—a plan to kill Castro, I'd be on my way to jail. You may have suspicions, but that's all. You don't have anything else. Isn't that right? Isn't the fact that we're sitting here proof that, really, no one's incriminated me?"

Trying to shake him with a steady stare, I didn't reply. I wished Friedman would return. A taut silence lengthened. Leo's eyes held firm—as firm as mine. It had happened to me before. A true believer or a madman can't be stared down. Finally I pointed to the phone.

"Tell me who you were talking to, if you've got nothing to hide. Give me the lady's name."

"Try to appreciate my problem," he said reasonably. "The lady isn't my wife, and she isn't my mistress, either. She's just a—" His sly smile shared a man-of-the-world joke with me. "She's just a casual friend, I'm afraid."

"Give me her name."

"I thought you were investigating an assassination plot, not the state of my love life."

I moved my head toward the door. "There isn't going to be any assassination, Leo. Lieutenant Friedman's taking care of it, right now. Castro's schedule is being changed."

The remark seemed to amuse him. "Really? In less than two hours, you're going to change his schedule?"

Now it was my turn to smile. The next point was mine: "How'd you know when his plane was landing?"

"It was—" He hesitated, but only for an instant. Then: "It was in the paper."

I shook my head. "Sorry. Try again."

"It was—"

The office door opened. Secretly, I swore. Friedman had returned. At the wrong moment. He spoke to me, saying "It's all set. No problem."

But I knew Friedman too well—knew he was bluffing. He couldn't order Castro's schedule changed. He could only request, and wait for his superiors to make the decision. And high-level decisions take time.

I watched him stride directly to Leo. Gripping the edge of the rosewood desk with both hands spread wide, Firedman leaned toward Leo. It was a comradely gesture, implying that they were about to share a secret.

"Now," Friedman said amiably, "we can talk. The reason I had to leave in such a hurry, I'm in charge of municipal security for Castro's visit. And I had to make, ah, certain arrangements. They've been made. So now we can talk, no sweat." Friedman remained braced against the desk for a moment, staring down at Leo Cappellani. Except for a small, tolerant smile, the other man chose not to respond.

Covertly, I glanced at my watch. The time was nine-twenty. I watched Friedman push himself away from the desk and sink down in an armchair. He sat for a moment in silence, staring at Leo—who readily returned the stare, unintimidated. Finally, in a light, bantering voice, Friedman began to speak.

"The arrangements I've made have, ah, de-fanged your plot, Leo, if you'll excuse the metaphor. There's no way you can kill Castro. So if I were you, Leo, I think I'd spill the beans. You're new at lawbreaking, I gather, so maybe I should tell you how the game is played. It's actually a combination of musical chairs and blindman's buff. Or maybe it's steal the bacon. Anyhow, the idea is to save your skin. You do that by copping. That's what it's called on the street. Your expensive attorney'll call it plea bargaining. But the principle's the same." Friedman paused for emphasis, then said, "Basically, the one who gets caught, cops. He blows the whistle on his associates, in other words. Whereupon the D. A. recommends that the judge go easy on you—which he does. Now—" Friedman leaned forward, driving home the point: "Now, that's what Rosten's done, see. He's copped—and he's left you holding the bag, or left you without the bacon, or without a musical chair, or whatever. In other words, you're stuck. So the best thing you can do is stick the next guy down the line. Or, preferably, *up* the line. See how it works?"

While Friedman talked, Leo had been studying him. The suspect's eyes revealed nothing, but occasionally his mouth twitched, as if he were amused. He sat with his chin supported on a judicious steeple of fingers. I noticed that he wore a star sapphire on his left little finger.

Finally he dismantled the finger steeple, to point at me with a languid forefinger.

"I've just told Lieutenant Hastings that I think he's trying to bluff me. And the same applies to you, Lieutenant Friedman. As they say on the street, you're trying to jive me. Aren't you?" Gently, Leo smiled.

Projecting an air of utter indifference, Friedman shrugged. "Suit yourself, Leo. I'm giving you a chance to salvage some of your expensive skin. Whether you do it or not, that's up to you. But I can tell you this: you aren't going to enjoy prison. A lot of inmates don't change their underwear often enough, and some of them have terrible table manners."

"I think I'll take my chances, Lieutenant."

"Hmmm." As Friedman appeared to think it over, he turned to me, slightly shrugging. He seemed to be saying that he'd done his best for Leo, and now it was time for us to get back to work. As he was acting it out, Leo spoke.

"You see," Leo said, "I have an advantage over you. I *know* Paul Rosten. And I know that he wouldn't cop, as you call it."

Again projecting total indifference, Friedman silently spread his hands.

"As for protecting myself," Leo said, "I've been giving that some thought while you were talking, Lieutenant Friedman. And I've got a scenario for you. Would you like to hear it?" His genial glance included us both in the question.

"Let's hear it," I said.

"All right." He paused a moment, as if to arrange his thoughts so as to make the most interesting story for us. "Let's say, for the sake of argument, that I'm in as much trouble as you suggest— that I'm deeply implicated in a plot to kill Castro. And let's suppose, also for the sake of argument, that he's going to be shot between eleven o'clock and noon. Now, if both those premises were correct, then your best move, it seems to me, would be to take me to jail. However, as I've already mentioned to Lieutenant Hastings, you apparently don't have enough evidence to arrest me, despite the fact that it would seem to be your logical move." He paused to look at us each in turn, then continued: "So what's *my* best move? Obviously, if I wanted to establish my innocence, my best move would be to do just what I'm doing now—" His gesture included the three of us, and the game we were playing. "What better alibi could I have than—"

"Let's go back to your 'eleven o'clock and noon' statement," I cut in. "I still want to know how you learned what time Castro's plane is scheduled to land."

He smiled. "I'm glad you mentioned that, Lieutenant. Because, when I think about it, I realize that you're right. I didn't read it in the newspapers. Perhaps someone told me about it. Except that I can't remember who, right now. Maybe it'll come to me."

As he spoke, I glanced at my watch. In an hour and ten minutes, Castro's plane would land. I looked at Friedman, wondering what strange game of brinksmanship he was playing. Because if he intended to meet Castro's plane, he'd have to leave within a half hour.

I watched Friedman rise to his feet. His eyes were cold, his voice harsh: "If you leave this office before one P.M.," he said, "you'll be arrested, and taken downtown and booked—and that, Leo, is a solemn promise, from me to you. The same applies if you try to leave town without notifying the police."

Friedman turned on his heel and walked out of the office, gesturing for me to follow him. I had no choice but to obey.

23

I followed Friedman through the receptionist's office and into the hallway outside, where Friedman walked quickly around the nearest corner, at the same time pulling his miniature walkie-talkie from inside his coat.

"What the hell're you *doing?*" I demanded. "Christ, he probably phoned an accomplice, the first time we left him. You're letting him—"

"*Shhh.*" He spoke urgently into the walkie-talkie. "Are you receiving it all right, Canelli?"

"Yessir. Everything came in fine. And a tape recorder finally got here, just this minute. So I can talk to you, no sweat."

"Are you sure the recorder works? Did you check it?"

"Yessir, I checked. It works fine."

"What's he doing now?"

"I think he left the office. Anyhow, I think I heard a door open, after you left. But I don't think it closed. So—oh, oh. Now it closed. I'm getting footsteps, coming closer. I guess the bug's a little ways from the door, eh?"

"It's under the front edge of the desk. Maybe twenty feet from the door."

"Well, it sure works good, Lieutenant. Those new bugs, they're really something, you know? Honest to God, I heard every little sound you guys made. It's too bad I didn't have the recorder, then."

"Don't worry about it, Canelli." As he spoke, Friedman gestured for me to check Leo's door. I stepped to the corner of the hallway, and peeped around.

"Stay there," Friedman said to me. "Keep looking." And to Canelli he said, "What's he doing now?"

"He seems to be walking around his office, I'd say."

"He hasn't touched the phone? Hasn't dialed?"

"Not that I heard, Lieutenant. Of course, the recorder probably got more than I got, especially since we're talking. Want me to play it back? I can—"

"No," Friedman barked. "Don't fool with the goddamn recorder."

"Well, jeeze, Lieutenant—" Canelli's voice trailed off into reproachful silence. His feelings were hurt.

Friedman sighed. "Sorry, Canelli. I—"

"*Hey.* He's doing it now. Dialing."

"All right—" Relieved, Friedman exhaled. "Just make sure the recorder's getting the clicks. That's the whole purpose of this."

"Yessir."

It seemed as if interminable minutes passed, but I knew less than thirty seconds had elapsed before Canelli's voice crackled:

"I got it, Lieutenant. But it isn't much. All he said was, 'Are you ready?' Then, after a second or so, he said, 'I'm out of it now. It's all up to you.' Something like that. Then he hung up."

We were already breaking for the elevator as Friedman spoke sharply to Canelli: "Play back the tape and get the clicks. Call the phone company and ask for Supervisor Diane Sobel. Tell her the number's for me. Tell her we need the location in seconds, not minutes. Got it?"

As I pushed the elevator's "down" button, I heard Canelli say, "Yessir. Got it."

"What the hell's keeping Canelli?" Friedman scanned the parking lot, then glanced at his watch. "Christ, it's five minutes after ten." He looked anxiously in the direction Canelli had gone searching for a phone.

"You want to go look for him?" I asked. "I'll stay here until we get some support."

"If the phone company's diddling him for a warrant—" Frustrated, Friedman tapped the roof of his cruiser with a clenched fist.

"Listen," I said, "you should be on your way to the airport, right now."

"I'm not so sure," he answered. "It might be better if I—"

Canelli came trotting around the corner of the massive brick building. Cheerfully smiling, he was waving his notebook at us.

"I got it," he called. "Sorry it took so long." He drew up in front of us, panting heavily and shaking his head. "Jeeze, I must be out of shape, or something." As he gulped for breath, he handed his notebook to Friedman. "That's it, Lieutenant. 501 McAllister. It's a pay phone on the first floor. In the lobby."

Friedman swore. "501 McAllister. That's on the corner of Polk Street." As he spoke, two black and white cars pulled into the parking lot, stopping bumper-to-bumper beside us. I nodded to the uniformed officers, gesturing for them to stay in their cars. Friedman was still earnestly swearing. He was, I knew, trying to make up his mind, struggling with a no-win decision. It was the only time he ever seriously swore. Finally he turned abruptly to me.

"I'd better go to the airport. That's my best shot. If I can do anything, it'll have to be on the scene—with the goddamn motorcade. I'll give a direct order to our men, and screw the goddamn bureaucrats, if they haven't made up their minds." He opened the door of his car.

"All you've got to do is route Castro away from that building," I said. "What's the problem?"

He was already in the car, starting the engine.

"The problem," he said, "Is that I think 501 McAllister is across the Civic Center Plaza from the City Hall steps, in easy rifle range. *That's* the problem. I can change the motorcade route, probably. I'll catch some flack, but I can do it. But I don't know whether I can do anything about changing what happens on the steps." As he spoke, he thrust his hand into a pocket. "Here— take these." He handed me a dozen small lapel badges. "That's your security identification. They work for the FBI and the State Department security team." He put his cruiser in gear. "You get down there, Frank. Collar the triggerman, and tell me when you've got him. I'll be on channel twelve."

Tires squealing, he pulled away.

"Park over there," I ordered. "Around the corner, on Polk." As I spoke, I checked the time: ten twenty-five.

Canelli started his turn, muttered when a woman in a bright orange Ford repeatedly blew her horn, and finally pulled to a stop in a loading zone. I reached for the microphone and got Halliday, in Communications.

"This is Inspectors Eleven," I said. "We're positioned at Polk and Golden Gate, on the northwest corner. Do you have our backup units under way?"

"That's affirmative, sir. Three units. Six inspectors."

"Give them our position. And tell them to hurry. Not code three. But hurry."

"Yessir."

I hung up the microphone and swung open the car door. "I'm going to the phone booth. You wait here until you've got all six men. Then come to the booth. If I'm not there, wait in the lobby. Bring walkie-talkies, but no shotguns. Clear?"

"Yessir, that's clear."

501 McAllister was an office building that had probably been built in the late twenties or early thirties. Standing on the sidewalk, I counted windows. The building was twelve stories tall, and faced the Civic Center Plaza. Friedman had been right: the front of the building commanded a clear view of the City Hall steps. The range would be about three hundred yards, optimum for a scope-sighted rifle. If the president were the visitor, every office facing the Plaza would have been evacuated, then secured. For Castro's visit, security was a little less stringent.

A team of four patrolmen were erecting crowd-control barriers: heavily weighted steel stanchions with rope threaded through their eyebolts at waist height. Now, the rope was slack, lying on the pavement. As the crowd gathered, the ropes would be pulled taut. Across the street, in the Plaza, a group of demonstrators was gathered in a loose circle around two men who were hammering wooden handles on anti-Castro placards.

I nodded to one of the patrolmen, entered the building, quickly crossed the small lobby and went directly to three phone booths located next to the two elevators. Canelli's information was correct. Leo had called the phone in the middle booth. Using my handkerchief, I closed the booth's door. At the same moment one of the elevators opened, and two patrolmen stepped out. Both men were strangers to me. I identified myself, explained the situation and ordered one of the men to guard the booth against destruction of latent prints.

"What's your name?" I asked the second man.

"Diebenkorn, sir." He said it sheepishly, as if the sound of his name embarrassed him.

"Well, Diebenkorn, you're my communications man." I ordered him to park his unit directly in front of the building. As I was hastily outlining Friedman's situation and coordinating communications channels, I saw Canelli entering the lobby, followed by six inspectors. All seven men were big and burly, momentarily evoking the incongruous image of seven football linemen dressed in business suits, shouldering their way through the doors toward bruising action on an imaginary line of scrimmage.

"Come over here—" I gestured for them to follow me into the farthest corner of the lobby, where they assembled around me in a loose circle. It was another football-style image: the huddle, everyone waiting for signals. As I handed out the lapel buttons Friedman had given me, I gave the orders.

"I don't know how much Canelli told you," I said, "but here's the situation. For those of you who don't know, Castro is landing at the airport in about twenty minutes, maybe less. He's scheduled to drive in a motorcade through the Golden Gateway and the financial district to here"—I gestured toward the lobby doors and the plaza beyond—"the City Hall steps, where the mayor'll welcome him. Now, Lieutenant Friedman is in charge of municipal security, and he and I have good reason to think that, somewhere in this building, there's someone who's going to try and kill Castro, probably when the mayor's welcoming him. So—"

I felt a hand on my shoulder. Turning sharply, I faced a tall, stooped, sad-faced man with a long nose, a prim little mouth and ice-cold eyes. He was dressed like a banker—and held a small badge in the palm of his hand.

"I'm Parsons," he said. "FBI. What can I do for you?"

I tried to explain the situation while my men shifted restlessly around me. At my elbow, Canelli was muttering something unintelligible. As I talked, Parsons frowned disapprovingly.

"I haven't got anything on this," he said. "I just talked to Mr. Brautigan. Just a few minutes ago. And he had no problems to report."

"Well, Lieutenant Friedman and I have been working with

Brautigan all morning," I said. "And half the night, too. And believe me, there's a problem. Have you got this building secure?"

Holding his chin disdainfully high, Parsons nodded. "We were here at eight, when the doors opened."

"How many men do you have?"

"Three," he answered. "Including myself. We checked packages —anything big enough to hold a rifle, or rifle parts. All deliveries to the building have been impounded."

"What about the offices facing City Hall? Are they evacuated?"

Parsons sighed. "We've checked them out. But they aren't evacuated. Those weren't my orders."

"Do you mind if I have them evacuated?"

Nostrils pinched, mouth pursed, he said, "This building is my responsibility, Lieutenant. The FBI's responsibility. I'll have to check with my office before I can let you evacuate those offices. And, frankly, unless Mr. Brautigan has gotten some new information in the last minute or two, I doubt if he'll issue the orders. I'd be glad to try. But—"

"Christ, I'm *giving* you new information right now. Right this minute." I looked at my watch. "And, right about now, Castro is landing at the airport. He could be here in a half hour, for God's sake."

He stepped back, glancing speculatively toward a phone booth. I moved toward him. Looking him hard in the eye, I dropped my voice as I said, "Listen, Parsons. While you're phoning Brautigan, I'm going to check out the offices for anything suspicious. I won't evacuate them. I'll just check them. I'm going to assign two men to each floor, beginning at the twelfth floor." Still holding his eye I said, "We've gone to a lot of trouble over this, Parsons. Including myself, I've got ten men here, solely on my authority. And I, personally, have lost a night's sleep. So I'm sure as hell not going to walk away from it. And you can tell Brautigan that. For me."

Still with his chin high, neck stiff, he shrugged. "Suit yourself."

"Are there any empty offices?" I asked. "Or any locked up?"

"Five or six empty, I'd say, and a few locked up. All of which, incidentally, we checked out. In fact—" He permitted himself a small grimace that could have been a smile. "In fact, we checked out everything but the ladies' room." He reached in a vast pocket and produced a set of four keys, which he extended to me with thumb and forefinger fastidiously pinched. "There are the master keys. One key is for the office doors. One's for the cleaning closet on each floor. The other two are bathroom keys."

As I turned to my men, I felt another tap on my shoulder.

"Don't forget to return those keys to me. They're my responsibility, you know."

I assigned my six men to the three top floors, ordering each team of two to check every third floor. Canelli and I, meanwhile, would investigate the locked offices, beginning at the top floor. We would coordinate our communications through Diebenkorn, outside. While the six men dispersed, I waited in the lobby until Parsons called Brautigan, at FBI headquarters. During the conversation I saw Parsons's face become increasingly glum. Finally, hanging up, he turned to me and curtly announced that he'd been instructed to "cooperate" with me. Trying to conceal the satisfaction I felt, I ordered him and his men to secure the lobby. Canelli, meanwhile, was holding an elevator for me. Going up to the twelfth floor, the elevator ride seemed interminable.

"This is a pretty old elevator," Canelli said. "Fifteen years, I bet. At least."

When we finally stepped out into the twelfth-floor corridor, a team of inspectors was already at work, briefly questioning each person they found in every occupied office. Canelli and I momentarily hesitated, getting our bearings.

"How about the cleaning closet?" Canelli asked, gesturing to a pair of small blind doors set next to a door marked "Stairs." "Should we check that?"

"Why not?" I stepped to the first of the small twin doors and tried each of my four keys, without success.

"I, ah, don't think that's the cleaning closet, Lieutenant. I think that's, ah, probably for the electrical panel. There's one for every floor. For the lights, and the elevator relays, and like that." As he always did whenever he corrected me, Canelli spoke softly, apologetically. Beneath his scruffy car coat, he was probably sweating.

As I was opening the matching door on a jumble of mops and pushbrooms, Canelli walked quickly down the hallway, rattling office doors. The time was ten minutes after eleven. As we searched the empty offices I repeatedly called Diebenkorn, checking on Castro's progress. The motorcade was now approximately two miles north of the airport, Diebenkorn reported, proceeding toward the city.

We'd worked our way down to the seventh floor when my walkie-talkie crackled to life. I could hear Friedman's voice, but the transmission was hopelessly garbled. A moment later Diebenkorn cut in.

"Are you getting that, sir?"

"No," I answered shortly, "I'm not."

"It's Lieutenant Friedman. He's trying to contact you directly. There must be interference."

"Get the message, then, Diebenkorn," I said sharply. "Get it and relay it to me."

"Yessir."

I was fitting key into a door marked "Vista Vacations" when Diebenkorn came back on the air. "Well, what's he say?" I asked irritably. I'd decided Diebenkorn was an officer who couldn't accept responsibility.

"He says that he's routing Castro around this building. But he can't do anything about the ceremony on the steps of City Hall, he says. Because of the media. They're going to televise the speeches, he says. So Castro won't buy a change of schedule. Neither will the mayor. Or the FBI, either, because they don't have a backup plan, I guess."

Swearing under my breath, I answered, "All right. Give him a roger. Tell him that we haven't found anything—that the building is about half searched."

"Yessir."

I slipped my walkie-talkie in my pocket and pushed open the "Vista Vacations" door. It was a small office, furnished with an oversized metal desk, a persimmon-colored plastic-covered couch and a matching armchair. Framed travel posters decorated the walls. A woven straw rug covered the floor, wall to wall.

As we'd done before, Canelli checked the office itself while I opened the clothes closet and the door to a tiny alcove containing a mirror and washbasin.

I'd just opened the lavatory door when I heard a sharp intake of breath. Whirling, I saw Canelli in a crouch, gun drawn, facing the metal desk.

"Hey," he said. *"Hey.* Come out of there. Slow and easy."

As I drew my own gun I saw a head of close-cut auburn hair rising form behind the desk. A face followed—a woman's face.

Shelly Jackson.

24

"Drop it," Canelli grated. "Drop the goddamn gun."

As she slowly straightened I heard a heavy metallic thud as a pistol struck the carpeted floor behind the desk. Now she stood at her full height. Ignoring Canelli, she'd turned to face me. She wore a two-piece tweed dress. Her shoes were alligator, matching her purse. The silk scarf knotted at her throat was green, highlighting her eyes. She could have been dressed for lunch at the Fairmont. A small, ironic smile teased the corners of her provocatively shaped mouth. Her gray-green eyes mocked me with cool, controlled contempt.

"Drop that, too," Canelli barked, stepping toward her. "Empty your hands. Put them on top of your head. *Now.*"

Instead, she moved a single step toward the big window behind the desk. She raised her right hand, fingers spread—showing us an empty palm. She rotated the hand, for both of us to see. She was pantomiming a magician's now-you-see-it- turn.

Then she raised her closed hand to waist height. She took another slow, measured step toward the window. In the closed left hand she held something small and square, the shape and size of a cigarette package.

"If he shoots," she said to me, "he'll blow up a lot of innocent people." She spoke in a cold, flat voice. Her eyes had never left mine. Now she rotated her left hand, allowing me to see what she held. It was an ordinary electronic garage door opener. When she was sure I'd seen it, she half turned away, aiming the opener at the window.

"There are bombs," she said softly. "There are two bombs. And if you don't do exactly as you're told, I'll explode them. Right now. With this." She lifted the small plastic garage door opener.

Cautiously moving between Shelly and the desk, with his revolver trained on the girl, Canelli stooped down behind the desk, reappearing with a blued-steel automatic in his hand. At a nod from me, Canelli retreated, holstered his gun and disarmed the automatic. The gun was a 9mm Browning, the best of its type. There'd been a cartridge in the chamber. The small knurled hammer had been cocked. She'd been ready to kill us.

"You may as well put your gun away, too, Lieutenant. You aren't going to shoot me." Her eyes moved away from mine as she stared out the window. As she leaned on the window frame, her face was profiled against the glass. Dressed in her expensive brown tweed dress, with the silk scarf at ther throat, her pose was aloof, detached. She lowered the electronic opener until it angled down toward McAllister Street, then rotated it until it lined up on the City Hall steps.

Her purpose was plain. She'd hidden explosive devices somewhere on Castro's route, either on the street or at the City Hall steps. When Castro appeared, she'd explode the bombs. It was a common terrorist tactic.

There was no rifleman. There'd never been a rifleman.

I realized that I still stood in a muscle-locked, self-defensive crouch. I straightened and holstered my revolver. With my eyes, I gestured for Canelli to step back, giving her room. In the silence, I could hear the sounds of a crowd in the streets below. Shrill voices were shouting in unison: *"Castro nunca, Castro nunca."*

"It won't work, Shelly," I said. "We know the whole plan. We got it from Leo, an hour ago. We've had Castro's car diverted. He taking another route. There won't be a speech, either," I lied.

Still with her face averted, staring down into the street, she smiled. It was a detached smile, eerily serene. Seen in perfect profile, the smile softened her face. She was a beautiful woman.

"Leo didn't talk," she said quietly. "Neither did Rosten."

I looked at my watch. The time was eleven-forty. In twenty minutes, bypassing the building, Castro would have arrived at the City Hall steps.

During those twenty minutes words were my only weapon.

"Why do you think we're here, if Leo didn't talk?"

"You probably tricked him," she answered. She spoke in a calm, reflective voice. "He might have let something slip, but he didn't talk. Leo's not really very smart. But he's dedicated."

"The perfect tool. Is that it?"

The small, curiously pensive smile returned. She nodded. "That's it." There was a short silence. Then, still looking down into the street, she said, "Has the motorcade really been diverted?"

Suddenly I knew why she asked—and suddenly realized that I'd made a terrible mistake, telling her that the route was changed. The electronic opener probably couldn't operate much beyond a hundred feet. Its signal probably couldn't carry across the Plaza, to the City Hall steps. The bombs, then, were close by, probably in the street below. So when Castro bypassed the building and reached the City Hall steps, three hundred yards away, it would all be over. She'd be defeated, vulnerable. The advantage would be mine.

But I shouldn't have forewarned her—shouldn't have surrendered the vital element of surprise.

"*Has* it been diverted?" she asked sharply.

"Yes." Letting my eyes fall, I tried to put a note of duplicity in my voice—tried to make it sound like a desperate lie.

Her face was still in profile. I saw her mouth tighten, and her eyes slightly narrow. Now she turned to face me fully, searching my face for the truth.

"How many policemen are in the building?" she asked quietly. "Besides the FBI men?"

"Just us. Canelli and I."

The ice-green eyes searched mine for a final moment. She was making her decision. She checked her watch, then again turned to look out the window. All the while, her thumb remained on the opener's square plastic button.

"We'll give it ten minutes," she said finally. "I'm waiting for a call."

"Who's going to call you?"

She didn't reply. But now I could see the first signs of tension working at her face. Her jaw was tightly clenched. Beneath the smooth, creamy skin of her neck, muscles were drawing taut.

"Are you worried about the getaway?" I asked. "Is that what the call's about?"

She didn't answer.

"If it's Leo you're waiting for," I pressed, "forget it. He's in custody. He told you so, on the phone—told you he was out of it." I let a beat pass before I said, *"Didn't he?"*

Still she didn't answer. Profiled against the window, her face was impassive.

But now a muscle was jumping at the corner of her mouth. Her neck was corded.

I moved a slow, cautious step toward her. I didn't have a plan. Certainly I couldn't wrestle the opener away from her before she pushed the button. But I wanted to be closer to her as I began probing for weakness:

"How'd you get into this, Shelly? I can figure Leo. He's a true believer. He's the nut—the one with the wild eyes. There's always one like him in an assassination. But you aren't a true believer. And you're certainly not a nut."

This time, her smile was genuine: a small, smug little smirk of pleasure. "No, I'm not a nut, Lieutenant. I'm a business person. I work for people who'll pay me a lot of money for this job."

"Which people? Right-wingers?"

The question amused her. "Right-wingers are amateurs," she answered contemptuously. "And it's the amateurs that cost you in this business. I tried to tell them—tried to warn them about Leo. But they wouldn't listen. Not until he had Howard kill Booker. And then it was too late."

"Who're they? Who's paying you?"

She didn't answer.

"Is it organized crime? Is that it?"

Again she refused to answer. But the small smile widened almost imperceptibly.

"Organized crime," I said. "The Mafia. They hired you for the job. You found Leo, who'll work for free. Then you turned up Mal Howard. He's always been for sale."

Still she didn't respond. But the truth was plain in her face. Years ago, the Mafia had vowed to kill Castro. And the Mafia never forgot. Castro had deprived them of their greatest prize:

Cuba, crime capital of the world. For that, they'd promised, Castro would die.

Here. In San Francisco. At the hands of a slim girl in a stylish tweed suit.

Trying to get her talking, to find a wedge, I said, "I should've connected you with Mal Howard. You were both in Florida at the same time. Christ, it should've been obvious. He has a background in explosive devices, too. It all fits."

She nodded indifferently. My theorizing didn't interest her.

"You're an enforcer," I said. "A goddamn lady enforcer."

She glanced at me. Once more, the smile teased the provocative corners of her mouth. Finally she spoke.

"You're lucky there were two of you," she said. "I would have shot one. But I couldn't risk trying for both of you."

She'd started to talk. I must keep her talking.

"Have you shot many people, Shelly?"

"Not many." As she spoke, she glanced sharply at ther watch. The time was ten minutes to twelve. She looked at the phone, still silent. The ten minutes she'd allowed herself were gone.

Suddenly she wheeled on Canelli. "Get back against the wall," she ordered. Her voice was harsh, her manner decisive. She'd made her decision. Instinctively, I knew she'd decide to cut her losses.

"Move, you fat slob." She gestured with the opener. *"Now."*

As he obeyed, Canelli's soft brown eyes reproached her. Canelli was sensitive about his weight.

She turned to me. "Come here," she ordered. She pointed to a spot on the floor less than a yard from where she stood. "Stand there. I want to show you something."

Moving slowly and deliberately, careful not to startle her, I obeyed. She pointed down at the intersection of Polk and McAllister. The intersection was packed with people. During the past fifteen minutes the crowd-control officers had raised their rope barricades. Two mounted officers rode on smartly prancing horses, patrolling the barricades.

"You were right about Mal Howard," she said. "You were exactly right."

Staring straight into her eyes, I only nodded.

"Howard made a bomb," she said. "Two bombs."

Still I didn't respond.

"Look down there," she ordered, pointing with her free right hand. "Do you see those two trash containers on either side of Polk Street? At the corner."

Following her gesture, I felt my stomach suddenly contract. Two small boys were sitting on one of the big metal canisters. Across the street, a pretty teenage blond girl stood leaning against a matching canister. She held a sandwich in one hand and a pop-top can of Coke in the other. She was squinting as she stared up Polk Street, trying to catch sight of the motorcade.

"Jesus Christ," I said. "You can't do that. You'll never sleep again if you do that."

Momentarily her eyes blazed. "You son of a bitch," she whispered. "Shut up. *Listen.*"

"But they're children. They—"

"Shut *up!*" Now her eyes were wild. Her free right hand was suddenly shaking violently. "I'm getting a half-million dollars for this. So *listen.*"

Holding the opener, her left hand was shaking, too.

She forced herself to speak slowly, choosing her words. "Those canisters," she said huskily, "both contain explosives. The explosives are inside two four-inch steel pipes. The pipes are closed on one end and open on the other. The pipes are packed with dynamite and shrapnel. They're like two mortars, pointing toward each other. We put the cans there last night, Leo and I. When Castro's car gets between the canisters, I press the button. Then I—"

"Shelly—Jesus. It won't happen. He's not coming this way. You —"

"If he comes," she said, speaking now in a low, deadly voice, "it'll be in the next five minutes. I was going to blow the canisters from here and escape in the mess. Leo was going to pick me up, a block from here. But you changed that, you son of a bitch. So I'm leaving. I'm going to leave this office, and get on the elevator and go down to the street. I'll blow the canisters from the street. And if you try to stop me any time between now and then, I'll press the button. I'll—"

"But Castro's not—"

"If you come after me, I'll press this button. Do you understand? So if anyone dies, it's your fault. Not mine. You're the one who'll kill them. It's your decision." Suddenly she stepped away from the desk, moving toward the office door.

"Listen, lady—" Canelli stepped cautiously toward her. "I can tell you that—"

208

"Shut up." It was a low, half-strangled shriek. "And remember, stay inside, here. Stay in this office. If you don't they'll die. All of them, down there—they'll all die. Because they're my ticket out of here. Those kids. They're my insurance." In front of the door now, green eyes blazing, she looked at me for a last long, terrible moment.

Then, while I watched, she transformed herself before stepping out on stage to play the part of a beautiful young matron, she drew a long, deep breath. She straightened her back, squared her shoulders, lifted her breasts. Magically, her face smoothed. She gave me a last small, smug smile—and stepped out into the hallway. Her shadowed shape lingered a moment on the frosted glass door, then disappeared.

Instantly, I reached for my walkie-talkie-just as Canelli brushed past me, bounding desperately for the desk.

"What—?"

"Get to the door," Canelli hissed. "Open it a crack. See when she gets on the elevator. Tell me when she's in it."

"But—"

"Do it, Lieutenant. I was an electrician. Tell me when she's in the elevator." At the desk now, he snatched up potted plant and emptied the plant and dirt on the floor.

"Listen, Canelli. You—"

"Shut up, Lieutenant. Just *do it."* Moving soundlessly, he sprang to the door of the lavatory and jerked it open. Now filling the pot with water, he turned to me, pleading: "Please, Lieutenant. Do like I say. I can stop her. Once she's in the elevator, the opener won't work. She'll be surrounded by steel and concrete. The signal won't carry three feet. Honest."

Three strides took me to the office door. One cautious millimeter at a time, I cracked the door until I could see her standing in front of the elevators. Above her head, a white plastic arrow lit up. One of the two elevators was coming up. She glanced impatiently at the arrow, then looked quickly back toward me. I held the door motionless, open just a fraction of an inch. I knew she couldn't see me watching her.

Behind me, I heard water furiously runing—then diminishing, finally stopping. Footsteps approached as Canelli came to stand close beside me.

"What's happening?" he whispered.

"Nothing. She's waiting for the elevator." As I spoke, I saw a red arrow flashing, pointing down. Gripping the opener in her left hand, holding the alligator bag with her right hand, she was tensed for escape. I heard the elevator doors come open. She threw a last glance in my direction, then stepped forward—gone.

"She's in the elevator."

Beside me, Canelli drew the office door slowly open. The moment the elevator doors thudded shut, he leaped into the hallway. "Come on, Lieutenant. *Quick.*" Hugging the planter pot filled with water close to his bulging stomach, with his muffler trailing behind, he was running awkwardly for the two small twin doors: one to the cleaning closet, the other to the electrical panel. Holding the planter pot out to me, he ordered, "Put your finger in the drainage hole."

Like characters in a comedy sketch, each trying to staunch the flow of water from the bottom of the pot with a clumsy finger, we juggled the planter between us. Finally, with his hands free, Canelli drew his revolver. "Watch the goddamn floor indicator," he said.

Holding the heavy water-filled pot, I stepped back. Over the elevator she'd taken, numbers were flashing as she descended from the sixth floor to the fifth.

Beside me, a shot crashed. Another. And another. Throwing down his revolver, Canelli was struggling with the door to the electrical panel, his fingers jammed between the door and the frame. I saw blood on his fingernails.

Above the elevator, the number "3" flashed—and remained lit. The elevator had stopped for passengers.

The door splintered and came open. Frantically, Canelli grabbed for his pistol, aimed at a locked metal panel inside, fired twice. As the panel door came open, the "3" blinked out.

"The water." Canelli held out his hands.

Number "2" winked on.

I handed Canelli the planter, saw him throw the water on the exposed bank of switches and relays. Instantly, electricity sizzled, sparks showered down on the floor around us.

The number "2" winked out.

But the "1" was out, too.

The elevator was stopped between the first and second floors.

"Whew." Shaking his head, Canelli stooped to retrieve his revolver. Still shaking his head—exhaling loudly—he holstered his revolver. Beneath the stocking cap, his face was sweat-streaked.

"I'm sorry I yelled at you, Lieutenant," he said earnestly. "See, I used to be an electrician, like I said. So I knew that—"

"Wait, Canelli." I raised my hand—and saw my fingers trembling. "Wait. Be quiet. *Listen* to me." My voice, I knew, was hardly more than whisper.

Gulping for breath, mopping his face with the end of his stadium-style scarf, he silently nodded.

"You've got to get the second-floor elevator door open," I said. "You've got to make sure she doesn't get out through the escape door in the ceiling of the elevator. And I've got to get the bomb squad out here. I'll send some men to help you. Clear?"

"Yes, sir, Lieutenant. That's clear."

As I watched him lumbering toward the stairway door, I wondered whether the bomb squad would find the two small boys still sitting on the trash canister.

Epilogue

The Private Detective

At ten past seven that Monday night Frank Hastings and I were sitting in a back booth in Marlowe's, a tavern on Bryant Street across from the Hall of Justice where cops and police reporters and bail bondsmen congregated. I had been there for fifteen minutes, nursing a beer, and Hastings had just come in.

He ordered a glass of tonic water from the waitress—for reasons of his own he did not drink anything alcoholic—and ran a hand heavily over his stubbled cheeks. He looked about the way I felt: tired, emotionally drained, in need of a dozen hours of uninterrupted sleep. I had spent all of last night and most of this morning answering police and FBI questions at the winery, and even though I had taken a four-hour nap after returning to San Francisco, it was going to be a while before my internal clock was functioning properly again.

"We just finished interrogating Shelly Jackson," he said.

"She gave us most of the story, on advice from an expensive attorney." His mouth quirked. "She's going to cop a plea."

"That figures," I said.

"Right. Everybody plea-bargains these days—except for fanatics like Rosten and Leo Cappellani."

"You didn't get anything from Leo?"

"Not a word. As soon as we arrested him and told him Shelly was in custody and Castro was safe, he shut up tight. Just name, rank and serial number."

I nodded.

"But like I said, we got most of the story from Shelly. Apparently both Leo and Rosten have been active in right-wing paramilitary politics for years—quietly and secretly. They were both recruited, if that's the right word, by Frank Cappellani when he was alive."

The waitress came back with Hastings's drink, and while she was setting it out I thought about Rosa. She had told us last night that she suspected Leo had followed in his father's political footsteps, but that he would never discuss the matter with her; neither would Rosten, who she knew was a disciple of her late husband. Whatever her feelings about Leo's involvement in the attempted Castro assassination, she had hidden them behind a fresh cloak of imperiousness. But I got the impression that, despite appearances, Alex had always been her favorite son and that she would not stand by Leo; his political fanaticism might be forgiven, his murder of Booker might be forgiven, but the attempts on Alex's life could never be.

Even with all the adversity I thought she would find a way to salvage her life and the winery both. With Alex's help, maybe. A man who has faced death three times and survived either learns to be strong or falls apart completely, and last night and today Alex had shown signs of a new maturity in his behavior with the police and the FBI.

When the waitress moved away, Hastings said, "Anyhow, everything with the Cappellanis went down about the way you reasoned it out. If it hadn't been for Leo's obsessive hatred for his brother, the whole damned assassination might have gone off as planned. And Castro and Chirst knows how many innocent people would be dead right now."

"Where does Shelly fit in, exactly?" I asked him. "Is she another zealot that Leo brought in?"

"No. It's the other way around: she's the one who recruited Leo, under orders from Miami. She pretended to be a zealot for Leo's benefit, but actually she's a mercenary—a Mafia enforcer."

I stared at him. "Mafia? The *Mafia's* behind it all?"

"That's the way it looks. They've had a vendetta against Castro ever since he threw them out of Havana when he took over; he cost them millions in gambling and other illegal revenue." Hastings sipped some of his tonic water. "Shelly wouldn't tell us who gave her her orders; she's too smart for that. She wants to keep on living while she's in prison and when she finally gets out, and she wouldn't stand a chance if she started naming names."

"How would a woman like her get mixed up with the Mafia?"

Hastings shrugged. "She wouldn't tell us that either. Blood relations in the organization, maybe. There are other ways too, if you're greedy enough and amoral enough."

Christ, I thought the Mafia—a Mafia enforcer. And I had liked her and considered having a relationship with her, and all the time she had been setting Castro's death for the powers behind organized crime. I had been wrong about people before, but never more than I had been about Shelly Jackson. Just thinking about it made me feel cold inside.

"Where the Mafia made their big mistake," Hastings said, "was in using amateurs for the job instead of people from their own ranks. I suppose they did it to throw the blame on Leo's right-wing group in case something went wrong—only they didn't figure on the whole operation coming apart the way it did." He shook his head. "The next time, if there is a next time, they won't make the same mistake."

"You think they'll go after Castro again?"

"If they want him badly enough. And I think they want him that badly. Someday, somewhere, Castro will leave himself vulnerable again and they'll put out another contract on him."

"That's a nice prospect."

Hastings said wryly, "I just hope they don't pick San Francisco again."

We were silent for a time, thinking our own thoughts. Just a couple of cops, one public and the other private, one in his forties and one just past fifty—working too hard, trying too hard, accomplishing a little but never quite enough. Little cogs in the big system, not unlike the cops and the private eyes in the pulps. Well, in one sense that was exactly what we were: a pulp cop and a pulp private eye. But in another sense we were both in better and in worse shape than those boys.

We could think in much broader terms and we could feel much more deeply—and we knew that when you deal with pain and death and human corruption, there are never any happy endings because there are never really any endings at all.

The Police Lieutenant

I watched Bill raise his glass of beer. He drank briefly and returned the glass to the table before him, thoughtfully rotating the glass on the wet formica. Even in the dim light of Marlowe's, I could see fatigue etched deep in the lines of his face. I wondered how much he'd charged the Cappellanis for risking his life to save Alex. Did his fee schedule include a multiplier for mortal danger? To myself, I wearily smiled. Because I knew there were no guarantees for this big, serious man. If someone caught him with a sucker punch, or a broken bottle laid open his face, there wouldn't be a partner to help him, or a dozen cars dispatched to run down the assailant. He wouldn't get hazard pay or sick leave. He'd never get a departmental citation. If he died a gaudy death, the story would make the back pages of the newspapers. But there would be no white-gloved policemen drawn up beside his grave—no volley of shots—no sound of taps.

That, then, was my edge over the private detective. If I got injured in the line of duty, it would be a front-page story. If I got killed, there'd be a parade at the graveyard.

I knew he hadn't charged the Cappellanis enough. And he knew it, too. Some men had an affinity for money, and a knack for acquiring it.

But not Bill.

And not me, either.

Even as a second-string fullback for the Detroit Lions, I'd made a good money during the four years I'd played professional football. But cars and taxes and a year's love affair with an heiress had taken most of the money—and a surgeon's bills for three knee operations had taken the rest. When football was finished with me, I'd make the mistake of marrying the girl—and compounded the mistake by taking a make-work PR job from my father-in-law. The money in the executive suite had been good, but it all went for country club dues I couldn't afford and interior decorators I didn't like. So I began spending too much money for too many drinks in too many bars—alone. A divorce lawyer had taken the final share, and I'd escaped to San Francisco, where I was born. A tough, jug-eared captain named Krieger got me into the Police Academy. I'd known Krieger since kindergarten; after our first fight, we'd been friends for life.

I was the oldest rookie in my class at the academy. On the obstacle course, the pain in my knees brought tears to my eyes. I'd felt tired and lonely and defeated. I missed my two children, in Detroit, but I knew I couldn't exist in the same town with my ex-wife and her father, both my enemies. So, during the days, I learned to be a policeman. At night, by myself in my apartment, I drank. At the end of every month, so my children would remember me kindly, I sent their mother child-support payments she didn't need. Then I borrowed money to get through the next month.

"You look tired," Bill was saying.

"So do you."

He smiled, nodded and sipped the beer. "I'm beginning to think it's a chronic condition."

"You, too?"

He nodded again. "Me, too."

I finished the last of my tonic water and looked reflectively at the empty glass. After I'd made patrolman, Krieger had knocked on my door one night and told me that if I didn't quit drinking our friendship was finished—and my career, too. He'd stayed in my apartment less than thirty seconds; he hadn't even bothered to close the door behind him. But, that night, I poured the last of my bourbon down the toilet.

Three years later, Krieger tried to disarm a young long-shoreman who'd killed his wife with a deer rifle and was threatening to kill his three small children. The longshoreman had shot Krieger in the throat. After the full-dress funeral, I'd signed up to take the sergeant's exam.

Across the table, Bill was shaking his head. "Jesus. A lady enforcer. It's still hard to believe."

"I know. But she's as tough and smart and as ruthless as any mobster I've ever known. I've never interrogated anyone with more brains or guts."

"In the past few years," Bill said, "the Mafia's turning up everywhere. When I was a cop, in the fifties, the Mafia didn't even have a toehold in California. Now, Christ, they're everywhere."

"Back east," I said, "the Mafia owns the politicians. That's the real secret of their power. And that's what they're trying to do out here. They're succeeding, too. Especially in Los Angeles. They've got crooked politicians and crooked lawyers in their pocket. It's a hard combination to beat."

"Does Shelly's lawyer have mob connections?" he asked.

"I don't know whether he's connected or not," I answered. "I do know, though, that he's rich, and he's got a Beverly Hills practice. I asked a friend of mine in Los Angeles to check him out for me. Just for the hell of it."

"I'll bet you a lunch that he's connected."

"No bet. But lunch is a good idea." I looked at the clock behind the bar. "I'd better get back to the squad room. Some reporters are waiting for me."

"And I'd better go home and go to bed."

We walked out of the bar together, and shook hands on the sidewalk outside. During the last half hour, a light rain had started to fall. The sidewalk glistened; cars threw up plumes of mist as they passed.

"The next time there's a poker game," I said, turning up my collar, "I'll call you. Try to make it."

"I'll make it. Thanks."

We smiled at each other, nodded goodbye and hurried off in different directions, both of us hunched against the rain.